"Superbly balanced and delightfully complex, with finely intertwined roots of mystery, romance, and the drive for personal redemption."

–Mark Pryor, author of the Hugo Marston novels

HARVESTING

Desired by Many

THE

Forbidden by a Deadly Few

SKY

KAREN HUGG

Woodhall Press
Norwalk, CT

PRAISE FOR KAREN HUGG'S
THE FORGETTING FLOWER

*"Karen Hugg is the rare author who
can blend wonder and suspense"*
—Emily Carpenter, Author of *Until the Day I Die*
and *Burying the Honeysuckle Girls*

"Intriguing and atmospheric, **The Forgetting Flower** *has
a fairytale quality, a journey into the sensuous magic of
plants. The florescent beauty at the heart of this eerie
story of sisterly love and redemption is the extraordinary
mountain hybrid Violet Smoke with its scent of burnt
apricot, as dangerously potent in Paris as it was in its
beginnings in Poland."*
—Deborah Lawrenson, Author of
The Lantern and *300 Days of Sun*

*"The delight and grit of Paris, the desperation of poverty,
the love of plants and family—all beautifully and
authentically told. The literary side of the novel brings
sensitivity and texture to the struggling characters and
their surroundings, and the thriller side kept me up late,
anxious to find out what happens next."*
—Sue Burke, Author of *The Semiosis Duology*

"Karen Hugg's **The Forgetting Flower** *instantly captures a
reader's imagination. A book for those who love not only
Paris and flowers, but also intrigue and danger."*
—Marty Wingate, Author of
A Potting Shed Mystery Series

HARVESTING THE SKY

KAREN HUGG

woodhall press

woodhall press

Woodhall Press, 81 Old Saugatuck Road, Norwalk, CT 06855
WoodhallPress.com

Cover design: Jessica Dionne
Layout artist: Wendy Bowes

Library of Congress Cataloging-in-Publication Data available

ISBN 978-1-949116-91-5 (paper: alk paper)
ISBN 978-1-949116-92-2 (electronic)

First Edition

Distributed by Independent Publishers Group
(800) 888-4741

Printed in the United States of America

ETHAN

"It seemed that we had finally passed this very difficult trail so that we could mount the horses and continue on. But suddenly from the cliff above the trail, two gigantic eagles flew out from a nest, circling on enormous wings. My horse shied and bolted, galloping along the trail and the overing. The rein was unexpectedly torn out of my hand and I had to hang on to the mane.

Above my head were cliffs but below me, 1000 metres down in the deep ravine, rumbled the beautiful, blue Pyandzh, the upper reaches of one of the great rivers of Inner Asia. That is the experience, which afterwards this traveller remembers best. Such moments steel one for the rest of one's life: they prepare a scientist for all difficulties, all adversities, and everything unexpected."

--Nikolai Vavilov,
1916, Five Continents

AUTUMN
CHAPTER 1

For months, Andre had imagined what the apple would look like and now as he crested the mountain ridge, he was about to find out. He doubted it would be truly white, the "pearl" Nes had described. He guessed yellow with hints of cream. That would be more realistic. Then again, what was realistic about a white apple that healed people in a matter of hours? He dragged his aching body through the rain, his heart beating with an excited tic as he followed Samal, the team guide. She seemed unaffected by her tall bulging backpack and heavy wool coat, ambling up the slope like a dragonfly zooming over grass.

In Kazakh, she said, "This way, soon, I think."

Andre's pack, heavy with equipment, pressed on his shoulder blades, bonier from walking thirty miles into the forest for three days. His stomach grumbled. He was ready for whatever ramen soup they had left and a good night's sleep.

At the ridge's top, Samal paused and pointed at a foggy light illuminating a cloudy opening, her black eyes alert. "Tengri!"

In the distance, the top of a tree, much broader than described, stood.

"Is that the tree? Are you sure?"

"Yes, very sure." Her favorite tin cup for cooking, eating, and washing bumped against her black braid.

He searched his mind for the Kazakh words to say the tree didn't quite fit the description but failed to piece them together, glancing back through the dense crowns for Vlad. The translator was plodding along sixty feet below, too far for earshot, and Nes, well, he was bringing up the rear to make sure Vlad didn't wander the wrong way again.

"Alright," he said, trying to lighten his voice. "Let's find out."

Soon, the forest trickled away to a field of artemisia and herbs, rolling gently downward to an expansive field. About a quarter-mile off, the Tengri tree stood exactly where the old villager had said it would be, on a small hill between a cherry thicket and crooked stream. Good God, it *was* there! Out in the open. For anyone to study. They'd struggled through wind and snow and searing sun to find it. Paid bribes at highway checkpoints, even smoked dirty crumpled cigarettes and eaten sheep's head soup out of courtesy for information. Now, he'd be part of the team that brought it to the Western world.

"Holy..." He dropped his head in relief. *What a gift.* He whispered his thanks "Raqmet."

As they wound their way into the field, he studied the tree. It grew sturdily with a wide trunk and sweeping crown, branches evenly spaced so it gained all of the light and air it required. No bare patches in the bark. No canker or cracking. Somehow it had survived decades of lightning and wind and late frosts without the protection of other trees. His dad would have clapped his hands and said, "Ah, what a lucky stick!"

Still, the leaves had turned a reddish-orange color. Late-season color, about-to-drop color. And where were the apples? He scanned the branches. None. A lump of worry solidified in his gut. The tree was going dormant. If it was going dormant, that meant it had dropped its fruit. If it had dropped its fruit, they'd have no apples to bring home and the project was screwed.

As he neared the tree, the hill's size grew, looming 30 feet in the air. The slopes sharply surged up, covered in tangled dense shrubs. They reminded Andre of the chaparrals near his family

He scooted toward the hill's edge, laying on his side, and sawed the root, the prickles scraping his face. The deep bellow of Vlad's voice and Samal's frantic one echoed, but he stayed spread out. His arm hung over the ridge, the blade bumping against the soil's pebbles. He almost had it. A spray of rain wet his neck. He breathed out. *Nearly there.* He sawed faster, faster, and finally cut through. The sapling loosened, but a small feeder held it back. He yanked it, felt in the soil with a finger. *Get closer.* He got on a knee to take out his pruners, still a hold of the sapling, when the rock under his knee slid and the root snapped.

His body dropped into a slide along the hill. Branches slapped his face. He grabbed at clumps of tarragon, feeling the wet leaves. With his foot he groped for a toehold, but only found gravel. If he dropped the Tengri, he could hoist himself up, but it would break in the fall. The herb slipped from his hand and he slid, his forearms scraping rock. He dropped into the cold air before catching in a hefty wild rose.

Ouch. Stillness. He grabbed a prickled cane. Ouch. Thorns poked his ear. He exhaled. Through the leaves, the field, green with the gray humps of boulders, swayed below. His foot pressed against the shrub's base, then slipped. His body jolted. Bump. Face hit a stone. His ankle too. Pain. Warm liquid. *Where's the saw?* More pain. *Is my tooth loose?*

Vlad and Samal exchanged high-pitched calls, repeating Russian phrases again and again, back and forth, negotiating in a panic.

Rain blew. He gripped a rock, the toe of his right boot still stuck in the rose. Crackling sounds. *Branches breaking? The fire?* He was unsure whether looking up or down worried him more.

Some twenty feet above, Nes appeared at the edge. "Brilliant. Now your arse's in a thistle."

"I don't know how..."

"Here, catch."

A clump of rope landed at his chest.

"Hold tight a sec." Nes disappeared for a minute, then threw a leg over the rope, gripping the taut line, and tapped around for a hard surface. The hair on his calf was blonde. His leg, pink.

The image blurred from blood. Andre blinked, unable to see, but felt the sapling in his hand, the trunk as solid as a bone.

"Nes, take the sapling."

"Andre, forget the sapling."

The wind kicked up the smell of wet soil.

"Nes, take it."

Carefully, Nes climbed downward, setting each foot by a rock or plant. "You're about to break your back, now let it go and grab the damn rope."

"If I hold it high, you can reach the roots."

"Andre, forget the sapling. Grab the damn rope!"

By the time Nes helped him onto the hill's edge, he couldn't see from his right eye. The blood was too thick. His mind in a daze, he stumbled around, pain shooting through his leg, a cloth at his head. He hobbled down to the fire where Samal's hands pressed his fingers, pinched his eyebrows, squeezed his foot. He slurped soup, though he had no appetite, and turned in. Later, he dreamt he was sleeping in the stream. His head lay on the bank, resting on a cool tuft of grass, his body immersed in the icy water. Every few seconds, he'd crawl out of the water and lie on the bank, but thunder clapped and his body would jolt into the water. A sharp ache pulsed at his leg. Rain pattered the tent in a grainy dusk. A flashlight haloed the canvas. Samal spoke soothing words—or was that Renia? A braid, smelling of smoke, hit his ear. She pushed a pill down his throat. He rolled over and fell into darkness until silver light flooded his eyes.

He woke in his sleeping bag, in shirt and jeans and knit hat, his ankle throbbing.

Voices mumbled outside. The words "leave" and "tomorrow" and "hell" and "road" bounced off his ears.

"No, too risky," Nes said.

Vlad's voice, hollow like an owl's hoot, said, "If we go, we find car or truck. I'm sure of this."

Andre felt thirsty, yearned for tea, water, anything. He threw on a coat, went to unzip the tent. His left pinky and ring fingers were in a splint.

The air felt warmer than the day before, windier, dry, the sky showing jagged slivers of blue amidst high clouds. By a small fire, Vlad sat on a rock like a giant on a tiny stool, a wrinkled map unfolded over his lap. His meaty hand rubbed his goatee. Nes leaned over his shoulder, studying the topography, saying, "...at least a 500-meter elevation."

The two looked up.

Nes's eyes widened, then retracted into a smile. "Well, your mug's a shade brighter. Feel any better?"

Andre blinked, his vision a touch blurry, his temple throbbing. A tight bandage was taped near his eyebrow. When he tried to stand, pain shot through his leg. He teetered, hopped a step, and sat sloppily on the ground. "Do you have hot water or...?"

"Sure, sure," Nes said. He took a tin pot from the coals and poured in water from a bottle. "Hang tight."

Andre eyed the Tengri, looming over the camp. Yesterday, he'd somehow grabbed the rope, then Nes's hand, then ... he couldn't recall. "Nes, do you have the sapling?"

Samal's voice cried out. She strolled jauntily from a western rise, speaking fast Russian, binoculars swinging from her neck. At seeing Andre, she clapped her hands, her tone switching to a slower warmth.

"She says she saw the swamp," Vlad said. "That way with the swamp is best."

"What?" Andre said.

Nes unzipped his pack. "Where's the bloody tea?"

Andre felt torn about whether to break camp. He wanted to wrap himself in his sleeping bag and lay still, in pain. "Are we leaving so soon?"

Vlad stood up. "Come. Sit. It's warm here."

The fire spit a chunk of wood.

Andre backed up. God, he hated fire. Burned his hand once as a boy and hadn't been able to roast a marshmallow since. "No, thanks."

Nes poured water in a cup and dropped in a tea bag, passed it to Andre.

He gulped the warm liquid. It soothed his throat, radiated to his chest, steamed his whole head. His mind reeled. *Too warm.*

He drank again. It tasted like hay.

"Bright news. Samal found a shortcut to a road," Nes said. "But not to worry, we'll lift off when you feel better."

He felt unsteady, nauseated. The ground lurched beneath his feet. "What about..." Food, what was the food supply? They'd been low with only two bricks of soup left. Could they pick huckleberries? He had half an energy bar. No, it was gone. But how? "I think I ate..." he said, his breath heavy. When he imagined the nuts in the bar, his stomach churned. Nes and Vlad skipped in his vision. His mouth watered. He fell to his knees and threw up.

"I think I better rest," he said.

"Sure, mate, it's only seven. Sleep a bit. Samal and I are off to look for more Tengris."

He crawled in the tent and dropped into a deep sleep. The wind whipped and rippled the canvas. Soon, more voices. He woke to staccato chatter, unsure in the fog of semi-consciousness where he was. A woman's voice. Had to be Renia. Months ago, she'd shaken his hand at the school greenhouse. She had a soft face, smelled like jasmine. She'd given him her joy, the *Saintpaulia* hybrid, to deliver to that Swiss lab. Then later at her shop, in July he'd helped her fill out more paperwork. Her eyes were the color of green beach glass.

"Not a goddamn chance!"

Nes's voice blared like a seagull. "No *focking* way."

Another voice pierced his ears. Was it Renia? Whoever she was, she spoke Russian.

Vlad answered in a low-pitched English. "She's right. He's hurt. And no more food."

"What the hell do you call all of this?"

"Yes. It's okay, but we must leave early."

Blackness. Crackling. More mumbling. Outside, voices cursed, then a pregnant silence. The canvas unzipped. He smelled flannel. The light from a headlamp shocked his eyes. Nes's gold beard. And just behind in the darkness, Renia's outline, no, Samal, carrying a bowl.

"Alright, mate," Nes said. His wedding ring glinted in the weak light. "Time to sit up. Come on."

"What is it?"

Samal slid a cold spoon in his mouth.

"Just ... cereal," Nes said. "Swallow, eh? That's it. Try and keep it down now."

He chewed. A mealy mush sluiced through his throat. "Nes, where's the sapling?"

Nes's eyes flashed, cooled.

Samal shoved in another spoonful.

"Nes..."

"How's the ankle? Do you think you can walk?"

He shifted it. "Ow."

"Alright then."

More cereal at his mouth. He tasted tart juice. "Wait a minute." He chewed, tasting mealy fiber, thin skin. "What am I eating?"

"We'd like to get you to a clinic. This might help."

Andre cringed. He was eating Tengri apples. *God damn it.* He pushed away the bowl. "How could you?"

"You can't walk, Andre."

"What are you *thinking*?"

Nes frowned, his mouth crooked like a bare branch in winter. "What am I thinking? I'm thinking we weren't going to get five pounds anyway. I'm thinking we have to get you on your bloody feet and walking if we all don't want to starve in the Tian Shan mountains. That's what I'm thinking."

CHAPTER 2

Five days later, Andre sat beside Nes in a conference room, feeling like a mouse in a sterile lab box. Tan walls, gray carpet, white board, projection camera, even a blank monitor. Pendant lamps hung overhead with sharp bulbs burning a clean white. Andre gripped the arms of his chair, tapping in a nervous rhythm, breathing in the silence. It all smelled like nothing, seemed to be nowhere, and was as unfamiliar as the tweed jacket and polyester tie he was dressed in.

He yanked his shirt cuff over the cuts on his wrist, a futile exercise since despite his formal clothes, his face displayed a mass of scars. They were road-rash-like scabs spreading from his left eye to his mouth. His fingers rested in a proper medical splint. His ankle bandaged, but better. A ghostly pain sizzled in his left temple by the prickly stitches. That morning while doing a pitiful job of shaving he realized with his wavy hair, low-set brows, and muddy eyes, he looked more like a creatural villain in a graphic novel than a human.

"It's been ten minutes," Nes said. "Maybe they forgot about us."

Andre stared at their reflections in the giant window. Two slumped saps in ill-fitting suits and hasty haircuts. "If we're lucky."

The glass door swung open and Monique Castel entered with a brisk determined walk. She was a slim, forty-something woman in a silk blouse and wool pants that hugged her figure without wrinkles or bulging. Tailored, clean. As clean as her walnut hair, which, in a short bob, framed a bland pretty face. She was the ideal image of a manager with a history of accomplishment spearheading a new natural medicines project—a reflection of her expectations for Andre and Nes's expedition. Expectations that hadn't been met.

She skimmed the display on the table: eighteen whole apples, two dozen partially-rotten ones, scion branches, and the sapling in a small pot at the center. Its few remaining leaves sagged. The plant was still in shock at having been cut and taken from home. But more than 60 branches lay in neat rows. *All healthy.* The wood was fresh but mature, able to produce fruit, each branch sprinkled with strong bud marks. Good for grafting into trees that would grow robust, medicinal apples. Andre thought Nes had chosen well.

"Gentlemen," she said. "I just spoke with Monsieur Bankole by phone. First, let me say how much I appreciate what you went through during the expedition." She gestured at Andre. "It seems the weather was uncooperative and I recognize the danger and difficulty."

Andre shifted in his seat, setting a hand to his forehead.

With two reluctant fingers, she picked up a bruised apple and turned it over. Nes had included the rotting apples in the collection, which seemed a pathetic decision now.

"But this," she said, "this is unacceptable."

With a sheepish groan, Nes said, "Well, we did warn you, Monique. We warned you in summer that—"

"And this is the only sapling?"

"Yes. The tree was on a hill covered in rock and—"

"You told me the forest is filled with hectares of these and you found only one."

Andre cleared his throat.

"As you've done before, Monsieur McFadden, you overpromised what you could obtain," she said.

"Not at all," Nes said. "There are hectares of apple trees, but only one Tengri. We know that now."

A heated discussion about terrain, the team, and the second trial ensued until a climactic silence when Castel paced before the window. Outside, Paris twinkled in the dusky blue of a late fall evening. At the left, the mirrored towers of La Defense reflected the setting sun, casting a copper glow, while at the right, the slanted roofs and limestone buildings of the Colline suburb absorbed the light and broadened shadows. She paused, seeming to take in the rickety rooftops and black lamps and clay chimneys, all barely visible in the mist.

"Gentlemen," she said, "I give you 15,000 Euro so we can have fruit to conduct a second clinical trial. But you returned with … sticks."

"The sapling will probably produce several. And if we still graft the scions," Andre said, "we could harvest a few apples by next autumn."

She folded her arms. A heavy ring with a large pearl hung off her finger. "Crop production comes later," she said. "Our goal was to introduce the sample apple *now*. You were to deliver sample apples *now,* so we could arrange the second clinical trial."

Castel had planned on gathering wealthy investors, medical officials, supplement company salespeople, politicians, even the mayor of Paris at a reveal party. All to present the Tengri. Eating one would prove its benefits. An ache in the back would lessen, a sinus allergy might clear, and overall, more invigoration. The first trial had proved that. But it was impossible to present rotten apples to potential clients.

She eyed Andre's scars, her face softening. "I was sorry to hear you were injured. How is your health now?"

The idea that he'd almost been injured in a more severe, expensive way made his stomach tighten. At least she couldn't see the gash at his ankle or nasty bruise on his shoulder. He paused, debating what to say. "Well..."

In Kazakhstan, after he'd eaten the apple mush, he'd slept in a strange relief and woke the next morning without as much pain. He felt well enough to put pressure on the ankle and hobble out, wash his face in the stream. Afterward, they packed and hiked to lower elevations until after ten exhausting hours, they set up camp near the swamp. The next day, they struggled around it and by sunset landed at the road Samal had seen. Hours later, a trucker stopped and they crammed into his cab, arriving by morning on the outskirts of Almaty. "Worth far more than three hundred Euros," Nes had said. Andre had waited in the medical clinic among tough brutes with sliced faces and broken noses. He'd fought a rocky slope that gave him five stitches in the temple, four in the chin, and a stone's worth of defeat in the heart.

To Castel, he said, "My injuries are healing. I feel much better."

She studied him a long moment, closed her eyes. As if to the far wall, she said, "Alright, thank you for coming. We're finished here."

"Finished?" Andre said. He swallowed. "Madame, this sapling is quite mature. I'm confident it will produce apples this year."

"Monsieur Damazy, Monsieur Alba and I signed a contract for apples and tissue material to produce fruit-bearing trees, which you and Directeur Bankole were to provide. You did not provide them."

A few days earlier when Andre had told Edo by phone of the expedition's outcome, Edo had been quiet for a tense minute. He'd negotiated hard for their names to be on the patent, for favorable financial terms for the three. Edo had even scheduled his own trip to a grower's conference in South Africa during the expedition, never guessing Nes and Andre would return early. Failure hadn't been in the projection.

Now, what would bring money to LaRoche Naturel and prestige to AgroPolyTech was in jeopardy. AgroPolyTech was a natural sciences university whose horticulture program, unlike the school at Versailles, was not high-profile. The Versailles school groomed famous landscape architects and commercial growers, but AgroPolyTech, housed in a small, three-story building in the Fifth Arrondissement, spawned mostly nursery workers and restoration experts, specialists who spent more time slopping in mud and carrying heavy plants than pointing and dictating notes. They needed a success story.

"The tree," she said. "Please take it away. And the branches."

Take them away? Where? If the contract was void, they'd have no funds to propagate. How many years could they wait? He imagined his mother gripping his father's arm as she inched across the kitchen, her foot dragging. Andre clenched his hand in a fist. *We should have asked the villager for apples from his cellar.*

"Now, let's not be rash," Nes said. "We found the tree. We know where it is now. We know it's tip-bearing, we know—."

She shot him a searing look, the heat in her eyes ready to light a match. "Do you think you're going back?"

"Well, I'm just pointing out—"

"Gentlemen, Monsieur Alba and I are not interested in risking an extreme amount of resources to fund a project that will fail. We'll take the apples per our agreement, but I don't have time to deal with the sticks. Thank you for coming. Monsieur Alba and I will discuss the matter and let you know soon whether our partnership has dissolved."

Out on the street, the air smelled of car exhaust and chaos. A potted boxwood at a restaurant leaned with brown foliage, roots half-exposed. Andre stormed to a round kiosk and kicked it hard. Again. He cussed. Marched around complaining until Nes shoved him toward the metro and assured him Monique would call the next day. But the next day she didn't call. She didn't call Andre, nor Nes, nor Edo. Nes caught the train back home to London and Andre began a frustrating check of his phone messages every other hour.

Though he left voicemail for Edo, Edo didn't return his calls. He tried not to read into the lack of communication and distract himself with school work, taking over his propagation class again and writing his expedition report for the university. He prepared the scions for winter storage in the basement lab. In the halls, he answered classwork questions from students, brushing off their concerned looks about his injured face. When they asked what happened, he lied, told them he'd been camping on vacation in the mountains. The contract forbid him from talking about it. His fibs worked mostly with everyone except the department office manager. Through the travel itinerary and receipts for reimbursement, she knew he'd hired a Russian translator and a Kazakh guide, knew he'd bought odd backpacking equipment, and more than anything, knew an experienced horticulture professor hadn't gone with his botanical explorer friend to dreary Kazakhstan for what he told the students was vacation.

As days passed, Andre ignored the smoldering gossip. One morning, a student asked him with wide eyes if he'd been on another plant-hunting expedition. He laughed off the idea though he knew they knew and could do nothing about the rumors. He even made the local student newspaper, which ran a short column about the "mystery trip" professor Damazy had undertaken to "somewhere in Central Asia," perhaps to retrieve a "new, one-of-a-kind, never-before-seen apple."

The talk spawned his own kernel of paranoia, where every morning he'd check on the scions in the lab's fridge before stopping by Edo's office to see if there was any word from LaRoche Naturel. Two days later in his office planning a lecture, he heard his boss' voice. He hurried down the hall, following the low Nigerian accent.

He rolled into Edo's office calling his name, but found it empty. The overhead lights blared, an abstract design bending across his laptop screen. Pen uncapped on papers. Andre checked behind the door where on a bookshelf, a vintage radio played Ethiopian pop. Slanted books, odd driftwood. A grow light hummed over a sapele table of desert succulents, its tube casting a purple glow. No Edo. By the window, a collection of *tillandsias* hung and a tall cactus covered in white, needled fuzz stood in a Mexican pot. Fela Kuti, playing guitar on a poster, reigned over the stillness.

"He's gone," the department manager said. She squeezed past Andre and put a file on the desk.

"For the day?"

She shrugged. "I think so. He went to an unplanned meeting with the dean. He asked me to lock his door."

Out on the street, the late afternoon air was warm, the breeze cool. Andre headed home, his leather bag across his chest, his black racer jacket zipped high. His mind churned with the threat of the partnership collapsing. *What a disaster.* He passed a man in a wool coat and knit hat, holding a little girl's hand as he scrolled on his phone. "Papa, everything will be okay," she said. A backpack, decorated with Japanese anime characters, bobbed on her back. "I hope so," the man said. His enormous hand enveloped her delicate one, able to crush it at any second. Big, tan, strong. The hand of Andre's father. Oskar had been an orchardist because trees were rugged. They were tough, built houses, fed people, gave them air, bettered one's health. Andre was a horticulturalist because each plant amazed him with its unique qualities. The Tengri was ultimate proof of that.

At his building on the Rue Rollin, he went up the circular staircase, trying not to remember his time as a teenager, trying to breathe out the tremor of shame in his chest, breathe through that other time when he'd encountered a special plant. Fifteen years ago. He remembered sitting on a stack of pallets at Suntime Orchards on a hot day in California, talking with Jason.

"I named it 'Zeus'" Andre had said.

They drank from water bottles, on break. The sun burned high and hot. Jason plucked the middle of his Metallica T-shirt to cool himself. Andre poured water on his neck. The two had finished fixing a sprinkler line in the citrus field.

"Who's Zeus?" Jason said. "Like a god or something?"

"He was the most powerful god in Greek mythology. And this pomegranate shrub is a dwarf, but the fruit is gigantic and super sweet. It's like the size of a god."

Jason rolled a stray avocado back and forth between his shoes. "Sounds cool."

"It's the sport of a *Punica* shrub my dad grows. I took cuttings and now I've got ten plants growing behind Field 22. But I hardly get any fruit from the darn things. I think it's because the winters are too wet. It needs to grow in a drier area." He watched a guy drive a tractor in the distance, blowing up a cloud of dust. "And I can't afford to rent a space."

Jason smiled. He had a chipped incisor, dots of acne on a ruddy face. "Dude, I got this. My grandma. Grandma Mel. She's got the house in the foothills."

"No ... would she?"

"Totally. She's my grandma, she'd do anything for me. And she knows your dad so it's all good. All good."

Now, in Paris, he crested the third floor, thinking how ironic Jason's statement was. It hadn't been all good. In fact, the opposite. But not comparing this experience to that one was like pressing a broken nut back in a crushed shell. He walked the short dim hall to his door. *I did all I could.* His keys slipped from his hand, collapsed on the floor. *Then why did someone die?*

He lifted a breath in his chest and went inside. His apartment was a small atelier with a tiny bedroom and snug kitchen. The walls peeled paint and the sinks flowed with stale water. Still, he found relief in shutting the door. The locks always kept out complications. And here, his plants never asked much of him. They didn't complain. They didn't vie for power or act with selfish intent. They didn't betray his trust. They didn't take one action, then regret it later. They were honest, predictable. Their ways, noble.

As he hung up his coat, he caught a whiff of the hoya's flowers. Sweet, cold. It had bloomed during the five hours he'd been at work. He'd waited three years.

The living room, a large rectangle with a wall of floor-to-ceiling windows, faced a roof deck, flooded with sun on a clear day and sheltered from wind by neighboring buildings. Despite the high ceiling, the room felt cozy. The seating area had a mid-century couch and a rickety rocking chair. A dining table made from a slice of burl wood sat piled with books about the rare plants of China, gnostic gospels, history of the Gauls, and what started his fascination with apples: *Five Continents* by Nikolai Vavilov. A fishtail palm stood in the corner by the windows, a bulky schefflera to its left, a tree fern to the right. These plants led into two arms of greenery he never tired of seeing: agaves, philodendrons, cycads, bromeliads, dracaenas. Varying shades of green, contrasting shapes. Andre had always thought of his little atelier as a shoebox diorama of a horticulturalist's life.

The patio door jiggled. Outside, Linus pushed on the pane. He opened it and picked up the orange rag doll cat, scratching his neck as he went to the kitchen. Every time he looked at Linus, he thought of his mom, Vivienne, who'd been Linus's best friend when she'd visited five years ago. Patient Mom, crippled from her mid-50s on. Maybe it had been from the stress of the family being shunned, he didn't know. She said it wasn't, but he'd always wondered. If only events had unfolded differently, she wouldn't have suffered so much. And if only the Tengri had been discovered then. They knew the apple's chemical couldn't work miracles, but it could help. If combined with other pharmaceuticals, other protocols, a person like she could move her limbs more easily, stand straighter, speak clearly, even smile a whole relaxed smile.

Linus roamed the counter while the watering can filled in the sink. He eyed the fridge where a photo of him, his parents, and grandmother hung, taken at his grandmother's childhood home in Bordeaux where his uncle now lived and cousin Delphine grew up. They were all by the fireplace, his parents' faces beaming because they liked taking family photos and his grandmother's more reserved face because she believed in looking noble rather than happy. He took the watering can to the patio. Containers of vegetables and vines and herbs crowded the roof deck, all arranged for practicality rather than aesthetics. A lone teak chair he'd picked up from the Clignancourt market waited just outside the door for what scant relaxing he did.

There, between a cypress and juniper, the sapling stood in its little pot. It had healthy scaffolding branches and a strong leader. Most leaves had browned and fallen off.

"Not as cold as Kazakhstan," he said, "but hopefully you'll adjust."

The black soil, a soil he'd carefully crafted to mimic the plant's native conditions but with extra nutrients, drank the water quickly. He made sure to flood the surface again, rotating the pot to give the biggest branch more space to elongate, worried about its teen stage. It could fruit, but its energy would deplete and the plant would not grow a sturdy branch structure. It could weaken, even die if a disease got in. Still, it was his best chance for producing Tengri apples.

He crouched down and removed a maroon leaf that dangled by a dried petiole, then brought his hands together, the branch between his palms. "Stay alive for me," he whispered, "people need you."

His phone rang.

Edo.

"I've news," he said.

"What did LaRoche say?"

"Well…"

"I mean, is it good news or bad news?" Andre said.

Edo let out a deep fluid groan, somewhere between worry and resignation. "Uh … just news. Meet me tomorrow in the Jardin des Plantes. Three o'clock at the labyrinth."

CHAPTER 3

On Tuesday, the sky threatened a thunderstorm, its clouds morphing from gauzy white to menacing pewter. Andre had gone to the Bois de Vincennes that morning to teach his plant identification class and, without time to change, arrived at the Jardin des Plantes in his canvas work pants, flannel shirt, waxed coat, and tool scabbards. His machete sat at his thigh, having hacked blackberry shrubs to get to native plants in a grove. Feeling too warmly dressed for the day, he unsnapped his coat, walking through the garden's courtyard of low trimmed boxwoods. They intertwined in a pattern that suddenly ended without logic. That irritated him. It was a botanical journey to nowhere, a design that didn't make sense.

Nor did it make sense that he and Edo were meeting at the Jardin des Plantes. Yes, AgroPolyTech partnered with the garden to do demonstrations. Oftentimes, graduates from the university even worked there, but it wasn't a place teachers or students visited for recreation. Why they weren't meeting at school perplexed him. Their offices were 30 feet from each other.

Along the main flowerbeds that led to the Natural History Museum, a dozen gardeners in green jackets worked, cutting away expired perennials. They collected stems and raked leaves into large piles on orange tarps. Visitors sat on benches along the paths, chatting, taking photos, playing with children. He caught a whiff of caramel popcorn then overheard an American couple discussing a nearby rose when he spotted Edo sitting on a bench outside the labyrinth, staring at a metal cupola whose weather vane spun wildly in all directions.

He was a Nigerian-born Frenchman with a tall lean frame and reassuring eyes. Yellow turtleneck sweater, dress pants, bald. His face seemed sculpted rather than born with high cheekbones and a long nose. Andre always thought he had a graceful way of moving, like a dancer.

"I was glad to hear from you," Andre said. "Why are we meeting here?"

Edo eyed the circular maze. "Because when I have a puzzle to solve, I often walk the labyrinth to think, to make a circle until I come to a conclusion."

"Why? What's going on?"

He lifted a hand at an *allée* of trees. "Come. Let's talk."

They headed into the more private shaded path. Edo's face contorted. "Madame Castel is very concerned about the expedition's outcome."

"Yes, she was clear about that at the meeting."

"So I called Monsieur Alba."

Castel's superior. "Ah. And what did he say?"

A cutting wind kicked up, bringing the smell of garbage to Andre's nose.

"Have you noticed today is the perfect temperature for growing an orchid?" Edo said. "Cold at night, then warming quickly with humidity during the day? The *Disa invertia* I had at university in Ibadan would adore a day like today."

"Edo, what about the contract?"

"Well," his eyes scanned a bed of irises weakly leaning into the shadows, out of bloom from the dark canopy. "What they want is *sakoso*."

They turned into the Allée Becquerel and passed the tall conservatory with its grand arched roof. Its bluish green windows rose in a geometric grid, almost as if it were a paneled, digital game in the soft openness of the walkways. "*C'est belle, n'est-*

ce pas?" he said. "This renovation has done the house wonders. Their team somehow created more space inside. Have you been there since it reopened?"

He was stalling. "I haven't had a chance," Andre said.

"It's amazing how with hard work, what was old can become better than new again."

"Edo—"

"Let's cross the esplanade."

They walked across the main courtyard, the sun heating Andre's face, the sudden wind cooling it. His phone vibrated. *Dad.* That was odd. It was six in the morning in California. Must have been a mistake. Sometimes his dad fell asleep with the phone on his lap. He silenced the call.

"The contract," Edo said, "required returning with a collection of edible apples."

They passed through the gate and into the Rue Buffon, Andre letting his fingers bump along the iron fence, its black pickets like the bars of a jail cell. They passed a brief patch of lawn, freshly mowed.

"Well, they sent us too late. We tried to..."

The smell of cut grass agitated his nose.

"Yes, I know. And I don't regret insisting you go. Directeur Bertrand is thrilled that one of our own was the first to document the tree. He liked your photos and report very much. He's already made an announcement to the local newspaper, which I disagreed with, but regardless... returning without apples has created new terms with LaRoche."

Andre's ankle throbbed with a faint pain.

"And now you and Nes," Edo said, "or in this case, you, must do what you can to make the partnership successful."

"Yes, of course, I tried. I mean, I will."

His heart beat fast. He inhaled a deep huff to calm down, told himself Edo still believed in him. They'd known each other for years. After Andre had graduated from Davis, he'd applied to teach during the summer at a horticulture program in England that Edo managed. Years later, when Andre published an article in a French journal about the outdated pruning techniques used

24

by Paris's parks department, it coincided with Edo's appointment as the horticulture program director at AgroPolyTech. The article had infuriated the mayor but impressed Edo. He wanted a teacher to pass on the latest thoughts on tree health and maintenance methods to students rather than avoid rattling the establishment. In fact, sometimes Andre suspected Edo liked to rattle the establishment in his own discreet way.

They arrived at a driveway marked "Allée René Jeannel." On the right, a modern four-story building stood, its plain façade resembling a medical clinic. To the left, a traditional apartment building rose, its windows facing the street. Across the driveway, a white iron gate. At the post, Edo punched in a code on the key pad. The gate slowly rolled aside. They went to a nearby trailer. A uniformed guard popped out, recognized Edo, and waved.

They walked along a bank of cedar trees and came to a fork in the drive. To the right was the clinic's rear, to the left, the driveway wove through a short stand of Leyland cypresses. At its end, a cluster of maples shaded a small parking lot and low brick building. At the left, a brief field with rows of crops stood with greenhouses lining the perimeter. The whole area smelled of manure.

"Is this part of the Jardin des Plantes?" Andre said.

"Yes, the growing field and offices. The workers call it 'L'Enclos Vert' or 'L'Enclos.'"

He searched his mind for a translation of what sounded like "Lawn-cloh." "The enclosure? Like a pen?"

"I think it's a nickname, a half-joke."

They ascended a few steps into the brick building. The room was a rectangular office with cheap gray wallboard and a few yellowing posters displaying the lavenders of Provence. It smelled of grass seed and lime grit. To the right was a doorway leading to a smaller office with three desks and a round table. Inside, people talked on phones and workers in boots signed paperwork. A fluorescent light on the ceiling blinked randomly. Out at the main counter, a man with bushy gray hair and a crumpled rain hat sat alone pecking on a computer. "*Bonjour,* Monsieur Bankole," he said.

"*Bonjour*," Edo said. In an extended overly polite explanation, Edo explained they'd received permission to survey "S2." The older man listened as he peered, seemingly mystified, at the computer. With a sidewise glance, he examined Andre, an aggressive frown stuck on his face, a frown Edo didn't seem to notice. After Edo signed a document, the man mumbled, "It's difficult to access, try the vent panel in the rear."

They went outside and into the field, walking past rows of witch hazel and shaved firethorn. In a patch of dirt, a pair of soiled leather gloves lay beside a broken pitchfork. To Andre's left, two hoop houses, covered in translucent plastic, held dozens of *buxus* shrubs, all emitting the usual urine scent. Before him, on the field's far end, two broad greenhouses stood and rising behind, the stairwell side of a six-story apartment building, bland and modern in the gray light.

They paused at the first greenhouse, a placard over the door: S1. Edo pursed his lips as if dissatisfied with its clean appearance. The expression slipped into an odd slump, almost pitying, directed at Andre.

"What is it?"

"Andre, LaRoche wants us to produce Tengri trees, but they're concerned, now that we're only grafting, that the Tengri material we do have will be as close to one hundred percent successful as it can be."

Andre smiled a faint smile. "It's never one hundred percent."

"Yes," he said, "but they don't understand plant production as we do."

Edo surveyed the greenhouse. It was a rectangular post-and-rafter frame, some twenty by sixty feet. Corrugated, fiberglass windows. Through them, Andre saw foggy images of baskets: ivy, red-berries, pansies. They hung from beams and sat on tables, each attached to its own slim watering hose. He guessed they were the holiday baskets to be installed on the Jardin's lamps in a couple of weeks.

"Andre," Edo said, "they want to grow the trees under cover."

"Under cover?" he said. "In a hoophouse?"

"Well, a greenhouse."

"Greenhouse? You can't be serious."

Growing any apple tree in a greenhouse would be difficult, let alone Tengri trees, which had never been cultivated. It wasn't impossible, commercial growers did it, but Andre had always imagined he'd be growing the trees in a field with irrigation where they'd receive ample chill hours and easy natural pollination from bees.

"It's not optimal, I know," Edo said.

"Not optimal? It's a set up to fail."

"Not for you."

Edo's settled mouth told Andre he was serious. Very serious.

"But there's a much higher chance a disease could damage the trees."

"I discussed all disadvantages with them. And yet there may be some advantages."

"They have to remain cold still, after they're grafted."

"Exactly, and a cooling system will do that more precisely."

Cooling system? He looked back at the field. "Can't I plant them over here, outside?"

"No, they are set on doing it indoors. They want a private, secure facility."

"A secure facility?"

"Yes. It's important, as you can understand."

"Are they worried about corporate competition?"

"Among other things."

Andre stepped around in a frustrated circle. Growing in a house meant succinct climate control and close monitoring for pests. The incidence of disease would be much higher. Scab. What about scab? Apples didn't want to grow inside, they liked the open air, they liked the cold. Kazakhstan, their homeland, was cold.

"And so, what?" he said. "You've brought me here because they want me to grow trees in this house after the baskets are installed?"

Edo set a hand on Andre's shoulder. "No, I'm sorry, they don't."

He led him to the farthest corner where stalls of gravel and sand and a small shed sat. There, another greenhouse of similar size stood dented and grimy with a faded placard over the door: S2. Rusty screws sat half-cocked in the metal frame's holes. Virginia Creeper had crawled over the west side and roof. Corners sagged with black mold. Roof panes hung precariously with various holes and cracks and the windows shown dull gray from dirt, especially toward the shadow of the apartment building. The entire pathetic structure sagged in a lonely silence.

"This is where you will grow the trees," Edo said.

"What?" Andre checked his face.

Edo's eyes shimmered with a strange solidity.

"This can't be real. This is ridiculous."

"I'm sorry. This is real."

The door laid more than hung against its hinges, covered by a thick blanket of ivy tangled with wild clematis tangled with Boston ivy. Tall sprouts of feverfew poked through a bramble of blackberry, leaves browning from the autumn cold.

Edo tugged at the vines. They didn't waver. "Let's try the vent panel at the rear."

They picked their way through dense brush to a side panel whose half-cracked condition allowed a view of the interior.

"I expected access and apparently we can't enter," Edo said. "But with a look, you can understand the space."

Inside, the room was large. High ceilings, rusted lights, damp scent of mildew. Wet mossy pads had grown in the corners of the concrete floor. A few gnarled metal tables sat awkwardly clumped together as if someone had hastily pushed them aside to carry something larger beyond. One was black with mold from rain that had leaked from a hole in the roof. At the back wall, clear plastic flopped down from a shoddy repair job. A window had broken and someone had tried to seal it. Now it crunched and shifted in the wind. Miraculously, there was no graffiti or rats.

"This is ridiculous," Andre said.

"It will need repairs."

He scoffed. "Repairs? It's a ruin." He stepped away, rubbing his eyes. "And there is no other greenhouse, no other space in all of Paris to use?"

"I'm sorry, no."

He waved a hand around as if he didn't know where to point or what to say next. "Why can't we grow them in the school field at the Bois de Vincennes?"

"Impossible," Edo said. "Urban Agriculture has been given a large grant to grow new greens there."

Hard to believe. Space at the school's suburban campus was always available. He looked at the ceiling, half-expecting to see a bird's nest in the rafters. "And they want a high success rate in that."

He peered through the broken panel, tried to imagine tidy trees growing in rectangular banks of soil. The room was certainly big enough to grow 60 or 70 trees but the work to restore it to a proper growing facility was outrageous. Not in his ten years as a grower, nor during the time he'd worked for his dad, had he ever faced a challenge like this. The more he thought about it, the more he resented LaRoche.

"You will have all winter to repair the house," Edo said.

"While I'm teaching?"

"Yes."

The one large drum fan had rusted. The watering system control panel was a model from 25 years ago. He ran a hand through his hair. *Crap.* "I can't possibly do all of these repairs myself."

"No, of course not, which is why I've secured a budget. You can hire the contractors you need."

"And what about when I'm teaching? I can't manage this *and* teach."

"It can be done."

"With what assistant?"

Edo was silent.

"I need an assistant."

"There is no budget for an assistant."

"Well, I can't be in two places at one time."

"I have managed several projects without an assistant."

He wanted to say, *Not everyone has a shiny new Kew facility*

29

either, but he didn't. Instead, he threw up his hands and said, "Look at this place." Anger roiled in his chest, heating him. The whole notion was an insult. LaRoche wanted to punish him. That they had suggested this garbage house felt like a personal slap. "Well, I ... I can't work in there. I can't do it."

His phone rang, startling him. *Dad, again. What was up?* Two phone calls in an hour.

"I'm sorry, do you mind if I take this?"

With arms folded, Edo said, "Please."

Andre wandered toward the field. The air had cooled with a low mass of clouds darkening the sky. Outside the poly tunnels, two gardeners leaned over a ride-on mower. The machine hood lay open as they discussed how to best fix the engine.

"What's up, Dad?"

"Andrzej, you busy?"

"Not too much, what's going on?"

"It's Mom."

"What about her? Is she okay?"

"Well..." his voice whiffed into the phone, "not exactly. I mean, yes. She's fine now, well, not fine but..."

"What happened, where is she?"

"Home. Home, *now*."

"What do you mean *now*? Where was she?"

"At the doctor. She fell and hit her head."

"Hit her head?"

"I wasn't home. I told her not to walk without me, but the mail came and she wanted to get it and—"

"Holy..." Their mailbox was at the end of a long, sloped drive-way.

"There was some bleeding and I didn't—"

"Bleeding?" Andre said.

"Yes, I didn't know what to do. She didn't want to go to the ER."

"Oh, Dad."

"I know, I know. Calm down. We're all fine. We went to the emergency room and I'm glad we did. She had a bump above her forehead."

He paced, scratched the scabs on his chin. "Is it big?"

"Yes, and there's a small cut."

"Is she there? Can I talk to her?"

"No. She's sleeping, finally. She didn't want me to call. She didn't want to worry you, but I figured your grandmother might mention it."

"Did the doctors say she'd be okay?"

The lawn mower rumbled to life, then sparked and died.

"Well, they're worried about infection," Oskar said.

"Oh, God."

"Don't worry. She's okay. But she has to stay put. She's always trying to get up, trying to walk, do her exercises without the therapist."

Andre rubbed an ear, pinched his forehead. She was like a slow-motion toddler. Always on the quiet move, in denial about her capabilities. "You need to tell her not to take any chances."

"I do. I do. But you know, she has a hard time not being able to do what she wants. Her spirits get low."

With the autumn days graying, Andre worried her mood would suffer. "How are they now?"

The lawn mower sputtered to life, the engine rumbling the air, smoke sprouting from the rear.

"Well, we've had a long cold spell and it's raining here. That's made her restless."

He imagined his father leaving for the orchard in the morning. Every weekday, for 30-odd years after his father left for work, his mother went to the same social services facility where she worked with depressed adults and teens. Now, she might slip into depression herself.

"Tell her to stay put," Andre said. "I'll call her. I'm in a meeting, but I'll call later. Don't let her get up without someone there."

Oskar's voice rang flat. "She won't. I took the rest of the week off."

Four days off during harvest season? *That's not good.* "Let's talk more later. I have to go."

He ended the call and hung his head in a hand. *Christ.* She couldn't afford to get injured. She could have hit her head and bled to death. Chills ran through his spine. *If she was only a little healthier, a little more able.* He exhaled at the sky, noticed a crow perched on the greenhouse's peak. Cold rain dripped on his face. Like melting glass, the house settled into the earth, slumped in the soil. The natural world with its weather and birds and brambles wanted to claim it. It could either sit here ignored for another twenty years or he could claim it. Take it. Use it for the Tengri. Breathe new life into the ruin so he could create new life inside.

Absently, he reached for his scabbard and pulled out the machete. With a quick hack, he sliced through thorny blackberry canes. The clean cut felt good, like an accomplishment. Then he hacked another, and another. The dried feverfew fell, the bindweed collapsed, thistle decapitated. With a few more frustrated hits, he cleared the tangle, reached the mat of ivy and clematis hiding the door. There he swiped down until an obvious crack ran through the greenery, grabbed the hacked ends and yanked hard. He ripped the woody strings until the door, half off its hinges, appeared in the clear. With a sure hand, he grabbed the rusted knob and swung open the metal panel. Dank air rushed his face. Mildew and mud covered the ruins of grimy tables and rotted wood. He stepped inside, breathing it all in, the foulness, the abandonment, the insult, and decided on determination, whispering, "You're not lost yet."

CHAPTER 4

A week later, Andre dove into the work of the greenhouse. He
dug out the bramble by the front door and leveled the soil. A
Jardin gardener offered lime grit to finish the area and he grate-
fully accepted. Inside, he cleared cobwebs and chipped away old
wasp nests. He hauled out the rusted metal tables and rotten
wood, tossed them in a pile that resembled the makings of a debris fire. A cleaning crew came and pressure-washed the house's
exterior and contractors installed new HVAC and irrigation systems. The units were state-of-the-art, Andre having made clear to
Edo and the LaRoche team that that's what was needed to make
the project "successful." He ordered automatic shades to close
over the ceiling panels to cool the trees and a handyman to hang
a security door. By the time, the electrician arrived to replace the
lights, he declined extending the system to the roof vents for an
alarm, his budget drained.

One night, he scrubbed the concrete floor with a deck brush,
getting on hands and knees to clean corners where moisture had
created swaths of mold and algae. He worked for the entire day,
taking a quick break to eat a baguette and cheese, before rins-
ing the concrete and repairing a deep gash in the corner. By ten
o'clock, he was about to wash up and leave when a text dinged
his phone.

Edo.

"Good news," it said. "You now have funds for an assistant. Bertrand approved a transfer in the budget."

Yes. He typed: "Will call Lucille right away."

A blank pause hung on the screen. "Lucille is already employed."

Lucille was the only assistant he wanted. The soft-spoken, reliable student with dreads and tattoos who'd helped him on his last two projects. She covered everything, never forgot the smallest detail, even foresaw what he needed. His ace.

He typed: "I need Lucille. Someone mature who can be discreet, handle whatever I ask."

"She took a job in restoration."

"Ugh."

"I'm certain you'll find another student," Edo wrote.

"We need to keep it private and secure. Young people can be flaky and like to gossip."

Rolling dots, and: "There are many responsible young people."

Doubt it. Andre wrote: "I'll contact her just in case."

"You must cast a wider net," Edo wrote.

Now, deep into the semester, most student workers were employed. "Impossible to find good people not already employed."

The dots on Edo's end, bobbed, then stopped, bobbed again. "Look beyond university. You know many hort folks? Former co-workers, colleague of Nestor's?"

Andre squeezed the bridge of his nose, slouching. Yes, he knew wholesale growers, he knew nursery owners, he knew restoration specialists, he even knew plant shop owners. Some people were in Paris but most were in rural locations. And they had staff who were already employed. He would have to fill out the lengthy job request paperwork through the university, post a listing, review resumes, interview candidates, wade through the clogged bureaucratic process, and as the holiday season approached. His spirit dropped like an egg to the floor. "All right, I'll submit a notice."

In mid-November, the assistant position posted in the university online system. A scattering of weak candidates replied.

They either offered limited hours or scant experience. Every day, after teaching class, he'd go through the resumes and conduct interviews. He met with slovenly students tardy to appointments, responsible students who weren't available in January, and other students who simply checked their phones too often during interviews. At one point, he'd thought he'd landed a strong prospect and offered the student the job only to have hopes dashed when the young man took a higher paying one. He phoned Nes and asked him for leads in Paris, of which he had none. Thereafter, Andre posted the job in a few community bulletins. The candidates were even worse, mostly waiters or taxi drivers with no horticultural experience.

On a Tuesday night, after helping a plumber clear the floor drain in the S2 house, he headed home, sweaty and exhausted, wondering if he should chance the position on a smart, but inexperienced, person. He passed Fleurs de Jazz, a flower shop that often stayed open late. A woman stepped outside. Gold hair, ponytail, slim, purse at her shoulder. She pulled a bouquet of twigs and holly from the stand. Mademoiselle Baranczka … *Renia*. But when she turned, he saw a sharper face, older, not Renia.

A drop of disappointment cooled his heart. Still, it gave him an idea. Wasn't there a woman who'd lost her job at Renia's shop? Yes. The Asian woman. A French biology student. *She* knew plants. Last August, after he'd stopped by to conduct the conference call with her and the lab about the second round of experiments on the *Saintpaulia* hybrid, she'd told him her boss had fired the woman unfairly, that she was an outstanding worker, and that after some temporary employment, she was again searching for work. *What was her name?* If he could hire someone like her, he could end this silly frustrating process before deliveries in January.

Should he call the shop? Or stop in? His stomach tightened. *Do you want to talk with Renia in person? Yes. Do you want to go tonight? No.* Why not tonight? *Not ready. What was there to be ready? Too tired. Not showered, in work clothes. I have to…* But as much as he tried to talk himself out of it, he talked himself into it. Did he like her? No, of course not. They were colleagues.

He'd helped her with the paperwork, been at the shop during the calls with the lab, but no more than that. He did find her attractive. Who wouldn't? And her passion for plants, it rivaled his own. He marched on. *You gave up on the idea a long time ago.* On that July visit, she'd been laughing with a man as Andre came in. A man in a gray suit and expensive watch, a banker or salesman type. *Probably a boyfriend. She's married by now. So? Less pressure, more reason to stop in and say hello.*

Instead, he went home and picked up Linus, snuggled with him on the couch and fell straight to sleep. The next morning, feeling clear-headed, he got up, his determination flickering into a steady flame. He showered and put on his favorite black button-down shirt, the shirt that fit him comfortably, but looked professional. He made sure to trim his nails and brush his teeth and not comb his hair too much so it got frizzy. Then, with his heart beating so hard he thought it might bust, he threw on his racer jacket and asked Linus to wish him luck.

Outside of Le Sanctuaire, the display had transformed from the purple and red dahlias of summer to autumn pumpkins and dried corn stalks and curly branches. A tiny bistro table held a plaid tablecloth, displaying a Victorian tea set and centerpiece of cabbage and mums. Fancy lady stuff. Some sort of violin concerto played on the outdoor speaker. Sad, but pretty. As he approached the door, he strained to see inside. It was a dim blur of leaves and wood edges and rustic artwork. Was she there? Or was it the older woman, the owner, today? No human form shifted amidst the amber lights and foliage. Only the fountain at the room's center trickled water from a stone goddess' urn.

The air smelled of leaves and moist soil and pear soap. The boldest plants like red cyclamen and dusky pink pansies stood at eye level and the more exotic houseplants with glossy paddles and odd fruits were tucked in corners under grow lamps. He thought it all arranged elegantly for those who wanted an escape into nature.

"*Allô?*" he called out. "*Mademoiselle?*"

Silence.

He moved around a cluster of statuary. On a table, a two-foot-high rendition of Rodin's *Je Suis Belle* caught his eye. His favorite piece. The woman's folded body, the bumps of her spine, cupped in the man's arms, his body arching back to heave her to the sky. The dramatic intimacy hypnotized him. Just as he reached out to touch the smooth stone, a child laughed.

Voices in the rear workroom. He wandered over. A pearly light washed through the doorway.

The rear lean-to was a long narrow space, bordered at the back and ceiling by windows, lined with a long counter and decorated with tropical plants. Several baskets with trailing vines hung over potted plants: prayer plants, peace lilies, iron plants, and a gigantic monstera, its large oval leaves crawling up the corner wall.

Just a few feet away, an elderly woman in a tan raincoat held the hand of a toddler, a little girl with fluffy coco hair and shimmering eyes wearing corduroy overalls. Crouching at the girl's eye level was Mademoiselle Baranczka in dark slacks and a cotton pink shirt, a delicate gold cross dangling from her neck. She handed the girl a small dragonfly of green and blue cloth, dangling from an elastic string. The girl yanked the string up and down so the toy bounced in the air. She smiled and sang out, "*Merci.*"

The woman in the coat reached for her purse. "How much?"

"Oh, no charge," Renia said. "It's yours to keep."

"Truly?" the girl said.

She nodded tenderly. "Of course."

The girl opened her arms and the two hugged, Renia's eyes skipping upward to Andre.

Feeling like a voyeur, he said, "*Excusez-moi,*" and backed up.

"*Ah, mai non,*" she said.

The woman in the coat expressed her thanks and said good-bye and nodded at Andre as she passed, a potted fern in one arm, the little girl in hand.

When the door's bell rang at their departure, Andre said in French, "Ah, excuse me. I didn't know you were busy—"

"Monsieur Damazy. Of course, not at all. We were finished."

Their eyes locked for a moment.

Seeming unsure what to do, she looked at her counter, an open bag of soil and half-potted plant, then simply held out a hand. "It's nice to see you again."

He took two strides and gently shook it. It was warm and delicate, like a newly hatched bird.

"It's nice to see you too," he said.

Her face unnerved him: emerald eyes, clear skin with a few freckles at the nose, hair like golden grass. Placid, but observant expression.

"So," she said, "How can I help you today?"

The sun bounced off her glossy ponytail and onto the plants surrounding her. The winding stems of a purple akebia, the chartreuse pothos, black oxalis, and the charcoal hosta he'd given her last spring. "Ah," he said, "I see you still have the hosta."

Her eyes flashed confusion.

He nodded at it.

"Oh. Yes. I love this plant." She went to the cornered windows and he followed. "The leaves are big and such dark purple. Very beautiful. Have you seen it bloom?"

"Bloom?" He couldn't recall. He'd grown another dark hosta, similar to this one though smaller in form. Vaguely he guessed the blooms were lavender but wasn't sure.

"The scent is so sweet," she said. "Last July, I had to close the door because customers kept inquiring about buying it."

He stared at the leaf's widely spaded shape, its corrugated texture, remembering how they had emerged with a dusty violet color. "It's one of the few that kept its color until frost."

Last January, when she'd brought him the hybrid *Saintpaulia*, she'd noticed it in the greenhouse atop AgroPolyTech. Her face had ignited. She praised it, pinpointed all of the reasons he thought it spectacular too. That made his heart burst. He had no choice but to give it to her.

Now, he was happy to see it thriving. "I'm still not sure of its hardiness," he said. "I haven't grown that many outside in ground soil."

"Well, this one will never touch the ground. I..." She stared at it, or was she staring at his hand, resting on the pot's edge? "It's precious to me."

Her eyes vibrated with an easy truth he'd never seen in a woman before. She existed neither to impress nor shun, only to exist as she was and let others do the same.

"Beautiful," he said, then realized he'd said the word aloud.

"I know, it is, isn't it?"

He smiled, relieved. She thought he'd meant the plant.

Her eyes shifted down in the awkward quiet.

"So, I've come to ask a favor," he said.

"Of course, what is it?"

Her Polish accent beneath the French words charmed every sentence she spoke.

"Your former assistant, uh, the biology student. Is she still looking for work?"

"Oh, Minh?"

"Yes. That's her name. I couldn't recall."

"No, she took a full-time position."

"Ah, yes." He clicked his tongue. "I thought it was too good to be true."

"To be true?"

"Oh, I need help, I..."

Crestfallen, he shifted in a circle, his heart shrinking. Where in the world would he look now? Nes again? No one would move from London to work part-time in Paris. "Shoot..."

Her eyes waited, tracking him like an unsure fox.

"I need help with a project," he said.

"A plant project?"

"Yes, I'm growing this apple tree; it's medicinal." He remembered waking in that tent in Kazakhstan, how serene his body had felt, how whole. "It really helps the body. In certain people, it has a positive effect in 24 hours."

"Oh, goodness."

"Yes, it's a wonder. And if I can create more, I can help ..." he thought of his mom, "people."

"Really?"

"Yes, well, some. People with conditions: asthma, arthritis, maybe even M.S. or stroke victims. They're just starting to see how it works with the immune system."

Outside the window, a magpie hopped from lower to upper branches in a tree.

"That sounds like it has great promise."

"Yeah," he said, "it could." *Am I disclosing too much?* "So, as you can understand, it needs security. We have a secure facility, but I need a helper who knows plants and who's responsible. Mature, you know? Because right now, it's not public, and it has to stay that way at least for another six months."

"Oh..."

"And the job pays. I mean, I'm offering above the usual rate but it's not that many hours. And interviewing students at AgroPolyTech, I haven't found one that matches my needs."

She nodded, her eyes the iridescent color of a hummingbird. *I'm yakking like a fool.*

She cleared her throat, folded her arms as if the conversation discomforted her. With a meekly inquisitive voice, she said, "How many hours does the job require?"

"About 15 to 20. Maybe five some days, three on other days, but the hours are flexible." He imagined himself hurrying from L'Enclos back to AgroPolyTech to get to class on time. "Although Tuesdays and Thursdays, at least in part, are a must because I'll be teaching."

Her expression settled like wet leaves on bare earth.

"What is it?" he said.

"I..." She shyly smiled, as if hiding an idea. "I can't promise, but..."

His heart chimed. "*You* couldn't ... could you?"

"Well, maybe. My hours here will be reduced after the holidays are finished. At least until spring."

Did she actually need the work? "Ah."

"This isn't a surprise, it happened last January as well. So..."

He broke into a smile. He imagined her reaction at seeing the white apples on the Tengri sapling. Her surprised face. "You would love this tree."

"And after all the help you gave me last year," she said, "I would like to return the favor."

A radiant light grew in his chest. "I'd be happy to have your help."

"But I'll need my boss's permission, which will be difficult."

"Of course," he said. Outside, the magpie, with its beak, flipped over leaves on the ground. "You already work here and of course that's the priority."

Her hand landed on his forearm, those slender fingers resting on his cuff, those pensive eyes brightening.

His pulse pounded at his wrist. *Can she feel that?*

"But I'll try," she said.

His face warmed.

"My boss," she shook her head, "she is like a lion, but," she shrugged with a shoulder, "some days, even lions are generous."

After their conversation, Andre walked to L'Enclos, feeling like a kite riding a wild wind. He'd gone to find an assistant and might end up with Renia herself. If it worked out, what a lucky break. Then again, if it didn't… He could only think about whether it might. The upsides. She knew plants and she knew him. He knew her, sort of. She was sensible, knowledgeable, strong, and more than anything, discreet. He knew that from her experience with the goons who'd tried to steal the *Saintpaulia* hybrid. Of course, she'd never told him the full story, just that two Russians had harassed her. Didn't matter, she and her smarts had outmaneuvered them. As he approached the S2 house, he clapped his hands, hoping with a sharp ache that it would work out.

That afternoon, he focused on the last work of the house, adding to the outside debris pile and sweeping up. He needed to prep the space for the carpenter who would deliver new tables in a week. He'd debated whether to order tables with metal frames and metal screens but decided on wood frames with metal screens. Wood could hold more weight and he hoped the trees would be heavy and robust by summer. He worked vigorously, tossing the last of the scrap onto the pile. Later, two students with a van pulled up. They helped load the lumber and pots and screening until all was packed up. By seven o'clock, Andre paid them cash and they drove off.

Drinking from a bottle of water, he watched their tail lights fade around the drive's curve, content to stand in the cold air since his body emitted heat. The sky had fully darkened. L'Enclos sat in a murky loneliness, save for the scattered, lit windows in the apartment stairwells bordering the yard. The office across the field sat like a squat possum, asleep in the grass. The parking lot, empty. The hoop houses stood closed and locked and useless on a winter night, waiting for spring. In the far distance, the steady hush of traffic rose from the busy indifferent city.

A thud boomed.

He checked the S2 house. The door, wedged open, showed the new lights, empty rectangular room, its scrubbed translucent panels.

More thudding. Steady and low.

It sounded like a ghost pounding a door to escape. Andre crept toward the thudding, rising from the house's left side. At the brick wall boundary, stalls of compost and gravel lay in individual stations separated by short, cinderblock walls. Beyond, a grassy path squeezed through a thicket of trees and shrubs to the yard's corner. There, an old shed stood.

Tin roof, shabby, about ten-by-ten feet wide with wood slat walls and a wooden door whose planks were rotted at the bottom. Flecks of paint hinted it may have once been white. Through the cracks in the boards and beneath the door, yellow light slipped. A large dead bolt lock warned people to stay out. But what things would one protect in such a sad little structure?

Moaning. A man's voice, mumbling.

Andre stopped. Listened. The pounding came from inside. Slowly, he approached, wondering if someone needed help, debating whether to call out.

"*Mon Dieu, mon Dieu,*" a man said, groaned in a low plea.

Andre inched closer.

"*Mon Dieu, mon Dieu … brûle en l'enfer!*"

Burn in hell? Andre blinked.

More thudding, as if the man stomped a foot on wood or pounded a fist.

Andre stepped to the door, his heart pounding. The night air chilled his neck, damp with sweat. He raised a hand, about to knock, when a fierce pounding startled him. The shack's walls trembled.

The man moaned.

He was either injured or insane. Either way, dangerous. But if he were injured and Andre walked away... he couldn't forgive himself.

"*Allô?*" he said.

Silence.

The cracks in the boards were too narrow to see through, the light too bright.

"*Allô?*" Andre knocked lightly on the door.

A chair, a bench, some wooden object suddenly slid against concrete.

Andre tried the doorknob. Locked.

The light went out. The slats, dark.

He backed up, his breath racing. He stared at the door, bracing himself, waiting for a person to emerge, but the door did not open.

In French, he said, "Is anyone there? Do you need help?"

Silence.

The whole area, the shed, the surrounding shrubs, sat in silence. To his right behind the greenhouse, the apartment building's windows glowed with weak utility lights. At the building's foot, beyond the cement wall bordering L'Enclos, was a parking garage entrance. Above it hung a red light that spun around whenever a car emerged, and a sign that said "Do Not Enter."

He gave the shed one last glance. It answered with a blank quiet. With a tight vigilance, he went back the S2 house.

Once inside, he closed the door and surveyed his to-do list. Last item: test the heating and cooling system. At the panel, he started the fans. Each one worked well. The louvered vents all opened. Satisfied, he grabbed a towel and wiped his face, deciding whoever was in the shed did not want to be disturbed. He tossed his tools in his leather bag and sorted through his new set of keys, then shut off the lights and went outside. As he locked the door, he debated whether to leave the light on for security, the one that hung over the newly scrubbed S2 sign, but decided against it. Nothing was inside yet. So, he turned to head home.

A man.

He jumped.

Old man. In overalls and oiled coat. Three feet away. The gardener Andre had seen on the first day with Edo. Thick frame, gnarled hands. His gray beard was long, almost too long to be practical, but not unlike beards Andre had seen on other men in the industry. Low-set eyebrows and a strong Roman nose, a bold face one might see on an angry king in a Romantic painting. His gray hair shot out in tufts from under a rumpled, canvas hat whose string must have broken and been lost years ago. The knees of his pants had faded from ground-in dirt. He held, in his gloved hands, a crowbar.

"Were you...?" Andre said and pointed to the shed.

"We will need a key to this facility."

Andre eyed the crowbar. "What? Why?"

"All managers must have keys."

"But... I thought Manu was the manager." Manu was a younger guy Andre had met the day before. He'd introduced himself as the grounds manager.

"I named Manu the manager, but I am the true manager."

Andre swallowed. *True manager?* The man stood like a sawed-off stump. Clearly in his late sixties but no frail chicken.

"I will give Manu a key in the morning," Andre said.

"You will give *me* a key now."

Irritated, he licked his lips and lied. "I don't have a copy."

"This is unacceptable."

Andre weighed walking around him. The man's eyes tracked his face. They were alert, unyielding. Andre had never been in a physical fight and wasn't about to start one now. "I'm Andre Damazy, I don't think we've met."

Suspicious stare.

"I need to leave," he said.

"You, nor any other guests of the Jardin des Plantes, a member of the covenant of the French parks system, in the city of Paris, France, do not have the right to break regulation. You must understand this. It's the law. If you do not give me a key, the director will ask for your vacancy."

Whoa. Recited straight from the bylaws, he guessed. Andre considered the options: tell the old fool off, kill him with kindness, confront him about his behavior in the shed, or just hand him a key. "I assure you, I'll resolve this with Manu straight away in the morning." He took three broad steps around the old man, watching him from the corner of his eye. When he didn't feel a crowbar hit his shoulder, he relaxed and mumbled, "first thing tomorrow," then hurried toward the driveway and its welcoming shadows.

CHAPTER 5

The next Tuesday, Andre taught his propagation class at the "high farm." On the roof of the university building, a small urban farm with raised beds, shed, and greenhouse provided hands-on training for students. It was where Andre taught most of his classes and conducted his own research. Despite the windy conditions and biting cold in winter, he'd created every successful hybridization experiment he'd ever done there: a lavender broccoli, mild chili pepper, longer lasting pole beans, dwarf onions. He'd even developed several unique ornamentals that lived inside the greenhouse, including his proudest success, a fully pink-leafed kiwi. Not only did he work in that small greenhouse, he read there, ate there, took appointments, puttered with plants, and generally hid away from the rush of school life.

After the propagation class, another teacher had reserved the rooftop greenhouse so he headed to his office to grade papers. In the tight box of a room, his desk faced the wall, back-to-back with his officemate Thierry Cloutier. At the office's rear, a casement window faced a dreary utility shaft. In the deep eastern sill, Andre had managed to grow a prayer plant and South African onion while Cloutier had grown decorative grasses in angular geometric pots.

Their desks were a study in contrast. Andre's bulletin board was jammed with notes, business cards, and photos. A bumper sticker of Plant Releaf hung beside a postcard of his grandparents' vineyard in Sonoma. Cloutier's board held one staff extensions list, neatly tacked with four pins of the same color. On Andre's desk, amidst the school assignments and department memos, was a collection of pencil erasers shaped like flowers, cacti, and trees students had given him. A rickety low lab stool doubled as a visitor's chair. One white orchid sat on Cloutier's otherwise empty desk and to the right, a framed photo of a desert garden in Dubai hung on the wall.

Cloutier taught landscape architecture for urban spaces, and worked with city governments and large corporations. He had the charismatic flair and important contacts built over two decades of working with high-profile politicians. Now, the chunky man in business pants and silk tie reclined with feet crossed on the desk, talking on the phone. His thick hair was tamed by gel so it sloped like an upward rollercoaster off his forehead. He wore a pinky ring and an oversized gold watch.

"*Voila, c'est ça!*" he said. His voice stung with a sharp reediness. Silence. He rattled off a quick efficient explanation about why decorative grasses were the ideal choice for a reflecting pool. Listened for a moment. "*Voilà, c'est ça!*"

Andre pulled out his chair, bumping Cloutier's.

They both lifted a hand in apology.

As Andre sat down and opened his book bag, Edo appeared in the doorway. "Do you have a minute?"

"*Oui, oui,*" Cloutier said. "*Voilà, c'est ça! Oui.*"

"Sure," Andre said. He rolled back, bumped Cloutier's chair.

They both lifted a hand in apology.

Once in the hallway with the door closed, he almost rolled his eyes, remembered Edo had mentioned Cloutier's reputation had saved the horticulture department a decade ago because of high-profile donations. "What's up?"

"I need you to sub for Fabron next semester."

He cocked his head. "A fourth class to teach?"

"No. I've removed Identification, Propagation, and Native

Plants. This is basic Botany. The only class for which you will be expected to deliver grades. It's a Tuesday and Thursday schedule."

"I guess I can swing that."

From behind the door, Cloutier's voice chimed. "*Voila, c'est ça!*"

"Have you found a candidate for the assistant position?" Edo said.

"Maybe. She's checking with her boss to see if she can fit it in."

"Her boss?"

"Yes. She's employed."

"How is this possible?"

"She's not working full hours in January. Do you remember Mademoiselle Baranczka from the plant shop?"

Edo's face was a blank.

"With that rare *Saintpaulia* hybrid, from last year? She'd initially called you about it."

"Ah, yes, yes. That was an interesting specimen. Well, if you are able, bring her on board sooner rather than later."

"I will."

"*Voila, c'est ça!*"

Edo turned to leave.

"Hey, I have a question. You know Manu? Is he the manager of the Jardin des Plantes crew?"

"Yes, why?"

"And that older man, the one with the gray beard. He's not the manager, right?"

"Brodeur? No, he is no longer a manager. What happened was—"

Andre's phone dinged. He checked it, smiled. "That's her."

"Her?"

"Renia."

"Renia Baranczka."

"That shopkeeper is truly interested in this job?"

"I think so."

Edo's eyes lowered, his lips curled at the edge. "Just keep it discreet, and professional."

"Oh, of course. This isn't—"

"Put Botany on your calendar," he said and walked away.

"*Voila, c'est ça!*"

Andre checked Renia's text. She said, "I'm available."

He clenched a fist. *Yes.* Typed: "Great. Let's talk and I'll fill you in on details. When are you available to meet?"

A long pause. A pulsing dot bounced over and over.

"This evening or Thursday morning."

He gulped. *Tonight?* He rubbed his mouth, paced a little. In what, six hours? That was soon. *Bring her on board sooner rather than later.* "This evening it is," he wrote, "seven, eight?"

Bouncing dots.

"Seven-thirty. At the university?"

His breath quickened. Seven, nearly dinner time. Was now a chance to invite her for dinner? No. This was work, about work. *Keep it professional.* He typed: "See you at seven-thirty."

He opened the door, hoping Cloutier would be gone by then. He had nowhere else to talk with Renia.

His office mate sat on the window sill, dress shoes bumping the radiator cover. With a snap, he said, "*Ciao,*" and ended his call. "Ah, Andre. I'm wondering if I might borrow your chair and stool tonight? I'm finalizing a presentation with two students this evening."

The library was too quiet. Classrooms, often occupied. The basement lab might seem creepy and the rooftop greenhouse had a class. So, he decided to meet Renia at the school café. It was inside the tropical conservatory, a glasshouse in the central courtyard of AgroPolytech, not a completely private space but not completely public either. As he entered, moist warm air hit his face. He went around the central rockery and its shushing waterfall, passed the brief counter and kitchen where a cook laid out cuts of meat on baguette slices. He wove through the palms and bromeliads. Ferns and mosses dotted the basalt edging the pond. Though the tables were hidden in the greenery, he found Renia, reading a book in the corner, camouflaged by a banana plant and bird of paradise. He thought her gray sweater blended nicely with the smooth ficus trunk behind. Her book's title slanted away from eyeshot, the toe of her dress boot bouncing, a silver ring with an amber gem on her middle finger, catching the light.

"An interesting read?" he asked.

49

She looked up, her eyes filled with the dream of the page's words.

He squeezed into the opposite chair, nestled in the leaves of a date palm, which seemed to lean far over his head as if eavesdropping.

"Yes." She held the book to display the cover. *The Rare Trees of Africa.*

"Ah," he said, jazzed at the choice. "I've read this. It's wonderful. Very comprehensive. And it reminds me, Edo, our director, started an experiment ten years ago with the Baylay Tree."

Her face broke into a surprised smile. "They talk about that tree in this book."

"Yes."

"There are stories of it enhancing fertility."

"Yes," he said.

"And the tree," she said, her eyes widening, "it's so unusual in form. Very narrow leaves. Blue. Wispy like clouds. I haven't seen anything like it."

He smiled. "Yes, I know it well." The leaves were like long skinny threads, so ghostly and ethereal. To see her excitement boosted his excitement.

"It's beautiful in such a unique way," she said.

"Exactly. It is. I've seen them. Not in the wild but… at the school facility, in the Bois de Vincennes. Edo grows a stand of them, well, hybrids anyway. But they have that pretty crown. Perfectly oval and yet somehow weeping. I can…" He thought of the trees at the edge of the Vincennes facility, fenced off with no public access, almost a forest now. "I can show you sometime."

Her eyes sparked. "I would love to see the tree."

That is, if Edo was okay with it. "I would love to show it to you."

She blinked, seemed to realize where she was and shifted in her seat.

He was leaning forward, hard, on the table, so he relaxed and glanced around for students who might recognize him. Thankfully, the only nearby diners were two graduate students he didn't know, involved in a conversation, behind a red tail flower.

"Do you want something to eat?" he said.

They went to the counter. He ordered a sandwich, she, the soup. When he paid, she protested, but he assured her he'd expense it. Then, as they ate, he awkwardly smiled and said he didn't know what questions to ask because he knew she was experienced and reliable and all of the qualities he needed for the project. And so, they wandered into a personal discussion of her childhood in Poland and his Polish-American family and how his father and her uncle fostered their passions for plants. By almost nine o'clock, they noticed kitchen workers washing pots and pans.

"We've forgotten to talk about this project," she said with a smirk.

"Yes, well..." He opened his laptop, which had sat closed on the table. "We have five minutes. I'll show you what we'll be doing."

The room felt self-consciously quiet without voices, only the rush of the waterfall masked their conversation. A café worker started turning over chairs and setting them on tables.

Andre wondered if he knew the worker. *Had she ever been his student?* He didn't think so, but then again...

"Well," he said, "here are the schematics for the production. It's..."

He waited as the woman moved to a table behind the water-fall.

"Sorry, we're trying to be discreet." He lowered his voice. "The company funding this wants it to kept quiet. And to be honest, so do I. It's... I'm afraid word has already gotten out through the school newspaper and other... sources." The idea that the dean had spread the word as well through that careless announce-ment worried him.

She didn't smile or swallow or even nod, remained steady. "I see. What is your security situation?"

"Oh, uh."

"Is your door made of thick material? Does it lock?"

"Yes, I ordered the heaviest one I could find with a lock."

"Ah, good. We don't want the trees vulnerable to theft."

"Yes. Vulnerable." He imagined his mother. The fall. He had to call his dad soon. Check on them. In a whispered tap, he said, "They..." he imagined the sapling, on his roof deck, standing in the open outside. Anyone with a ladder could climb up there and take it. "They all need a safe place to grow."

Slowly, she scanned the room, checking the kitchen, the counter, the tables, searching for eavesdroppers. It seemed she knew to check every crevice. "If these are the circumstances," she said, her tone business-like, "then perhaps we should plan a list of precautions to keep it safe."

"Yes." Relief mixed with surprise washed over him. "I've already started one right here."

Later, as they walked into the main floor lounge, he checked his phone, noticed it was almost ten o'clock, and offered to walk her home. She brushed off the offer, saying her apartment was too far but that she didn't mind taking the metro. He insisted on fetching her a taxi. After she was tucked inside and he'd paid the driver and tipped him to ensure he'd wait until she entered her building, he shook her hand. She smiled with a tender affection that sent shivers through his chest. As the taxi pulled away, he stood there like a fool, gazing at the back of her head before remembering where he was and going in the building. He tapped up the stairs, whistling lightly, his heart bursting like a ripe tomato. Renia would work with him on the Tengri. *God, the conversation couldn't have gone better.* They had so much in common. And she thought about the project exactly as he did. He mulled over her interest. Whether the encouraging expression was politeness or attraction, he didn't care. The bottom line was he had a reason to see her again.

Upstairs, the faculty corridor, with its carpet and dim lights, sat in a mute seclusion. Everyone had gone home. As he passed through the reception area, he smelled the faint scent of printer ink. Behind the office manager's desk, the postal cubbies stood. A dense pack of mail blasted from his box. Of course. He couldn't remember the last time he'd checked it, maybe right after his return from Kazakhstan. While most of the wood compartments held a lone envelope or stray memo, his contained a bulge of mailers, catalogs, and paper, so he grabbed the pile and took it to his office.

He plunked down in his desk chair and sorted. Two seed catalogs, press releases from botanical organizations, a survey, irrigation supply ad, and on and on. In a mechanical motion, he went through each piece, setting what he wanted on the desk, tossing what he didn't need in the recycling box. There was an ad for a non-profit that harvested homeowners' produce for the homeless. A bulbs catalog. Paperwork from the university for his medical visits. He came across a plain envelope, letter size, addressed simply to "Andre Damazy, AgroPolyTechnique University, Paris, France." He thought it was a note from a prospective student. Sometimes people wrote if interested in a horticulture career. But it was postmarked from Brittany, no return address. He stuck a finger inside to tear the flap.

A rectangular card fell out, an index card, the kind for flash cards or recipes. In faded letters, as if someone had used an old typewriter, it read in English: "Monsieur Damazy, you work at a university and you live alone, so maybe no one has told you what you are doing is wrong. You think you're special, about to create a new apple, but others have spent an entire lifetime to learn it's wrong to tinker with nature. Don't pretend you can improve perfection. You must stop this despicable experiment. If you don't, we will stop it for you. We are watching you—with many eyes. *Per mortem, salutis.*"

CHAPTER 6

Andre read the note again and again, checked the back as if other, more informative words might appear. "…you work at a university and live alone." How did the sender know that? Someone had indeed watched him, or researched him. He tamped down the alarm he felt at seeing the words "we are watching you —with many eyes." How many was "many?" And who were they? That old gardener, Brodeur? He rubbed his forehead, trying to think logically, suppressing alarm. The Tengri was a "despicable experiment." He wanted to reason with the person, explain he wasn't out to "improve perfection," just wanted to help. But what really disturbed him was the phrase, *per mortem, salutis*. A phrase he'd seen before but couldn't remember where: *Through death, salvation.*

Was that a coded threat? Whose death? *His?* He picked at the scabs on his forearm. And how had they discovered the Tengri project? Of course, the person hadn't mentioned the apple's name. They'd simply called it a "new apple." That ruled out anyone in his immediate circle. That circle was small anyway: Nes, Samal, Vlad, Edo, Monique Castel, her boss Monsieur Alba, and now Renia. That was it. Wait, Directeur Bertrand knew too. He'd announced it publicly but no news outlets had seemed interested. He scratched his head, his mind churning with worry.

Outside the door, the silent hallway unnerved him. "We will stop it for you." Somehow the gossip floating around school had spread. Was it the newspaper article? He searched through the mail and his papers for the school paper, couldn't locate it. As he remembered, they did question whether he was searching for a "new apple." He had let that slip when talking with a student one afternoon.

The time on his phone said ten-thirty. *Call Edo? Too late.* He had to get home. Was Linus outside? Yes. He stuck the note in his bag and sprung from his chair, making sure to lock the door.

The next morning, he called Edo. No answer. He tried the house phone and his wife answered. She said he'd arranged a rescue, so Andre wrote the address and headed to the metro. In the 7th arrondissement, he found an ornate monolith on the Rue du Bac. It had large plentiful windows and elaborate cement work from the Beaux Arts era. He went through the driveway tunnel underneath and came into a courtyard. Its four ancient walls, decorated with reliefs of leaves and grapes amidst woven iron railings encircled a dusty construction zone. Broken concrete chunks and hacked shrubs lay scattered. In the corner, a hunk of tree branches and root balls sat beside neat stacks of brick. Two mounds of dirt and gravel stood like sentinels at either side of a circular fountain. A statue of a Roman god held a spear. The god had been shut off and bubble-wrapped from head to toe.

In the north corner, near what seemed like a demolished, raised planting area was a long-bed tow truck. On it lay three twenty-foot araucaria trees. Two African men wrapped the scaly branches in swaths of burlap. Another African man, tall in a straw hat stood nearby, his dress pants tucked into rubber boots, his black slicker glossy from the morning rain. He frowned at an electronic tablet, pressing multiple buttons as if it wouldn't cooperate.

"Edo..." Andre said.

He looked up.

"Your wife told me where you were."

His eyes were unsurprised. "Is there a problem?"

One of the workmen called to Edo in Yoruba and Edo answered, gesturing to a block of rope atop the hood of a compact truck.

"Where are these going?" Andre said.

"Monaco," he said, his eyes on the workmen. "Fortunately, I found a home for them, but, unfortunately, these men are inexperienced with tree transport. It must travel on the highway."

"Take a look at this." Andre handed him the card.

His eyes moved across the words. And again. He turned the card over. "Where did this come from?"

"Brittany."

"Brittany," he mused. "How peculiar." He rubbed his chin.

"What do you make of it?"

"Hmm. It seems someone has discovered the Tengri project."

"But who?"

"I'm not sure yet."

"What do you mean yet? Do you have an idea?"

Edo handed him the card. "Well... I'm not certain."

"You're not certain?" That Edo wasn't surprised, almost expected this, made Andre's breath quiver. "Should I be worried?"

"Perhaps. Maybe... somewhat."

"Somewhat? Why? What do you know?"

The workmen were tying the burlap. He called out in Yoruba, frustrated.

Andre said, "Are we growing the Tengri at the L'Enclos facility for more than just privacy?"

"So to speak. LaRoche prefers not to garner any negative publicity."

"Negative publicity?"

"They are concerned about the news becoming public before they're ready."

Well, it's public now. "You told me it was corporate competition. Is there something else?"

He was quiet, eyeing the workers at the truck.

"Edo."

"It's nothing for you to be concerned with."

"Edo, I'm growing the damn things."

56

His boss pivoted. His body shadowed Andre. In a low steady voice, he said, "Last spring, during the initial clinical trial, one subject was convinced he'd been poisoned and pursued LaRoche Naturel legally in admitting this."

"Poisoned?"

"He was not poisoned, of course. There was no poison. But you know how apple seeds contain cyanide? It seems with the Tengri a certain level of the toxin, combined with the cytopro... cytopro, what is it? I can't remember, but that which boosts white blood cells. This man didn't understand this. He was convinced he'd been poisoned. He and LaRoche went back and forth until he sat down with their researchers and they explained the science. When his blood test came back normal from his own doctor, he dropped it. But before that, he threatened to go public with a what-do-you-call-it, a smear campaign."

"A smear campaign?"

"Yes, but all parties settled the conflict."

"You mean, like with attorneys – and money?"

"I'm not entirely certain what was involved. There was a non-disclosure agreement. I don't think he has broken that agreement, but that's what I have to investigate. If this note is his, he would be breaking his agreement."

Andre chewed his lip. "Nes never mentioned the guy."

"I don't think he knew. Madame Castel simply emphasized the point during the negotiations she and I had."

Andre paced in a circle. "Why didn't you tell me before?"

Edo motioned to the workers, to wind the burlap down the trunks. "Because it wasn't necessary for you to know. Now it is."

Andre stared at the note. It didn't mention anything about the first trial or poison or being harmed by the apple previously. It simply accused Andre of behaving immorally. "Is that why you wouldn't let me work at the Vincennes campus? Is that why you chose the greenhouse in L'Enclos?"

"We need to take precautions."

"I'm going to the police."

"And I didn't want to alarm you."

"I'm going to the police."

Edo caught his arm. "I'd rather you didn't. No crime has been committed, Andre."

"But this is a threat," he said. "In writing. In Latin it says, 'Death through salvation.'"

A worker came around the truck bed to tie down the root ball.

Edo led them toward the corner. "Andre, the sender does not specify exactly what action he, or she, will take, and until this person does, we cannot act..."

Andre tapped the note against his palm. "I can't believe someone wants to stop the production of a fruit that helps you get well."

Edo's face relaxed into sympathy. "Sometimes people are suspicious of what's new. They don't trust it. And some might consider the Tengri... freakish."

"It's not freakish."

"The apples are white, Andre."

He'd always thought the unusual color was its most beautiful quality.

"Alors," Edo said, "I will research more on the test subject's background—as much as I can without drawing attention. But the last thing we need is for LaRoche to discover this and panic. They would have no trouble voiding the contract and sending another botanist to obtain Tengri tissue."

"Hah, well, they don't know where—"

"In the meantime," Edo leaned over, "I urge you to carefully consider your next steps. And above all," he waved a finger, "don't lose your nigboya."

"Nigboya?"

"Bravery."

After his meeting with Edo, Andre walked the streets aimlessly. Convinced he had to at least leave a record of the note, he went to the Préfecture. Inside the bright station, a police officer, a middle-aged woman, took him to her desk, which was decorated with a framed drawing of a watchful, wide-eyed owl in a tree, the moon glowing through eerie clouds. She examined the note, squinting at the faded letters, waving a magnifying glass over the blank areas. Before filling out a report, she asked a few questions about where and when and how he'd received the note. As they talked, it was clear she was more interested in his background than the anonymous note or what any of its words might imply.

"So, you were born in America, but you live here," she said. "Do you have family here?"

"Yes, my aunt and uncle and two cousins."

She studied the envelope, held it up as if she might see a secret code in the light.

"Any relatives in Brittany?"

"No, they're all in Bordeaux, except my one cousin. She's in Paris."

"No, distant cousins you don't get along with or something?"

"Don't think so. My other cousin is in Bordeaux."

"No ex-wife who may not want you to succeed in your job?"

"No, no ex-wife," he said. He and his last girlfriend, Claire, had faded apart a year ago, after she'd moved to Ireland. Neither held lingering regrets.

"And no family in Brittany? You're certain?"

Her eyes reminded him of an alert squirrel, listening with a frozen stance.

"Not that I know of."

"Ever vacation on the coasts?"

"No."

"No distant friendships? Someone from there that you might have met during a summer? Someone you didn't get along with during a vacation?"

He searched his mind. One boy who went out with his cousin Delphine had disliked him because he was American, but that had been at least ten years ago, in Bordeaux.

"Well," she leaned into her chair, folding her arms, revealing a bracelet that said, "Vivons chaque instant." It was either tarnished or antiqued purposely, Andre wasn't sure. "You might want to double check with your family about the Brittany connection. We often find things like this are linked to one's past actions."

Andre left the police station with his head hanging, his hands in his jacket pockets, a hard rock of guilt in his heart. One's past actions. His past actions in California hadn't been perfect. In fact, terrible. Ever since he'd left there, he'd made it his private goal to always help others, be kind, neutralize disputes at work or among friends. Yes, he'd failed in California and that failure had burrowed in his heart like a scrawny mole. It bit at him from time to time. But he didn't have enemies. At least he didn't think so. He took a breath, trying to exhale the tension, and turned to walk up the Rue Geoffrey Saint-Hilaire. *Give yourself a break. You work hard. You haven't screwed up since. Your closest friend shared the biggest discovery of his life with you. Because you're a good person. You're not a coward. And you're not going to blow it this time.*

He took out his phone and called his dad. "Does our family know anyone in Brittany?"

"Andrzej?"

"Yes, do we know anyone in Brittany?"

"No, I don't think so."

"We don't have any French relatives there?"

"No, your mother has a great aunt in Nantes...."

"Really?"

"Yes, but that's not really Brittany, is it?"

A woman in high-heeled shoes teetered across the street, carrying a child, two bags of groceries, and a hefty purse on her shoulder. The child played with a yellow plastic duck.

"What about Mom or Mémé?" His mom and grandmother and all French aunts and uncles had been born the children of a Bordeaux vintner. He didn't think they had any connection to Brittany.

"I can ask them," his dad said.

"Does Mémé know we went to find apples in Kazakhstan?"

"Your grandmother? I think so."

He closed his eyes. *Hell.*

"It does in involve her daughter," his dad said.

No, it didn't. Well, yes, a bit. The idea that his grandmother knew about the Tengri unnerved him. She was on the local

Rotary board, the Sonoma County Arts Commission Board, the Northern California Vinters Assocation Board, a Southwest Business Consortium, not to mention her church, that rigid church. Everyone knew her. Her network of elderly rich people stretched all across California. "Why did you tell her?"

"She wanted to know why you were on an expedition."

"And who told her?"

His voice softened. "I'm afraid your mother did."

He swallowed. Great.

"So, I was thinking about that apple tree, being high on the hill. Unprotected like that. I'll bet it had the sturdiest trunk you'd ever seen," his dad said. "Survivors like that grow strong without help around."

He smiled. His father. Oskar. Only he had pride in a tree's strength. He was a simple, working-class Pole from a family of simple, working-class Poles, most of whom had been skilled workers in San Francisco. His dad's choice to be an orchardist was a way of escaping a career as a plumber or contractor. Then in a practical next choice, he'd married the daughter of a long-established vintner in Sonoma Valley, becoming wealthy enough to invest and grow his orchard business. But later came payback: a son who was an indoor science nerd. As a child, Andre liked to slice plant stems open and explore their inner workings. He loved to dissect seeds as they sprouted. By eleven, he was already grafting plants to create new ones. His father took great pride in teaching him how to chop wood and repair machinery, but Andre's most satisfying accomplishment had been crossing two salvias to create a third whose purple bloom was so dark, it seemed black. Now, that Andre found such a strong apple tree made his dad shine with pride.

"Are you there?" Oskar said.

"Yeah, I'm here. The trunk was sturdy. For sure. The apples weren't in such great shape but the tree was healthy."

A limp depression settled on his shoulders. Andre is doing brilliantly overseas. Andre's a professor at the agriculture university in Paris. What his father said to his friends, his family, to his colleagues.

"So, how's Mom?"

Behind him, two women marched against the wind, one pressing her sweater closed, one struggling to flatten her hair from flying wildly in the wind.

"Well," Oskar said, "she's better. Healed completely from that fall. Now she's working on lighting a lighter. She has to roll the wheel and light the flame. She can almost do it. But getting back to the tree project... are you still the principal horticulturalist?"

His heart beat faster. "Yes, yes, don't worry."

His father's breath whiffed into the phone, fell into a gravelly acquiescence. "Well, I'm sure this project will be a success, I'm sure of it." He spoke reassuring words with an empty tone. "Not like... I'm sure it will be a success."

Andre picked at the last scab on his chin. Not like that other project.

"Dad, you know what, my battery is running low. Can you ask Mémé if she knows anyone in Brittany?"

"Sure, sure."

"Thanks," he said and killed the connection.

That other project. In California, when he was seventeen. They were dwarf pomegranate shrubs. The fruit shiny, red, the size of small baseballs. The seeds were as sweet as sugar with a spicy aftertaste, which made them unusual, and marketable. When Oskar ate them for the first time, he gasped at their taste, literally slapped Andre on the back, then cupped his chin. "My boy," he'd said, "you need to show your mother."

His mother, fully well before the stroke, already ate pomegranates for the health benefits. She bit into the seeds and laughed in delight, her smile lifting at both sides. She tossed a seed up and caught in her mouth, tap danced a little. "When can I buy some?" Andre had even swung by Jason's house with a clamped excitement, ready to show him what he'd been instrumental in creating, considered giving him a percentage of the income, but whenever he stopped by, his mom, Teri, said Jason was playing darts at a bar or racing cars or catching up on his sleep.

On Sundays, Andre sold pints of the fruit and small bottles of juice at the orchard's stand in the Santa Rosa farmer's market. They became popular and customers raved. Soon, a regular customer, an older man from Stockton, offered to bring the Zeus pomegranate to a chain of organic grocery stores. He was a buyer for Green Valley Distributers. Andre would have to deliver fruit regularly but confident he could, signed a contract with nervous delight. His father and mother were skeptical. "I thought they were just for fun," his mom had said.

"I'm growing a plant that's never been grown before. Totally on my own, Mom."

As the weeks went on, the pressure intensified. He had a contract to produce dozens of pounds of pomegranates. Twelve stores were expecting big sweet 'Zeus.' One store bought six bottles of juice every week. He had no patent. No formal growing operation, no crew. But he managed to fulfill orders by himself until some of the fruit ripened too quickly. Just when they'd arrive at stores, the skin would split. A few weren't as sweet as others. Within two months, the friendliness of the distributor evaporated. He called often, wanting specific updates on the progress until he threatened to break the contract, which of course, a month after the funeral, he did.

Now, years later in Paris as he walked home, he worried about another potential implosion, before he'd created one tree. He zipped his jacket against the wind, noticing a street sign that said Interdit! Iron fencing topped with spikes. Ancient cracked stone, a crumbling shutter, a roaring lion in cement. Over the years, he'd convinced himself that living in France was better than living in the valleys of Sonoma with its small-minded people and sweltering weather. He didn't mind it. He was of French descent after all. And Delphine was here. Her family, his family. He'd achieved a fair amount of professional success. Still, after all these years, when in a market, restaurant, or friend's home for dinner, the sight of a plain red pomegranate reminded him why he'd moved to Europe in the first place, and it stung.

He took the building stairs two at a time, anxious to get to his apartment. Once inside, he tossed the keys on the kitchen counter and picked up a meowing Linus, thankful Edo had chosen L'Enclos. LaRoche Naturel might have offered their own facility . outside of Orléans but that disgruntled test subject probably knew the facility and Edo, with his usual foresight, considered that. At L'Enclos, Edo could keep an eye on the project. It was far from the busy, more public, school facilities in the Bois de Vincennes, hidden in plain sight in Paris, locked behind a wall and watched by a guard, impossible to know about unless you worked at the Jardin des Plantes or lived in one of the few adjacent buildings. As safe as safe was.

Still, the crazy old gardener. Andre wondered if he was one of the "many eyes." Possibly. Otherwise, why had he been at work into the evening the other night?

In the living room, he cracked open a beer and sat down, the sapling in view outside the deck door. On his coffee table, a slab of salvaged molding with a glass top, a scattering of work lay: the project notebook, his budget, receipts, even the book that had led to this dream. Five Continents by Nikolai Vavilov. He'd found it at a rare bookstore one afternoon years ago. It traced how the first apple trees had evolved in Kazakhstan. Now, his heart surged at having the opportunity to add to that history.

The family photo, him, his parents, grandmother, lay amidst the mess, reminding him he might fail. You won't. He rubbed his eyes, focused on the image of his mother. She crouched at the fireplace in a winter sweater, one arm around his dad's waist, another holding a wine glass, her body leaning in as if she'd dashed over for the photo at the last minute. You're doing it for her. If some unfeeling fool with a typewriter wanted to destroy his work, then by God, let him try. If an insane duffer or ignorant test participant wanted to fight him, let them try. He'd be right there, ready, now and for months. No, Dad, this won't be like last time. He wouldn't fail. It wouldn't go to hell. With that, he got up and went to the buffet drawer where he stored dead batteries, bits of wire, burnt candles, and old scraps of reminder notes, laid the photo on the detritus of his life, and slid the drawer shut.

WINTER

CHAPTER 7

A few weeks later, the holidays appeared in Andre's life like an unwelcomed visitor. Eager to get through them and start grafting trees, he avoided the jet-lagged journey to California and caught a ride with his cousin Delphine and her boyfriend Charles to his aunt and uncle's house in Bordeaux. On Christmas Eve, Delphine and Charles announced their engagement, delighting her parents and spawning a last-minute party for New Year's Day. Andre enjoyed the time off enough, visiting friends from childhood summer vacations and helping his uncle repair a fence, but yearned to get back to Linus and the Tengri sapling.

On the first Monday after the new year, he went in early to get his employee paperwork in order and put Renia's name on the gate's security list. At the office, Manu sat on the building stoop, writing on a clipboard. He was a broad-shouldered Spanish-Frenchmen whose blocky, even smile and groomed black hair seemed like it could lead him to television if his horticulture career fell through. He often cracked wise with colleagues and worked late. Andre explained to him his strange run-in with the old gardener who'd insisted on obtaining a key to the S2 greenhouse.

Manu rolled his eyes and said, "He doesn't need a key, but I'll make him one."

"I didn't catch his name," Andre said.

"Albert Brodeur," he said. "He was head manager for eighteen years. Now, he works part-time, mostly for companionship."

A grump wants companionship?

"He's strange, but he's reliable," Manu said. "He was injured a few years ago in the garden when a branch he was cutting cracked and hit his head."

"Wow. No hard hat?"

"Yes, but somehow it fell off and he suffered a concussion. He hasn't been the same since."

As he opened his mouth to ask what "the same" meant, a gardener in the field called to Manu. Andre waved a quick thanks and headed to the greenhouse.

His phone rang.

An "Unknown" call.

He answered.

Silence.

"*J'écoute,*" he said. "*J'écoute.*"

Silence.

He hit the End button and blinked, wondering whether the call was a solicitation or an intended sign.

On Tuesday, Andre woke before his alarm, excited about taking the sapling to the S2 greenhouse. Now, after weeks, the house waited, repaired and ready. The HVAC system worked instantly, the fans spun smoothly, lights were bright, and sprinklers sprayed with strong pressure. Even the tables, rimmed by well-constructed wood, were clean and neatly arranged in rows. As he crossed the field at L'Enclos, he waved to a passing gardener, then unlocked the giant deadbolt on the security door, whistling. The house welcomed him with its vast space, its optimistic light, its clean wood counter along the wall, a glossy stainless-steel sink. He set his bag on the counter and the sapling on the nearest table, feeling an odd angst. It was too soon to put the plant in the smaller interior room where he'd grow select trees for fruit. Too far from the main work area. So, he kept it nearby and unpacked containers and mixing potting soil.

Later, at about ten o'clock, as he finished hanging a clock on the wall, he saw the outline of a person through the translucent walls. They coasted on a bike toward the S2 house, hopped off, and walked out of view. Soon, they heard a soft knock on the door.

He froze.

Renia. She was here. He tiptoed down the ladder, quietly set his screwdriver on the counter, and paced in a circle, running a hand through his hair. *What to do, what to do...*

Open it, stupid.

He set a hand on the knob, wiped his face, and opened the door.

She stood with a lowered head and cautious smile, wearing black jeans and a purple flannel shirt, gray jean jacket, and green Doc Marten boots. The sunlight glinted off a jeweled bobby pin in her hair as if sending a silent code of flashes, a code hiding a secret intentional message.

"*Salut,*" she said. Her voice padded softly at his ears, her slim hand resting on the strap of her bag. It was a large sack made of burlap and fabric whose central panel displayed a black tulip. He wondered if she'd sewn it herself.

He invited her in and she moved like a cat walking a narrow ledge, her face vigilant but self-possessed, her eyes, unafraid but observant.

Unsure what to say, he blurted, "I'm glad you're here."

"I'm happy to help." Her eyes shifted around the room, landing on the sapling. "Is this the Tengri?" Her gaze followed the length of its gangly branches, especially a new shoot that had crossed through the others.

He stood there, lost in her pure expectant face. Its fair edges and puckered mouth reminded him Fiaschi's sculpture, white marble, "Bust of a Young Woman."

"What? Oh yes," he said. "This is it."

"What a teenager," she said. "All limbs."

"Yes, it really is."

She inspected the tips, the bark. "Did it have fruit when you found it?"

"Yes. Well, it had. There were two expired apples on the ground."

Her mouth dropped in a smile. "It produced fruit already? You must be excited by this."

He nodded loosely, blinking like an idiot. "Yeah. I am."

"And what was the soil like there? Were you able to conduct a test?"

"The soil? Well, I couldn't conduct a test, I..." *How much to tell? I fell off a hill. Sprained my ankle.* "I couldn't, but my friend did. And we..."

Her eyes landed on the faint scars by his brow.

His train of thought evaporated. "We found..."

"And so, do we need to create that mix in this container? Or perhaps you've done it."

"I have. I've been... here." The door to the interior room stood wedged open. "I'll show you the fruiting room. The plan is to grow ten specimens for fruit for another clinical trial."

"Ah, yes, I remember."

"The other trees we'll grow for better structure and later fruiting. It's not ideal, of course, to grow apples this year, but we have to. Our patrons expect it so..."

She peeked in the smaller room where eight empty tables stood. "And so, these fruiting trees must be monitored more closely."

"Exactly," he said. "It's sort of an incubator. A dedicated space for the babies. We don't want to push them too hard or um, they may get too..."

"Weak? And maybe catch some disease?"

"Yes."

"And become ill. You don't want to lose any, I'm sure."

His voice was breathy. She already understood. "Yes."

They were quiet.

"Will you keep the sapling from Kazakhstan here as well?" she said. "The little appling you rescued?"

He smiled. *Appling.* He liked that, a made-up word. "Yes. It's

68

the appling's best chance."

"Of course. It and the others will be like tiny chicks in a nest. Very delicate and relying on us for their care."

"Yes, the sapling in particular, I mean appling. It'll be far from the main room."

"Oh. Does the door lock?"

"Just the outer one."

"If we put a padlock on the handle, then no one can push the handle down and open the door to this chick's nest."

"That's a good idea."

Her gaze skipped from the louvered windows to the fans to the ceiling vents. "These openings are small, but desperate people can be crafty. Do you have an alarm system?"

"Afraid not."

She eyed his knotted hands, her face softening. "Well, you will check when you're here and I will check when I'm here and together we'll take care of all the babies in the Chick's Nest."

"The Chick's Nest, yes." He hesitated, then said, "Does that make me a rooster and you a hen?"

Her face lit in a warm smile.

That was dumb.

"Ah, this reminds me." She unhooked her bag and opened it. "I brought a box of latex gloves, two soil thermometers, some alcohol wipes, and this, in case it's needed."

She pulled out a digital thermostat. "It comes with an app so you can check the temperature on a phone when you're not here. Then, if the electricity goes out from a storm or something like this, the device will alert you."

He examined the package. The brand was his favorite. He'd installed two digital thermostats, but neither had a remote app. "Wow, thanks."

"My uncle," she said, "he owns a perennial nursery. He finds them quite useful."

"This looks great, I've been thinking about getting one."

His eyes met hers.

She shyly smiled.

"It seems you've brought all I needed," he said, but he

wasn't referring to gloves or wipes or a sophisticated thermostat. He wasn't referring to any object at all.

They dove into the work of the day. They sterilized dozens of containers. Sixty-five in all. Then when he mentioned setting the pots on the tables to dry, she arranged each one with a foot of space between for maximum drying and minimum bacteria, as he would have arranged them himself. Next, they talked growing mix, deciding on soil percentages, he showing her the math he'd done in his notebook, she looking over his shoulder, offering a small suggestion about bone meal. When they'd finalized the best mix, they broke for lunch, deciding to get out bags of soil and peat and all else afterward. He offered to buy them lunch on the project budget, but she assured him she'd brought her own, so he reluctantly left for some kind of takeout, feeling guilty that he wouldn't return with anything for her, then feeling anxious that she might interpret a free lunch as flirtatious. Ultimately, he decided to grab a savory crepe and eat at the stand so she wouldn't be on her own, and perhaps lonely, for too long.

His instincts were spot on. Later, when he returned, he found Brodeur inside the greenhouse, in dirty overalls and soiled hands, pointing at Renia, lecturing loudly. He held a hefty bottle of plant food in his arms, as he listed the reasons for securing supplies and storing them properly.

Renia politely listened, unafraid to make eye contact with the brute though she braced her arms around herself.

"What's going on?" Andre said.

Brodeur's face hardened.

Renia's melted in apology. "Nothing to worry about," she said. "Monsieur Brodeur was introducing me to the way supplies are stored here at L'Enclos."

"L'Enclos Vert," he corrected.

"L'Enclos Vert," she said. "He believes it's much safer to store supplies in the outdoor storage house."

"It's not just safe, it's regulation," he said in a stern snap. His bushy eyebrows wrinkled. "She's not very experienced in such practices."

Renia stared at the Tengri appling, as if waiting through his words.

"Her name is Renia," Andre said. He made introductions, deciding to divulge her last name at the last second. If Brodeur didn't appreciate her non-French name, that was his problem.

"Regardless, you both need to practice keeping supplies properly secured in the storage house," Brodeur said.

A miffed irritation surged in Andre's chest. *The 'storage house?"* He meant his old shed. "Normally, we might," he said, forcing his voice to sound stable, "but we need this often for our project."

Brodeur cocked his head, seemingly irritated. "I don't care how often you need it. This is what's required by the parks system."

"Yes, but it's not volatile. It's natural. And once open, fish emulsion might attract pests. It's better stored here. We can put it under the counter, out of the aisles and—"

"All of the amendments for this or any other project must be put in the storage house," Brodeur said. His tone deepened, his mouth crinkled. "That is the rule."

"Monsieur," Renia said, "we're concerned our supplies may be used by others and we're on a limited budget."

"You can store it apart from the other fertilizers."

"But Professeur Damazy paid for it. It's not part of the garden's supplies If it's mistaken for a..."

Brodeur shook his head in a violent snap.

Andre lifted a hand. "Okay, we'll leave it in the storage house. But I'll need frequent access to it, sometimes in the evening when neither you or the staff are here."

"Manu is here until the evening on most days," he said.

"But I'll be here on Sundays."

His face crumpled. Andre guessed Brodeur hadn't expected him to do such a coarse thing as work on a Sunday.

"So, *I'll* need a key as well, to the storage house."

The old man's head twittered. "This is impossible. We cannot make you a copy of the key."

"You can't or you won't?"

"It's against regulation."

He exhaled. Brodeur thought it okay to have a key to Andre's greenhouse with its expensive equipment and precious stock, but Andre couldn't have a key to his crumbling old shed. *Ridiculous.*

"Well, then I'll need your home number so I can call you on Sundays and you can meet me here and open the storage house."

A smirk slipped onto Renia's face.

Brodeur scoffed. He glanced at Andre, then Renia, then Andre, then Renia's sparkly hair pin.

"The shed will be locked on Sundays. You, nor any other *guests* of the Jardin des Plantes, a member of the covenant of the French parks system, in the city of Paris, France, will not have special access. It is against regulation."

He turned to leave, the bottle still in his arms, then stopped. "And, what's more, your repairman insisted I move my vehicle because he couldn't access a panel. We store the cart and trailer behind the greenhouses every night. Is that clear?"

Andre suppressed an exasperated look. "Oh. Okay. Yes."

"I don't answer to a repairman or any of those scoundrels. He doesn't know how to do carpentry any better than I do, and yet he charges outrageous prices. No, I won't. I won't stand for it."

"I don't expect you to."

"And I must have a key to this facility. If you do not provide one, I will request one through Emmanuel."

"The key is already in process."

"Good." With that, Brodeur stomped out. Andre gently closed the door, leaned on it, letting his body relax into the cool metal.

"I can speak to him when he's calmer," Renia said.

"You don't need to bother with that."

"I don't mind."

"Well, if you really want to, but be careful. He's like a pile of kindling beside a roaring fireplace."

That night, Andre locked the door to the S2 house, exhausted. After lunch, he and Renia had sanitized all of the tables and counters and tools before going over the growing schedule and responsibilities. They'd numbered 63 pots with white marker. They hadn't encountered Brodeur after the initial meeting, but Andre still had no solution to accessing the old shed on weekends. So, he went in the office and found Manu at his desk, tapping out numbers on a calculator, and asked about a getting a key to the storage house. Manu agreed to make a copy, but because it was on garden property, he'd need a formal request from the university. "It might take a while."

"I'll get one," Andre said.

Once outside, he texted Edo, his fingers hovering over the letters, about to snidely mention that the silly shed might collapse at any moment but decided against it. *Keep it professional.* As he put his phone in his pocket and crossed the field, he noticed another short drive off to the right where a small garage stood. Inside were jackets and equipment and tools. Yet Brodeur went in the smaller shed at least three times a day. Andre often saw his stout body and crumpled hat walk along the translucent walls. Renia even mentioned she'd noticed he'd stayed inside on one visit for 25 minutes.

Renia. My God. Was he putting her at risk? If many eyes were watching him, were they watching her as well? And how? *Per mortem salutis.* Death, salvation. He shivered. *Don't worry.* Buildings and trees completely encircled L'Enclos. Only one gated drive led in and out. There was a security guard. Of course, behind the Brodeur's shed, there was a grassy path. *Where did that lead?*

As he walked in the dark to the gate, he watched for people. Empty. In the field, a lone lamp illuminated the grass, casting a sickly glow on a container of white pansies and black grass. The apartment building windows threw a dim greasy light on the driveway, the conifers along it casting exaggerated shadows. Far off, beyond the gate, the Rue Buffon lay brightly lit and active with cars and people though the security office stood dark and abandoned. The guard, Moussa, was done for the day. At the keypad, he punched in the code and the gate rumbled open like an irritated bear. What was the use of a security guard who didn't work in the evening? Anyone could hop the gate and get in. Even harassers who wrote threatening notes. He reassured himself that he'd only been sent the one note. Still, there were those silent phone calls: one that day, three previously. From an unknown number. With a tired body and even more tired mind, he headed home, deciding not to worry about it. The note incident was a fluke, he told himself, like a weed that shot seed and would die soon.

CHAPTER 8

A week later on Wednesday, the rootstock trees arrived at L'Enclos. He helped the delivery driver unload dozens of tall boxes that held banded apple saplings of the same genus and species as the Tengri, which Andre hoped would help pollinate the flowers. With a branch graft, the scions from Kazakhstan would hopefully meld to these high-yielding dwarves and produce white apples. *Hopefully.*

After inspecting the branches and roots and deciding all looked healthy, he got out his tools, eager for the solitude of the work ahead. First, he cleared the counter, hooked his bag by the door, and potted up the trees with soil, clustering a few at his feet like children listening to a story. He spaced out the other trees on the tables, trembling with excitement at how the room, with its woody stars, had transformed into a grower's greenhouse. His hands shook at the idea of making mistakes while grafting. It had to be done with precise attention. A few slipped cuts and he'd lose apples. Every grafted tree needed to survive.

He found his wax block and coffee cup warmer and washed his hands. Though it was related to *Malus sieversii*, no one had grafted the Tengri, so there was no research to consult. No failures to learn from. He was creating the history, right there, at the age of thirty-three in Paris—a history that would birth a fierce new cultivar or a failed dead experiment.

He inhaled a worried breath and exhaled centered air, then whipped off his racer jacket, washed his hands again, and got out the new grafting knife he'd bought just for this. He rubbed it thoroughly with an alcohol wipe, cleaned his pruners, and took the first scion branch in hand.

Thin, delicate, its wood still golden. *Okay, this is it.* With his pruners, he trimmed it and with the knife, carefully sliced the branch's end to a flat sloping point. On the rootstock tree, he sliced the branch's end. Inside, its tissue was white, as supple as a caterpillar. Gently he spread the branch apart and wedged the Tengri scion into the V, as male to female anatomy, making sure the buds were above the graft line. When he was satisfied all was straight and snug, he wrapped the connection with grafting tape and painted it with wax to hold in moisture.

LaRoche Naturel wanted apples by next fall. He and Edo had promised thirty, though privately they agreed if all went well, they could probably produce more. So, he grafted carefully into the evening, focusing on that precious wood, forgetting he'd missed lunch as the gray day outside faded to an inky night. His stomach growled. He ignored it, dipping his brush in the hot wax of the coffee cup to paint the last graft seal. *Almost done.*

In a sudden drip, wax hit his knuckle. Ouch. A burning sensation. He blew on it. Edo had once told him a story about how a vengeful tribal chief in Nigeria had harassed his parents when he'd been a boy. The chief had set fire to his parents' pineapple crop because they'd made too much money. He'd wanted in on the profits. "Those experiences," Edo had said, "taught me never to panic but always plan for the worst."

With that in mind, Andre examined every waxed seal and re-waxed one he thought might be loose, then washed his tools and ate a few crackers. His phone rang. He dug it out of his bag by the door.

Delphine. His cousin. He hadn't seen her since the holidays. She usually called on weekends, sometimes up to three times if she was in the mood to pressure him into being social. It was as if she thought his introverted nature was like a tough piece of candy you had to bite into and crunch in order to enjoy the soft core.

As he answered, he remembered he'd agreed to meet her and Charles in the Marais for dinner. "I'm working late. Sorry, I can't make it tonight."

"What? Oh, too bad. We're going to a new sushi place." Her voice bounced like a small brightly colored, rubber ball.

"Yeah, I have to finish here."

"Do you want to go dancing later?"

He half-smiled. She often urged him to come out for late-night concerts or dancing or even gallery openings. Probably because she was seven years younger than he and liked to actually spend time with people. He liked to spend time with plants. "No, too tired tonight."

"Are you alone in that big drafty greenhouse?"

"Well, it's not that drafty, but yes."

"That's creepy. Is it safe?"

He smiled at the question, imagining her friendly face. Button nose, wide slash for a mouth, sharp mahogany eyes always focused and watching in an expectant, almost childlike manner. Her chocolate hair, medium length in a long bob, was as straightforward as her speaking style.

"I'm fine," he said. "I won't be too late."

The lights went dark.

That's weird. His eyes adjusted to the dim. The tables stood like large gray nests, the door a ghostly portal. Beyond the walls, a vague light glowed from the lamp in the field. Nearby, the shadow of a tree branch formed a jagged silhouette.

"That was odd," he said.

"What?"

"The lights just went out."

"Really?"

He listened. Outside, no voices, no car engines, no buzz of equipment, nothing.

"Who's there?" she said.

"What do you mean? No one's here. I'm here."

"Are you sure you're alone?"

Am I? "I think so." He cracked the door and peeked out. The field's grass shone as a coarse yellow, as if dried, in the lamplight. All was still and quiet. The two hoop houses sat like cresting whales in the grass. *Is Brodeur still about?*

"The lamp in the field is on," he said.

"Should we come by?"

"No, it's okay. But I have to go out there and figure out what broke."

"Don't go *outside*."

"Why?"

"Well, there might be someone out there."

"I'll be fine."

"Andre—"

"I'll call you back." He tapped the red dot, chewing his lip, and checked his bag for a flashlight. The lamps burst on. White fluorescence illuminated the house.

Strange.

His bag wiggled on the hook, slightly creaking. He pushed it. The lights went off. He took the bag from the hook and saw the switch, frowned, and tapped it. The lights went on. He put his bag on the floor, sighing at the silly worry he'd felt.

In the white luminescence, his phone rang.

He answered. "My bag was on the switch. It's fine."

Silence.

"Delphine?" he said.

Silence.

"Delphine? Allô?"

No one replied.

That night, Andre dreamt about the sapling. He sat in a train with it between his feet on the floor. Outside, a mountainous countryside rolled by. Quaint villages with white houses and brown roofs and magenta geraniums. A man in a gray business suit sat across from him, reading a newspaper. "I'm taking this to a lab in Switzerland to be studied," he said. The window's lower panel was open and wind blew at the sapling. Its leaves flattened in the breeze. Andre got up and slid the panel shut, but once he sat down, the man in the suit opened the window and read his newspaper. Andre got up and closed the window. They exchanged the action three times. Finally, the man rolled up his newspaper and with a pinched mouth, as if the sapling had insulted him, hit the tree until its leaves fell off.

He woke in a hot sweat, his heart pounding, pushing away the fur at his arm, forgetting Linus lay curled at his shoulder. The cat chirped, jumped off the bed. He sat up and wiped his neck with a hand, went to the kitchen and splashed cold water on his face. Outside, the faintest light of dawn brightened the roof deck. On it, his potted shrubs and conifers stood in a loose circle, protecting an empty space. *Where's the sapling?*

Relax, it's at the greenhouse.

He got dressed and ate breakfast, waiting for the clock to hit eight. Once it did, he called Nes, who he knew left for the nursery around then. As Andre gathered his jacket and bag and keys, he gave Nes a not-too-coherent update on the anonymous note and Brodeur and the pressure he felt from LaRoche Naturel. Nes listened with short responses, the sounds of a roaring bus and clanging metal in the background. As Andre pet Linus and locked up the apartment, he thought cheery Nes would smooth over the situation. He usually did.

Instead, he roughed it up.

"Well, all of that nonsense with the old codger and LaRoche, to hell with that," Nes said.

"Right," Andre said.

"But this with the note. This is not good news, mate."

"Well, no," he tapped down the stairs. A tiny ant roamed in a lost circle at the corner. "But nothing's come of it for weeks."

"It's not a good sign."

"No? Well, yes, I know that." Andre said.

"No, I mean bad. As in really bad."

He thought of the silent calls. "I know."

"I don't think you do."

"I do." *More than phone calls?* "Wait, what are you talking about?"

"Do you remember Jack Mahone's email?"

Jack Mahone was an East Coast nurseryman they both knew, Nes better.

"I remember Jack," Andre said. "Not an email."

"He sent us an email last spring with a link to an article about a grower he knew who was vandalized in Oregon."

Andre stopped, his hand on the railing, the triangular stairs spiraling down in a vertiginous drop. "Vandalized?"

"At the university there. Some blokes sprayed two acres of apricots with glyphosate."

"Two *acres*?"

"Right."

"Why would anyone do that?"

"A panic about hybridizing."

"What?"

"Yeah, I know. All of a sudden someone reads a blog and decides it's bloody time to take action. The papers called it eco-terrorism. There was a phrase spray-painted on a wall, but no one seemed to know what it meant."

"A phrase?"

"Yeah."

"What was the phrase?"

"I don't remember."

"Was it *per mortem salutis*?"

"Was it what now?"

"A Latin phrase."

"Latin? Don't think so."

"Oh."

In the foyer, the mail woman cranked the lock shut on his mailbox, offering a side glance as she left. He paused, worried about its contents, reached to the box's brass panel, then lowered his hand. "Not now," he mumbled.

"What?"

"Nothing."

He rubbed his fingers together, got courage, and unlocked the box. One electric bill. He shoved it in his bag and went outside.

The air shocked his face with a chill, the smell of tar hitting his nose.

"Well, the researcher," Nes said, "Lisa... Lisa Wright or Wight, told the press she was mystified because the damn project was done to study allergy treatments."

"Really?"

"Yeah, can't remember the name of the tree variety."

"What a loss."

"Yeah, to say the least."

Soon, the scent of roses floated out. He approached Fleurs de Jazz. A chalkboard with a price list in pink cursive stood beside a bin of bouquets in water. Cut, red roses perfumed the air on one side of the door, a pot of live daisies reeked on the other. The daisies were nestled amidst antique objects: a flecked tin pitcher, an old child's bike, a wooden pelican, a rusty birdcage. "I'll bet LaRoche knows about that incident."

"I'm sure they do. It was in the Euro press. I'll bet they're worried someone's going to damage the Tengris."

Andre slowed, paced between the white daisies and red roses. Live daisies, cut roses. Live, cut. Live, cut. *What about the guy from the clinical trial?* Finally, he walked on.

"Listen, mate," Nes said, "if I were you, I'd get a big lock and put it on that greenhouse. A big one."

"You really think I could be targeted?"

"Well, it wasn't your mum who sent a threat."

His mother. *My God. What's going on with her?* They hadn't talked since New Year's Day.

"*Crap.* This is exactly what I *don't* need," Andre said.

Edo had never found the troublesome man from LaRoche's trial. He couldn't locate his whereabouts online. He might have if he had contacted Monique Castel, but he hadn't wanted to ring any alarms. "Do you think a test subject would leak information to a newspaper? Edo mentioned something about a disgruntled guy from the first trial."

"No one mentioned it to me, but it could happen, I suppose. The guy probably talked to a friend, a sister, an aunt who knows? Maybe wrote about it online. Rumors leak, that's for damn sure."

They talked more about the note, the Latin phrase, and how he'd received a string of anonymous calls until he arrived at L'En-

clos. Moussa, the guard, hadn't started his shift, so
Andre punched in the code and headed down the driveway. As he
rounded the shady curve, Brodeur drove toward him in the utility
cart, his hat low on his forehead. Andre waved. Brodeur passed,
meeting his eyes but not waving, his hands solidly on the steering
wheel.

As he approached the S2 house, he thanked God he'd sprung
for the more expensive steel door and hidden hinges. A sturdy
deadbolt.

"Well, I'm not going to worry about it for now," he said. "This
a good project, it's about helping others. If some people can't understand that, that's their problem."

"That's exactly what Lisa Wright told the press from the hospital."

"Oh, God. She was in the hospital?"

"Yeah, it seems these clowns took it upon themselves to stab
her in the stomach—three times."

CHAPTER 9

A ndre hurried to L'Enclos, feeling crumbled and anxious. He checked the street, checked the people passing by. Did an ecoterrorist send that note? How did they find out? *Rumors leak, that's for damn sure.* Nes was right. But most eco-terrorists didn't send anonymous threats. They were proud of their actions. Whoever they were, at least they didn't know where the trees were being grown. They knew Andre worked at AgroPolytech and they knew his cell phone number, but that was it. As he approached L'Enclos, he eyed the nearby apartments. How many people lived up there? And who could gain access to the buildings? He picked at a loose cuticle at his nail. Well, at least this guy didn't know what he looked like. He kept a low profile online, didn't submit portrait photos when publishing in journals. Although there was that one photo, his official school portrait from the website, blurry and from a distance.

At the field, a gardener mowed the lawn. Two workers trimmed potted topiary shrubs outside the hoophouses. Were those topiaries spears? No, fleur-de-lis. A woman pulled a small magnolia on a wagon to the office where another drank a cup of coffee and talked on the phone. All seemed usual. Beyond the field, the two greenhouses gently reflected the morning sun.

Vapor curled up from the roofs. The temperature was warming. Someone had noticed that because they left the S2 house door open for air. *The S2 house. That's my house. It's* open.

He leapt forward, stopped. A diesel truck roared to a stop before him like a giant rhino blocking his view. Startled, he searched for a way around the gray box. The truck revved again, backed up a few feet, squeaked to a stop. A man called out in French, "Can't see..."

He jogged in a wide arc around the truck's hood. "That's not the basket house." The house door, the heavy solid security door was wide open, propped ajar with a wooden wedge.

What in hell?

Inside, the greenhouse was empty. No one about. The grafted trees stood in diagonal lines on the tables, as he'd left them. Delicate, helpless. And the appling? The door to the Chick's Nest was shut, but the main door... open like a friendly invitation for anyone to enter. *We will stop it for you.* As he struggled to kick the wedge from under the door, the wind gusted. His hair obscured his sight. *Who did this?* He kicked the wedge, kicked harder. Finally, the wood spun loose and the door fell shut into stillness. Inside, leaves, grass clippings, even dirt was scattered on the floor. He swore and checked the Chick's Nest. The ten fruiting saplings and one appling stood on tables, potted, leaves intact, watering spikes in soil, all untouched.

He let go a breath of gratitude, whispered, "Time to buy a padlock."

Later, after he'd swept up and checked the trees for insects, he went to find Manu. Outside, by the larger garage, he and Brodeur crouched over a workbench. Manu wiped the end of a metal framework with a rag, maybe a trellis, then held it steady while Brodeur flicked on a blowtorch and soldered what looked like a joint. He didn't wear a face shield or safety glasses. Wasn't *that* against regulation? Andre waited for them to finish, the smoke of charred metal billowing. After Brodeur shut off the torch, Andre excused the interruption and asked about the open door.

Brodeur's face collapsed as if Andre had blared an inappropriate remark. "I didn't go anywhere near the S2 house."

Manu shook his head a little, staring off toward the greenhouses. "How long has it been open?"

"I don't know. It was open when I got here."

"That's strange. I didn't see anyone around this morning. Natalie was here, but we were working together."

An awkward silence hung.

"I'm certain I locked it last night," Andre said. "I thought..." He debated whether to point out that Manu was the only other person with a key to the door. "I mean, did you make any copies of the key for..." he glanced at Brodeur, swallowing, "anyone?"

"No, I haven't gotten to it yet. The master is in the drawer of my desk." To Brodeur, he said, "And you haven't seen the key?"

Brodeur's face wrinkled like a drying apple core. "You accuse me of stealing the key? Me? A loyal employee of Parisian parks department?"

"No, Monsieur, no one's accusing you," Manu said.

Brodeur gestured with the torch at Andre, its metal tip nearly poking his chest. "He left the door open and simply doesn't remember."

Andre stepped back, wondering if the tip was still hot. "Well," he said. The eerie ring of the silent phone call echoed in his ears. "I'm sure I locked it. I was worried about a break in."

"A break in?" Manu said.

"Well, I—"

"A break in?" Brodeur said. "There has never been a crime committed in L'Enclos." He frowned, his eyes shifting from Andre's boots to his jacket to his leather bag to his hair.

Manu held his hands out to calm Brodeur. "Now, let's just—"

"I'd like my crop to be safe," Andre said, an annoyed heat rising in his chest.

"It is safe. Moussa has guarded L'Enclos for six years," Brodeur said. "Are you saying he does not do his job?"

"No, I—"

"Apparently, you think L'Enclos is a dangerous location in which to grow your dainty little apples."

85

Andre's heart raced. *Dainty?* "I walked into dirt and—"

"My staff keeps a world-renowned public garden—"

"Your staff?"

"He means *our* staff," Manu said.

"A historic garden maintained to an impeccable level every day and you accuse us of running a shoddy operation in a crime-infested area."

"It's not crime-infested, I just want everyone to be careful. That crop of trees is valuable and—"

"And the historic Jardin des Plantes is not valuable?"

Andre soured. "Of course it is."

"I'll check with the other gardeners." Manu said.

"I only meant our partnership with—"

"If L'Enclos does not suit your university needs," Brodeur said, "you're free to find another location. I'm sure there are farms in the country who would rent you a field."

With that, Brodeur flicked on the blow torch. The flame poofed to life, blue and hissing. "Even if someone did unlock the door, I'm sure they did so to check on vital equipment."

Manu rumpled his lips.

Through Brodeur's flames of indignation, Andre saw a flicker of guilt. A faint glimmer. Then again, maybe not. Either way, the torch's fire prompted him to leave. He spun around and walked away from the heat, unsure whether the hissing sound was coming from the torch or Brodeur.

Inside the S2 house, he slammed the door and swore. Manu was about to make a copy of the key to his greenhouse for this maniac. He stalked around, whispering to himself. Then again, what choice did he have? He hoped Brodeur would be appeased and would never need to use it. *I'm sure there are farms in the country who would rent you a field.* He scoffed. Brodeur didn't know Andre had once done that. Rented a piece of land, though "renting" was a formal way of putting it. Absently, he went to the first row of Tengri trees and felt each's soil for moisture. He hadn't *rented* per se, only borrowed the land for a time. From Jason's grandma, Melody, or who her family called Grandma Mel.

She had a sweet acre with beautiful soil. A sweet acre for a sweet-ly tough woman, the memory of which made his gut clench with shame.

He remembered the house, a small, Mediterranean bungalow on a dusty road that led into the hills. The land, nestled in the boundaries of a neighboring ranch, was a square acre, and at several more miles inland, perfectly dry in summer and mild in winter for pomegranates. He could still smell the cistus, hear the gravel crunch in the driveway, see the sun on the oaks and rocky hills behind. How the sheer curtains blew from the breeze in the open windows.

Once Grandma Mel had encouraged him to grow his shrubs there, Andre chose an unused section of the backyard along the fence. The southwest corner had ample sun and perfect drain-age, removed from Mel's own bed of roses on the east side. Over the course of two days, he dug out a long bed, tested the soil. More acidic than alkaline, teaming with worms. He amended it with compost and a few other minerals and turned it by hand to aerate, raked it to a rockless silty consistency, and planted the pomegranate shrubs.

Every few days in spring, he'd stop by and water or feed the plants before chatting with Mel, who often wandered onto the back porch to smoke a cigarette. She'd throw a plump leg over the railing and sit atop, one cowboy boot hitched to a lower rung. She had speckled gray eyes, a hoarse laugh, and tussled hair the color of driftwood. She launched into long stories about her adult children, one of whom, Teri, worked for Andre's father at Sun-time Orchards. Mel often said, "you know how he is," or "you've seen her do that I'm sure," as if Andre knew all of her adult kids intimately. Sometimes she'd talk for longer than interested him, but he didn't mind. Despite three adult children and four grand-children, she spoke with a melancholy twang, as if she were lonely and squinting at the rolling horizon soothed her. When she ran out of words, she sat humming and watching Andre loop up the hose or pack up his little truck while some game show blared inside on TV.

One afternoon, she'd said, "That fool Jason got himself arrested again last night."

Andre mixed fertilizer in a giant plastic watering can by the deck, the sun beaming on his bare back, droplets splashing on his sunglasses. He stopped. "Again?"

"Yeah," she said, took a drag on her cigarette.

"For what?"

"Bar brawl."

Andre remembered Jason asking to borrow a hundred dollars a few days earlier at the orchard. He'd given him twenty.

"He owes his friends some money. If you can call those rats 'friends.'"

Andre debated whether to ask if this was his second arrest this year. He thought it was. Instead, he said, "Is he still there?"

"Nah, his silly mother bailed him out again. I told her to leave him in there a day or so and teach him a lesson, but she wouldn't."

Andre hadn't met Jason's friends, but he'd heard stories: stories about betting on car racing, betting on sports like basketball and boxing, even betting on scoring with women. Once, Jason had told Andre he'd gone to Las Vegas and married a girl he'd met on the internet. They'd spent the weekend losing twelve hundred dollars in the casinos. Who knew how Teri, his mother, had reacted then. She always seemed to forgive him.

"Yeah, Teri's a softie," Andre said.

"And his brother, you know, Karl, I told Jason, 'Karl already went through this. Until he found the Lord, he was lost. You need to learn from his example.'"

Andre thought of Jason's brother, Karl. A mean drunk who'd almost died in a car accident. He'd found God and straightened his life out, worked his way up the Walmart ladder to manager, got married, had two kids.

"Jason keeps shooting himself in the foot. I told him, 'learn a damn lesson from your brother. Your life doesn't have to be hell so *behave*.'"

That night, Andre went home, determined to contact Lisa Wright. After he ate a quick dinner, he searched online but found little about her. An outdated networking page with her job listed at the university in Oregon. He went outside with his phone. Often long-distance connections were clearer if he stayed in the open. Linus followed him onto the deck. Andre sat on the edge of the teak chair with the cat in his lap. Eight o'clock now, which meant eleven West Coast time. People were sure to be at work. He tapped in the number for the Oregon State University Agricultural Research Program and waited.

The phone rang.

Finally, a woman answered, "Research."

"I was hoping to speak with Ms. Lisa Wright," he said.

An unsure pause. "Do you mean Lisa Wight?"

"Yes, excuse me. Lisa Wight."

The woman's tone stiffened. "Who is this?"

He swallowed. "My name is Andre Damazy, I'm an American researcher in Paris. I wanted to ask Lisa about one of her tree projects."

Silence.

From below on the Rue Rollin, voices boomed up. Linus hopped down and wandered to the roof's edge.

In a cold removed tone, the woman said, "Lisa Wight no longer works here."

"Oh. Well, do you know where she works?" He let go a quick cringe. *What else to say?*

"No," she snapped. "I mean, yes, I do, but I'm not telling you."

His voice fell. "Sorry, I... I just wanted to ask her a question."

"I'm not allowed to give out private information. I can't, for her protection."

"Of course."

"Who are you again?"

"My name is Andre Damazy. I'm a horticulture professor at AgroPolytechnique University in Paris. I teach and do horticultural research."

"You're in France?"

"Yes. I'm growing some… trees that are similar…. I'm doing similar work to Lisa's. Do you know her, if she's still working?"

The woman cleared her throat. "Enough."

"See, honestly, um, I've been harassed some and I wanted to see if her experience was similar to mine. Of course, I know it's not, to a certain extent, but I'm growing medicinal trees and I'd like to have her… insight."

An audible breath shushed out.

A long car horn blared. His heartrate surged. He plugged an ear. He waited for the blaring to stop. "Sorry, that's traffic," he said. "So, I know she experienced a horrible act of vandalism and I don't mean her harm at all, but—"

The woman said in a flat command, "Tell me your name again."

"What?"

"Your name. Tell me your name and number one more time. I'll pass it on. Wait a minute, who do you work for? Do you work for Monsanto?"

"No, no, of course not. I'm a professor, at AgroPolyTech, you can check it out."

"Alright," she said.

"I hope her health is okay."

"Well, yes. We almost lost her last year, but it had nothing to do with those assholes, she changed jobs and got diagnosed with cancer and it was a rough patch there, but she's better now, and working at… wait a minute, just give me your information and if Lisa wants to contact you, she will."

"Thank you. Could I have your name?"

Her voice was business-like. "No, you can't. But I'll let her know you want to speak with her."

Andre gave her his number and email. As he recited the last letters, he heard a man on the street below, shouting. He went to the deck's edge and leaned over the low iron railing. Outside the pharmacy, a young man in a T-shirt stumbled, trying to throw a punch at another man in a skull cap with a neck tattoo. In slurred speech, they rattled off each other's faults.

"You slept with her," the T-shirt guy said.

"You broke my car!"

The guy in the skull cap clumsily batted his friend's fist away, calling him the French words for butthole of the world.

Andre struggled to remember his phone number, "Um... 3696."

"Get off!" the guy in the skull cap shouted. With both hands, he gave a hard push to his friend who stumbled into an orange roadwork barrel, knocking it over with an echoing boom.

"Woh," Andre said.

Linus crouched, peeking through the railing's ironwork.

"Is someone there?" the woman said.

The man in the sweater looked up, noticed Andre. "What do you want, idiot?"

Andre shivered, backed up.

"Your cat's a little idiot too!"

"A tasty treat," his friend said.

"No, no, I'm fine," he said to the woman. "We're fine. Just a drunk ass on the street." He regretted saying the word "ass."

She repeated the information to him and he thanked her and ended the call. As he tentatively glanced over the railing, Linus meowed. Below on the street, the man in the T-shirt shot him the middle finger, yelled, "Come down here! Come down, I'll give you a show." Andre stumbled backward, bumping a potted juniper, grabbing the prickly shrub as he fell against the chair. It skidded. Linus darted behind an urn, shrinking into the shadows.

"You stupid idiot!" the man shouted.

Andre scrambled to his feet. Linus's green eyes glowed widely, watching for danger in the darkness. Andre crouched, gently picked up the cat so as not to get scratched and nestled it deep in his arms before slipping through the door and into the living room. As he locked and bolted it and pulled all of the shades, he whispered, "Time to lay low for a while."

CHAPTER 10

A month passed. As Paris slept in the bare dormancy of winter, so did Andre. He limited life to his apartment, Botany class, and the Tengri project. Every day he made sure Linus was indoors before he left for class, then checked his mail at the university for anonymous notes, went to the S2 house, hoping no one had left the door open or unlocked. Lisa Wight hadn't returned his call and he interpreted that as she being too traumatized to talk about the vandalism. So, he stayed vigilant while caring for the trees, waiting for the scion tissue to meld with the rootstock branches. After two inactive weeks, where the waxed branches seemed like a sculpture rather than a living organism, he fretted the grafting was a failure. Days later, the branches plumped. Growth buds swelled. Within a week, tiny rolled leaves poked their tips out like delicate beaks.

Excited at his success, he strictly monitored temperature and humidity and fertilizing and watering while praying against disease. On Tuesdays and Thursdays, Renia checked the trees while he taught class. She dutifully logged in all of her activities and measurements in the project notebook. On Thursdays, her arrival hour varied and sometimes their time overlapped and they worked in tandem for one or two hours. During those times, he liked to bounce ideas off her and she had small strategies for encouraging healthy growth or saving money. Together, they discussed what might be wrong with a tree whose scion hadn't melded or so vigorously grown. When bored, they played a guessing game about how many apples they might actually harvest in fall.

During February on class days, he'd leave right after it finished and rush to L'Enclos, chomping an energy bar so he wouldn't miss seeing her. Sometimes, he'd enter the S2 house and she didn't notice him. Through the leaves, like a hidden raspberry, he'd spot a sliver of gold hair, a glimpse of auburn sweater, a flash of feminine unadorned hands. She'd be quietly concentrating on measuring a branch or inspecting a leaf, her settled lucid presence piercing him with a longing that, as the weeks went on, grew as brilliant and dark and solid as an acorn.

He hid it all and channeled his energy into the trees, focusing on what the two had done and still had to do. When they worked together, they'd chat about their families, his father's orchard, her uncle's nursery, their favorite plants, and favorite gardens in Europe. He felt as if he'd known her for years, sliding instantly into conversation, thinking similarly about the Tengri. When he considered repositioning a tree closer to a west or south exposure, she was already mentioning the idea aloud. When he went to the office to fetch hot teas, she'd be waiting with macaroons on a plate. They referred to the Tengris as if the trees were children, saying, "N21 hasn't been growing as quickly as her big brother, N23. Do you think she would like a bit more water?" or "Sapling 8 is looking like it finally appreciates that boost of emulsion, don't you think?" For weeks, the relationship flowed like a robust waterfall.

One Thursday night in late March, after they'd finished late, they strolled together to the L'Enclos gate, Renia walking her bicycle. He offered to hail her a taxi since night had blanketed the city but she refused, saying she wanted to ride since the air was warm. Just as he reminded her it was after eight o'clock, she patted his shoulder and reassured him she'd be fine.

That lovely hand.

"I know you want to spread the tree branches tomorrow," she said. "If you want, I can help for a couple hours in the afternoon."

Their task was to separate the Tengri branches so they'd grow strong intersections where each branch met the trunk. That she was free to help lifted his spirit. "Yes, I'd like that very much."

She smiled, said, "So would I," and pushed off on the bike. He watched her ride away, her tapestry coat fluttering like butterfly wings.

His phone dinged. A text from Cloutier. "The hallway is being painted tomorrow. Building Department said to take what's needed for the weekend tonight."

Shoot. He had paper lab reports to grade. In a stack on his desk.

"Coming now."

He walked briskly to the university and upstairs to the faculty offices. The tiny reception area was dark and abandoned, the two desks empty, a lamp on the printer table dimmed. With a rote glance, he checked his mailbox. Nothing inside. A mild relief. The mail had been unimportant for weeks. Down the hall, light spilled from his office. He headed to it, thankful Cloutier had texted since his only free time to grade papers landed that weekend. As he was about to go in, Cloutier came out. He was in a tan raincoat, russet fedora, slick portfolio case at the hip. They nearly bumped chests. "Oof!" Cloutier smiled. A Mercedes fob jingled in his hand. "Shall we dance, Monsieur Damascus?"

He thought Andre's name was rooted in the Syrian city when in reality it was a short form of Damazyn.

"Ha, yes," Andre said, "thanks for texting about the painting. I need my students' lab reports. That saved me." He pointed to his desk, shifted inside.

"No problem," he cheerily snapped, *"Bonne soirée, Andre."*

"Bonne soirée, Thierry."

The lab reports were in a loose stack, one whose top page had been flipped over, revealing a diagram where he'd started reading earlier in the week.

"Oh, Andre." Cloutier spun around. "Speaking of communication..."

Andre counted the reports, making sure he had all 22. "Yes."

Cloutier tapped a finger on his lips. "There was an odd gentleman whom I spoke to today."

"Oh? A student?"

"No, he wasn't a student. I inquired about that." Cloutier fluttered his eyelids in thought. His voice rang with a sharp reediness. "He was a man who didn't seem to know where he was. He examined each of nameplate on each office. Marie was gone for the day, everyone was gone for the day. So, I asked him after he looked at our door, if I could help him."

Andre swallowed. His name plate had fallen off the wall and he'd never bothered to tack it back up.

"He said he wanted to know where Damazy's trees were."

Andre went cold. "My trees?"

"Yes. I told him I didn't know what he was talking about."

His heart thumped. The lab reports felt dry and stiff in his hands. "Did you tell him we share an office?"

"No, because I had no idea what *your* trees meant."

"What did you tell him?"

"I said, 'Are you interested in enrolling in a class to study trees?' He said 'No.'"

Andre's breath shivered in his lungs.

"He was very shifty, uncomfortable. Anyway, I said, 'Are you interested in learning about trees?' He said, 'No. I want to know where the Kazakh apples are grown.'"

Cloutier giggled.

Andre licked his lips. His ankle faintly throbbed in pain.

"I said," he winced with laughter, "I said, 'Well, the Kazakh apples grow in Kazakhstan, of course.' I mean, how ridiculous is this?"

Andre feigned a smile.

Cloutier's face darkened. "But he was very intent, very serious. We went around a bit on this. I told him I didn't know where Kazakh apples grew. Maybe in Austria or Germany or some place cold like this. Anyway, then he said he had a message for Damazy, the so-called 'botanist-scientist.'"

"'So-called?'" Andre said. "He said those words?"

"Yes."

"What did you tell him, Thierry?"

"Isn't it curious?"

"Yes. Very. What did you tell him?"

"I told him that..."

Per mortem salutis. Andre bit his fingernail.

"Now, you must understand," Cloutier said, "he was dressed in soiled blue jeans, as if he'd worked on an oil drill, very soiled. Stains unlike earth materials like compost or lime and such. Nothing a student wears. And a very worn T-shirt with words, bright words and a flashy race car or something. And his hands, also very greasy."

That Breton had come to the office. The guy was so bold, he'd come to the office. If that nameplate had been tacked up...

"Also, his face," Cloutier said, "he had a pronounced scar at his lip. Of course, I don't mean to offend," he motioned to his own temple area.

Andre touched the scar at his eye. "Oh, none taken."

"And so, I was unsure of this appearance. Especially in a professional workplace. Even the students," he raised his eyebrows, "with their piercings and tattoos and such are never this shabby."

"Of course, of course." Andre stifled his breath, his heart beating fast. "Thierry, did you tell him this was my office—or give him my number?"

"*Alors*, I beg you to forgive me."

"Why?"

"I mean, if I've errored."

"Errored?"

"If I've errored on the side of caution. But I followed university protocol."

Andre released his clenched fingers, focused on the brass tie clip that Cloutier wore, the ornate carved clip Andre had always thought so ugly but now could have kissed then and there.

"I didn't divulge your number or say this is your office."

Andre let loose a grateful sigh, bumping into a head nod.

"What's more, I told him you were on a field assignment this semester. This is correct, right? You're working on a corporate project, aren't you? But then tonight, you said you have these lab reports to deal with so..."

"Well, I'm subbing in Botany, but that's all, I am on a field assignment."

"Oh okay, well, hopefully, you don't need to speak soon with this gentleman."

"No, I don't," Andre said. "I don't at all. I don't know him. And frankly, he sounds intimidating."

"Yes. This was my impression as well. He rubbed me the wrong way."

"Thanks, Thierry. I..." his chair squeaked uneasily, "I am growing trees for this corporate partnership, but it's confidential for several more months."

Cloutier's hazel eyes beamed with an unsure worry. "So, there is a tree project?"

"Yeah, but he has nothing to do with it." *Mention the threatening note?* Andre felt beaten down, hunted and beaten down. "I don't know what he wants," Andre said. "Maybe he thinks I'm someone else."

"Yes, of course."

"And if he comes back, feel free to let Edo know."

"I will. And actually, Andre, I think at least for now, I will keep our office door closed and locked."

"Yes. Yes, I don't mind at all."

"*Ah, voilà. Bon. C'est ça.*"

Outside, Andre walked up the Rue de l'Arbalète, the night air cool and damp. *What a close call.* As he walked home, he shook his head at how close he'd come to bumping into the thug. As he churned over ideas to make the S2 house more secure, he noticed a man about fifty feet behind, walking in the same direction. At first, he dismissed it as coincidence, there were millions of people in Paris, but when Andre went north on the Rue Mouffetard, the man followed. The guy was brawny, tall, wearing a charcoal hoodie beneath a trucker jacket. Lowered tan cap. It couldn't be... *him.* So soon? Cloutier hadn't mentioned exactly when the guy had stopped by the offices, but he might have been right outside the building, watching, waiting the whole time. Andre berated himself for not asking what the Breton had been wearing. Clothes. More description. Now, the cap shadowed this guy's face; his body bobbing in and out of shadows, making it impossible to see any grease marks on jeans or facial scars.

Andre tightened with panic. The man didn't have a backpack or bag or anything in tow. Not a student. He simply walked at a rapid determined pace with hands in pockets. As a test, Andre went right at the Rue Ortolan, hooked left into a pedestrian passageway. With a snug garden of shrubs on one side and burned-out street lamps on the other, the passage lay in a foggy claustrophobia. He hurried through, checking over his shoulder. As the walkway spilled into the Rue Saint-Médard, he eyed the stairwell behind, his body about to leave the corner, pausing for a breath.

The man appeared. Andre moved on. *Per mortem salutis*. His body tensed. Now, if he went left and right again into Mouffetard, the two had essentially traveled in a circle, with no destination. He quickened his pace, cutting through the Place de le Contrescarpe, using the giant empress trees and tumbling fountain as cover to wait and see. In a moment, the guy jogged in, stopped, scanning the square. Andre beelined toward the Rue Rollin, knowing now the man *was* the thug from Brittany. The phone caller. The note writer. The man who'd given Cloutier the creeps.

It will be stopped for you.

He hurried, his building across the street to his left, the cross of the pharmacy radiating green light. Almost home. He pulled out his keys, checking which was the one for the outer door. He needed lamp light so as he passed underneath, stretched his palm flat and eyed the keys. There it was. The largest. *Got it.* As he approached the door, he checked the street. The thug was right there, on his side, thirty feet away with only an orange construction barricade between.

No. He slipped the keys in his pocket and walked on. The last place he wanted to lead him was his apartment. Where to go? The metro? The confines of the subway unnerved him, so he took out his phone and opened the app for a taxi, marking the pick up at the Hôtel Saint Christophe. Hopefully, by the time he got there, the cab would be waiting and if not, he could wait in the lobby. A semi-public, well-lit lobby. He hurried down the Rue Monge and by the time, he rounded the corner for the hotel, the cab pulled up to the entrance.

How far to go? He settled on the Mitterrand Library. When they arrived, he paid the driver, got out, pretended to be interested in taking photos of the architecture, and watched pedestrians roam for twenty minutes. *How long to stay?* He was hungry. He walked along the Seine a while, passing a party on three moored boats, the music booming into the night, then headed into the Latin Quarter, stopping at a brasserie he never noticed before and went inside. Le Jardin Noir had darkly purple, almost black walls, and murals of vines. He sat at the bar and ordered a brandy and sandwich. As he lifted the wide glass, his fingers shook. *Gulp.* He ordered another. And another. Chatted with a couple from America until he finally relaxed. At midnight, he felt loose enough to hail a taxi and go home, though he told the driver the pharmacy address not his building number, which he didn't want recorded in any database.

At the pharmacy, the cab drove off and Andre checked the narrow street. Empty, save for a couple walking hand in hand far down. A few lights in the building across the street glowed, one with a ceiling fan spinning in a lazy circle, another with a scarf throne over a lamp to redden the light. He was alone and drunk and coldly depressed, still faintly dusted with fright. Once in the foyer, he jumped up the stairs two at a time and swooped into the apartment. Linus galloped across the living room at the sudden sound, crouching behind a fern, his reflective eyes observant. Andre locked the door and set a dining chair under the knob.

SPRING
CHAPTER 11

The next morning, his phone rang at six o'clock. He ignored it, breathing into the deep relief of sleep. The rings persisted. As his eyes unstuck and opened, he remembered last night roaming the streets, cabbing to the library, drinking at a bar, and being petrified to come home. How, during the night, the chair he'd precariously wedged under the door knob, fell and crashed and scared the cat, who knocked over a plant stand. A clay pot crashed and shattered on the wood floor. With blurry vision, he'd stumbled out of bed to find the problem, dirt scattered in the harsh moonlight, a pothos laying sideways, a sturdy plant he knew wouldn't die in hours. He checked the cat for injuries, stacked the shards, and collapsed in bed. Now, with a pounding forehead, he scrambled for his phone from the nightstand, unable to pinpoint what day it was.

"I left you three messages last evening," Edo said. "Madame Castel is bringing Monsieur Alba to L'Enclos in one hour. They are eager to see you and the Tengri project."

"But it's..." *What day is it? Friday.* "Okay." His mouth tasted like dry burlap. "They can't come at nine or ten?"

"This is their only availability."

After months, they were finally interested. "I'll be there."

He ended the call and took a quick scalding shower, shaved in a fast scrape, stuffed a croissant in his mouth while dumping kibble in the cat bowl, and left. His hands felt swollen and his jaw ached, but his headache subsided once he downed two pills and a bottle of electrolyte water.

Outside, the daylight was still faint and the streets empty save for a stray jogger. Rain fell. Light and cool on his warm, worried face. He turned south at the Rue Monge, hearing the sound of his own breath in a calm, trafficless city. The sidewalks were empty, the metal screens shut. He checked around. Clusters of green recycling bins sat like hunched trolls on the curb. At the corner, a truck idled. A man in a blue uniform emerged, rolling a handtruck stacked with boxes of soda into a shop. He'd love to grab one of those, preferably with caffeine. The smell of baking bread hit his nose as vines, hanging from window boxes, dripped icy water on his scalp. He turned left onto the Rue Lacépède and realizing it was already quarter to seven, jogged to the Allée René Jeannel.

At the L'Enclos gate, a gray BMW waited in the driveway, blocking the sidewalk. Behind the tinted window, Castel and Alba sat together in the backseat, a driver Andre didn't recognize at the wheel.

He pulled an old napkin from his pocket and wiped his face, then waved and called out a happy greeting, ignoring the sweat rolling down his spine.

Monsieur Alba raised a hand in return. The window slid down. In a smart navy suit, the executive extended a tan manicured hand, revealing a Rolex on his wrist. Andre shook it, apologized for being late, and assured them he'd punch in the code so they could park by the greenhouse. Castel's face tilted away as she talked on the phone animatedly, her gold rings chunky on her slim fingers. Her hair was fluffed and sprayed so it framed her face like an inky cloud.

After they parked in the lot and Andre led the two to the S2 house, Castel said, "We'd assumed you'd forgotten." Her expression was bold. "We were about to leave."

"No, just delayed by… by…" *By what, a late night? A broken planter? A startled cat?* "The usual. Do forgive me," he said, "Shall we go in?"

When Andre opened the door, he saw the Tengri project as if for the first time. The greenhouse stretched in a long tidy rectangle, bright from the clearing sky. Rows of trees filled the space on a diagonal trajectory, 50 some trunks now with several branches each, all sporting whole, unblemished leaves. They stood on secure wooden tables with screened beds, neatly lined in arrays of eight trees on each table, arranged for best air circulation and growth space. Together the trees formed an organized pattern of at-attention soldiers, silent in their existence, yet taking in light and water on instinct to make food. Their task was to grow and they knew that. They were direct in their pushing out of branches, pushing out of leaves, silently offering themselves to the world for what they did. Make apples to move seed. Move seed to procreate. Survive. Live on.

Andre relaxed with a slight pride once he saw the faint smiles on Castel and Alba's faces. He and Renia had created optimal conditions. He showed them around with confidence, noticing a few crumpled wax wrappers he hadn't thrown away from a lunch. Perhaps the scraps of unkempt detritus would signal he'd been too busy to eat out, which was ultimately true.

Madame Castel followed him obediently, careful to keep her hands clasped, her chin tilted upward and eyes never landing on anything in particular, as if examining the trees betrayed her concern for the project.

Monsieur Alba swiped his hands together, closely studying the trees. He was a shortish man with a slim frame and tightly combed hair. His suit was smooth, his black shoes shined, his nails trimmed and clean. His gray eyes darted from tree to tree, listening and nodding animatedly like an alert mink as Andre described what he and "his assistant" had done to encourage successful grafts and early blooming.

"This is impressive," Alba said. "You must be very proud." He had a fatherly air, on the verge of condescending, but not quite.

Andre talked about the philosophy behind growing apple trees, making sure to mention optimal conditions were outside before showing them the state-of-the-art temperature and ventilation systems, the lighting, the irrigation. He noted how lucky he was to work in a facility in Paris. If it hadn't sounded amateurish to say, "LaRoche's money has been well spent," he would have mentioned it.

"*Alors*, how many trees do we have?" Alba asked.

"We have 60 so far. And the last three may be late in waking up," he said, though he knew they weren't.

"This is extraordinary," Alba said. "All of these plants look very well-tended." He held out a hand to Andre. Andre felt reluctant to shake because he didn't want to spread contamination, but after a second, he felt embarrassed, so he shook.

Alba smiled an adoring smile at the nearest sapling, then reached out and rubbed a leaf between his forefinger and thumb. "The leaves are very supple."

Andre cringed. Whatever was on Alba's hand, or Andre's hand, was now on the leaf, and could be taken into the tree's vascular system. Discreetly, he looked for the tree's number, T43, and made a mental note to pick the affected leaf off later.

Alba wandered toward the Chick's Nest. He was about to grip the door.

"Wait, please..." Andre said.

They both stiffened.

"The trees are very delicate," he said. "Like infants. We have to sanitize—even our shoes. I have a sanitation thing over here." He looked around for hand sanitizer but realized they'd just run out so he slid the mat from beneath the counter to the doorway with his foot. Both guests stepped on it as he clicked the combination to the padlock.

Inside the Chick's Nest, ten saplings and one appling stood on four tables in a similar pattern to the trees in the main room. "We've created plush conditions for these saplings. The air is warmer, the lamps shine longer, the trees are watered and fertilized more often." He shut the door.

"These are the fruiting trees?" Alba said, he leaned over, pinched a leaf between his fingers and sniffed it. Andre was about to warn they didn't have any special scent when Castel said, "They haven't fruited yet. It will be a few more months, correct?"

"Well, yes," he said, "several, to let the apples develop to maturity."

"Monsieur Damazy," Castel said, "will these trees bear fruit of the same size that Monsieur McFadden brought us last spring?"

I hope so. "Yes," he said. "I'll be pinching off some flowers so the trees can channel their energy into a lower number of fruit that will mature to a larger size."

"A lower number?" Monsieur Alba said. He looked alarmed at Castel. "I thought we were growing as many as possible."

"We are," Andre said, "but asking these young trees to bear fruit on such a young structure is like asking a girl to bear children. It will strain the trees."

Alba's delicate eyebrows furrowed in doubt.

Castel's expression remained blank, her eyes as cool as coal, as if Andre were on his own to argue the point.

"We all decided," he said gesturing to her, thinking of Edo, remembering the speaker phone conversation they'd had a few months ago, "that thirty apples was a safe number to aim for. Otherwise, we risk harvesting small weak apples or even losing the entire crop."

Andre's phone rang.

Dad.

He silenced the phone and slid it in his pocket.

Monsieur Alba eyed a large leaf cluster on a sapling. "Yes thirty, well..." he said, his fingers jumping from leaf to leaf, rubbing affectionately. "Madame Castel and I were wondering if you can produce the apples by July."

Later, after the two LaRoche managers left, he inspected the leaves for pests and bruises. When Alba had said the word "July," Andre had stifled a laugh. They were dead serious, wanting to rush nature. The truth was he would have the tiniest of apples in July, perhaps larger ones if he injected ethylene into the greenhouse air, but that carried risks. So, he'd blinked as if to reset his angst, and said, "Unlikely, but we'll do our very best." They accepted the answer, thankfully. Now, as he picked off the contaminated leaves Alba had touched and collected them in a bucket, he shook his head at how clueless they were. Nature couldn't be rushed except when money was involved.

A steady buzz cut the air. Outside the house, the outline of a woman coasted to a halt on a scooter. *Renia?*

He opened the door.

She flipped the kickstand and parked a shiny Vespa on the grit. In a forest green leather coat, she lifted off her helmet and retied her hair in a ponytail.

"Wow. Is this yours?" he said.

"Yes," she blushed. "This is why I wanted to ride my bike last night. I knew the scooter had arrived at the store."

The Vespa was black, a new model with a double seat and roomy footboard. "It looks like a 250, with lots of power."

"It is."

"It even has a windshield."

"That's my favorite part." She pinched her lips, suppressing a smile. "Want to go for a ride?"

His mouth dropped. He realized he had a bucket in his hand. "Yes. Let me throw these in the compost."

After he tossed the bruised leaves, he threw on his jacket, smiling at the scooter, forgetting the morning, forgetting the previous night. She offered him her helmet, but he refused. As she started the Vespa, he sat snugly behind her, worried for a moment where to put his hands. He felt around behind, but the luggage bar was too low so he put his hands on his thighs and stiffened his body. *So tired. Gotta stay upright.*

Cautiously, she drove down a grit path to the driveway, passing Brodeur who plodded along with a wheelbarrow full of soil. Renia waved. He frowned. As they neared the gate, Moussa smiled and opened it. They zoomed onto the Rue Buffon. With the wind blowing her hair, he could smell her shampoo, a tea tree oil, icy and fresh. When they hit a bump, he jostled, losing his balance and grabbed her hips without thinking.

She didn't react.

He lifted his hands. "Sorry," he called out.

She slowed to a red light, swiveled her head, smiled. "It's fine."

They waited.

"Are you hungry?" she said.

"Yes." He nodded in case she didn't hear him.

"Do you like the Antonia Café, for lunch?"

That was a school hangout. *Is that wise?* Then again, two employees sharing lunch wasn't controversial. They weren't going home and hopping into bed. "Okay."

They flew through the neighborhood, she adeptly steering and braking as if she'd been on a scooter before. The wind felt freezing but refreshing on his face. He needed to perk up, counter his haggard, hungry state. They parked at the restaurant and took a table outside. As they sat down, her leather jacket crunched. He noted her noisy jacket. She laughed, said it was best for protection. They ordered and chatted about the bike.

"It's partly a present from my parents," she said.

"That's a really nice present."

"Well," her eyes shifted to her salad, "it's for my birthday."

"What? Oh..."

She crossed her hands, "No, no, it's—"

"Today?"

"No, Saturday."

They were quiet, him eating a sandwich, she eating a salmon salad. He wanted to ask how old she was but didn't want to seem intrusive.

"I'm thirty-one," she said. "Which reminds me, I'm going to Poland to see my parents this weekend. But I'll be back Monday evening."

"Oh, well, I guess we should take advantage of your time today."

"Yes."

They finished eating, he wondering if he should get her a birthday gift. Some plant-related bangle that would make her smile. A keychain? She'd seemed embarrassed to divulge the birthday, so he didn't mention it any more, feeling a slight chill in his chest. As they finished lunch, he sneezed into his arm.

"Are you okay?"

"It's strange. I'm a little cold."

"Did the scooter give you a draft?"

"No, I'm fine."

"Let's order some tea."

After they finished their tea, she rode more slowly back to L'Enclos where they parked and went in the S2 house, he zipping up his racer jacket to his chin, fighting off shivers, a swelling throat dogging him.

She watched him sneeze in his arm, apologize.

"Are you ill?" she said. "Your face, it's gray."

"Really? Yeah, I suddenly feel kind of lousy. I probably look lousy too."

"No, I didn't mean..." Her expression dropped.

He'd made her uncomfortable. *Fool.* "Sorry, I mean, I didn't sleep much last night. The LaRoche people came early to tour the house this morning. I'm... I'm..." He felt worn out, sleepy, like he could lay down on the concrete right there and sleep. His heart trembled. He wanted to confess that he was barely holding it together. That Alba had touched the leaves on the Tengris. That he'd been traced to his office, stalked by a thug, threatened with an anonymous note. He didn't want to worry her, especially on her birthday weekend, tell her that someone was out to ruin their project. "I'm stressed from work."

"Maybe we should postpone?"

He cleared his throat. It felt raw. "No, you made a special point to come today. And I'm sure you have to get ready for your trip. Let's get started."

They needed to separate each tree's branches so they ran more horizontally than vertically. A more ninety-degree branch crotch would allow more sunlight in and grow sturdier branches. They'd be more able to hold the weight of fruit. He brought over the box of wooden spreaders. There were three- and four-inch pieces, flat pine with small circular cuts carved in each end. A friend of Delphine's who was a carpenter had made them in

December. He'd used a Dremel to burn the size numbers into the wood: 3", 3.5", 4". They washed their hands and set about working.

At the first sapling, Renia said, "This one's branches have grown too closely upward."

"Yes, let's try a four-inch piece."

She found a spreader and set the wooden stick delicately between the branches.

He felt the remains of exhilaration from the Vespa ride and lunch and their talk. Now with a full stomach in the quiet of their work, his body settled. He kept a few feet away in case he was sick, still catching her scent of lavender soap and tea tree shampoo. As she bent over the branches, her ponytail fell to the side, exposing her neck. Smooth, gold with one brown freckle two inches below the ear, a secret curve where he yearned to hide and lose himself.

"What do you think?" she said.

He blinked, waking from his admiration. "Perfect," he said, then spun away to sneeze in his arm.

"Andre, you're not well."

"I'm better than I sound." *That was a lie.* He felt twisted and dry and barely able to stand straight. He wiped his mouth with his cuff, embarrassed at his lack of bodily control.

They shifted to the next tree. "I'm unsure about this one," she said. Gently, she tugged a soft branch down.

"Let's see," he motioned between the trunk and the branch, "between here and here, that's about 60, so let's use a three-inch." She took a stick and set it so the branches were propped open.

He rooted around in his shirt pockets, "Let's check how accurate I am." He pulled out a protractor and measured the distance: 57 degrees.

"You estimated perfectly," she said, her smile melting his concentration.

"Well, after you do it a thousand times, you learn to eyeball it."

He turned and sneezed with a loud cough.

"*Naz drowie*," she said.

"Thanks."

"I'm worried our ride gave you a cold."

"I'll be fine."

"Do you need a tissue?"

"No. Well, yes."

She plucked a small box from her bag and handed it to him.

"Thanks, sorry," he said, stepping away and blowing his nose, feeling like a sick goof.

They went to the next tree and set another spreader. He sneezed again, went for a tissue. Renia set two more branches and two more as he surrendered to simply standing a few feet from her and watching while he wiped his nose and sneezed.

"You estimate every angle beautifully," he said. A bulging soreness fired his throat.

She pursed her lips in an embarrassed smile. He wanted to compliment her on how thoughtful she was and how he appreciated her close inspections when they checked leaves, but he felt like praising her would be like trying to pet a fly. It would smash under the pressure. Besides, he didn't want her to think he was flirting even though he was ready to flirt if she flirted with him first.

"It's strange," he said, "I haven't been ill since Kazakhstan last fall."

"I can't imagine that was fun."

"No, it wasn't," he said. He remembered how despite a sprained ankle and smashed up face, he hadn't caught any flu bug.

"I wish..." she said, "I hope the Tengri can help with common illnesses like colds or skinned knees and such."

"That would be amazing, wouldn't it?" he said, then reddened with the shame of concealing a truth from her. "Well, I know it will. I... I actually ate some in Kazakhstan."

"Ah. Because you were injured?"

"Yes," he said feeling sheepish.

"I remember the cuts on your face."

"Yeah... and I sprained my ankle, and fractured a finger."

She frowned in concern. "And the Tengri helped you?"

"Yes, it did." At the memory, excitement surged through his chest. "It really did, Renia. I mean, I'll never forget how I felt after eating the apples."

Her eyes beamed. "It's as if it's the medicine of God."

He smirked at her religious reference. Then again, she was right.

"It's true. It's like the feeling is subtle, but it's there. The way you feel after taking a solid nap. Refreshed. An ache you feel goes away. Pain subsides. You feel more aware, kind of like those energy drinks, only natural. It wears off after a while, but I'm hoping with more studies over a longer period of time, researchers might be able to apply some version of it to more serious situations."

He thought of his mother. He hadn't called his dad back from this morning.

"Like your mother's condition," she said.

Had he told her about that? He must have. "Yes."

Renia's eyes lowered. "I admire what you're doing, Andre."

He shivered with the compliment, wanting to hide. "Oh, thanks."

"In fact," her eyes locked on his, "I've never encountered such a heroic person."

Stunned at her admiration, he swallowed, then winced at his searing throat. He wanted to take her hands in his, kiss them, toss all professional caution aside and confess that he wanted to be with her.

"I'm the one who admires..." His nose tickled. He spun away and sneezed.

"Andre, you need rest. Please go home. I can finish here."

"No, I'm just..."

She went and got his bag from the counter and brought it over, gently lifting the strap over his head so it lay across his chest. A sly smile spread over her face. "Go home."

"But the trees."

"I will do as best I can and you will check them on Monday."

"Well, I'll stop by tomorrow or Sunday for a few minutes."

"If you want, but I'd rather you sleep."

"Alright." He did feel like a wrung-out rag. "I will." He turned to leave, paused. "And oh, one more thing."

"I'll make sure to lock all the doors."

"Renia? Happy birthday."

CHAPTER 12

When he came home, he fell face first on the couch and slept until five the next morning. He woke with his boots on, his comforter wrapped around his body, the television flashing a soccer match. After slinking to the bathroom and swallowing acetaminophen pills, he fell asleep again, Linus curled at his stomach, only to wake later with a high fever. The hours passed with him popping fever reducers, sleeping, feeding the cat. At moments, he felt a touch better and convinced he could go to L'Enclos, went to shower before detouring and napping. On Sunday, Delphine brought him hot lasagna and stayed to chat, telling him she and Charles had decided to move in together before the wedding. It wasn't until Monday that the fever broke and he slept an extended, blacked out sleep.

At about three o'clock, he woke, feeling rested. Thinking he'd ask Renia to check on the trees, he called her. No answer. She always either answered or texted a few minutes later. He showered, thinking he'd stop by the S2 house, but afterward felt so weak he had to sit on the bed to catch his breath, then rolled himself into a blanket and slept. When he woke, he was hungry. Hungrier than he'd been in the last three days. He heated the leftover lasagna and after calling Renia again, scolded himself for bothering her. She was still in Poland.

On Tuesday, he felt strong enough to work, but thinking he might be contagious, decided to cancel class. Instead, he dressed and took a taxi to the S2 house, sucking on cough drops. At the door, with his key in the lock, something felt strange. The deadbolt didn't move, as if it had been already unlocked. Inside, dry curled leaves sagged on sticks. An entire row of trees held dead leaves—and some in another row. With a panicked step, he scanned the tables, the counter, the trees, pounced at the nearest trunk and scraped the bark. The tissue was brown, revealing dead wood.

God in heaven.

He whipped out his phone and texted Renia: "Do you remember locking doors on Friday?"

A minute later: "Yes. I set the padlock on Chick's Nest handle and locked outer door. Double checked both. I kept temp settings and set timer to water on Sunday."

Who'd been inside? Brodeur? A garbage man? It must have been Brodeur. He and Manu were the only other people with keys.

Renia texted: "Why?"

"Just wondering. Safe travels."

Andre examined every tree in the house. Plants T18 through T26 were dead. Plus, T9 and T16. How had that happened? There wasn't a pattern. Not a virus, he'd only been away a few days. Not water. The soil was moist. Couldn't be bacteria because the leaves had no spots. They wouldn't curl from scale. But an entire table had been affected, an entire cluster, rather than a pool at the aisles or a clump at a corner. It was throughout Table C, with two trees presenting a few curled leaves on Table B, and two trees lining the center aisle. He scratched at the bark layer on each. The cambium on most were brown. Gone in three days. It had to be the work of a living person. That thug had sprayed them with herbicide.

He cringed, clenched his fists. Swore up and down. *So many gone.* As he paced around, he noticed a clue. Someone had sprayed the plants on Table C, then only sprayed T9 and T16 at the tables' ends, as if in a final gesture on the way out.

113

He gave a small scrape to the bark on T9 and T16. The cambium layers on these two were lined with a faint green color. They were alive. He wanted to grab the trees and dump the soil on the floor and wash the roots with a hose over the drain, but suddenly thought of the appling and rushed to the Chick's Nest door. The padlock was still intact. Inside, the saplings still sported their whole green leaves, the temperature held steady, the fan still hummed. He hung his head. *Thank God.*

He shut the door, thankful for the padlock, and washed the half-alive trees' roots over the floor drain, picked off their lost leaves, and repotted them in fresh soil. Watered well. Still, they might die. They had no leaves to make food. The light of life went out of a plant in silence, without fanfare, with only wilted leaves as its last signal. For all he knew, these had taken their last botanical breath days ago.

As the shock lifted, the despair settled in. Nine plants, possibly eleven, were destroyed. How vicious. They were harmless plants. It had to be that Breton thug. Was he an ecoterrorist? An anti-corporate fanatic? Andre yearned to speak with Lisa Wight. She still hadn't returned his call weeks later. Should he try again? It hardly mattered. That Breton had accomplished what he'd set out to do... at least in part. Why, Andre had no clue.

He left the dead trees as they were, wanting to collect them in the corner. They were no longer trees, only brown twigs with crunchy leaves. Glyphosate was painfully effective. The plants took it into their veins like humans absorbed alcohol in the blood stream. It circulated throughout the system, the plant feeding itself as if the toxin was food. His heart sank as he thought of their suffering. He preferred cutting down a plant at the base, simple decapitation. But herbicide made it suffer longer. Not too much longer, but enough to struggle for a day or so.

He searched the entire greenhouse, struggling to figure out how the guy had broken in. The front door showed no sign of forced entry. The deadbolt was still intact, even the louvered vents. He must have exited through the door, unable to lock it from the outside. Andre examined the drum fans but none had been bent or removed, not even in the Chick's Nest. As he reset the padlock, he felt a draft on his ear. Ten feet above and a few feet away, a roof vent lay open. The translucent panel stood at an unnaturally upright angle, yanked and stuck in the open position, half-cranked to the side, one of the armlike hinges bent, the other ripped off.

The T18 through T26 trees had stood beneath the vent. That the table was moved diagonally a foot or so told him the intruder had fallen against it. Andre wondered if the thug had jumped from the ceiling, lost his balance, and stumbled into it. He may have even fallen onto the table itself, though no dirt was scattered on the floor. Perhaps, that had made a noise, a noise that had alerted Manu or someone working nearby.

He called the police. They asked if he was safe and unharmed, asked about damage. He agreed to wait for an officer on site and hung up feeling restless and unsure what to do. He opened his laptop and searched on Lisa Wight's name. A news article about the vandalism in Oregon appeared. Those trees had been also sprayed with herbicide. He rubbed his forehead. Should he try calling again? In a fit, he found the OSU number and did. She wasn't available. He left a message and hung up, grabbing the hose from its holder and watering the healthy trees in case they'd been hit by stray spray. He winced. What would he tell Alba and Castel?

A figure passed by the house's front wall. He hurried outside. Manu was unlocking the door to the S1 house. A woman with light hair and a tall frame talked about moving perennials into the demonstration garden. Andre stopped himself from charging them.

Manu made introductions. Andre asked if he had a minute and they went in the S2 house.

"I was curious if you were in over the weekend."

"Not Saturday," Manu said, "or Sunday." His eyes examined the floor while he removed his suede gloves and stuck them in a back pocket. "But Brodeur was here on Saturday."

"Really?"

"Yes. He told me he came in to install a small replacement tree in the garden."

"Do you know when he was in?"

"I would think seven or eight o'clock. He prefers to come in early and leave early."

"So, he was here Saturday morning?"

"I think so. Why?"

"Someone broke in and sprayed my trees."

Manu looked around, his gaze landing on the dead trees, his face contorting in disgust, then sympathy. "Why?"

"Not sure. But here's another question. Do you know if Monsieur Brodeur ever visits Brittany?"

"Brittany? Yes, I think he went there a few years ago *en vacances*."

"Really?"

"Yes, his niece lives there."

"She does?"

"No, wait, that's Belgium. Or is it? I can't remember. You know, you can ask him. He's in the Art Deco garden right now, but he'll be back soon."

A half-hour later, a police officer arrived on a motorbike. Officer Kateb was a slight lanky man with a short, military-style haircut. His face, with its large eyes and narrow structure, resembled a boy's, but he wore a mustache and spoke with a deep voice. His eyes were probing, yet Andre found him amateurish. He rested his hands on his belt and jiggled a leg when he spoke. Still, he had an alert nature that seemed like he might spot a significant clue or deceitful person and seeing how he was the only officer that had come, Andre had no choice but to talk to him. He explained the break-in and plant spraying. Kateb took notes on a small pad with a stoic shorthand. He neither nodded nor said much, instead focused on the story. Andre explained that he might be a target by an ecoterrorist campaign, similar to the one in Oregon, with which Kateb wasn't familiar. As they talked, it seemed Kateb barely knew apples came from trees at all and just as Andre was about to dismiss the encounter as useless, Kateb started circling the roof vent.

Carefully, his eyes scanned the frame, the panel, the floor area, the shifted tables. He took photos from every angle and said though the crime of damaging eleven plants wasn't exactly significant, he thought it worth studying the entry point.

They walked the perimeter of the S2 house, a floor of packed grit at the front and east, flattened grass at the west and back. When they came to the broken roof vent, Kateb noticed a dent in the S1 greenhouse and asked for a ladder. Andre hurried to the shed to find one. It was locked. He jiggled the door, cursed, then ran to the S1 house. Manu was watering flower baskets. He apologized for the key request still being tied up in paperwork and lent him his own.

As Andre was about to set it in the shed door's lock, Brodeur popped out, clearing his throat and wiping his mouth with a handkerchief.

"*Bonjour,*" Andre said. *Just the person I'd like to speak with.* But he didn't have time. He searched his mind for the French word for "ladder." *Echelle.* In French, he asked for a ladder, explaining that the police were waiting for it.

A cold suspicion burned in Brodeur's eyes. "Police? What in the world do they want?"

"My house was broken into over the weekend. Someone got in through a roof vent and sprayed some of my trees."

"*Your* house?"

"Well, the S2 house."

Brodeur tucked his handkerchief in the breast pocket of his windbreaker. "Yes, I heard him."

"What?"

"I heard something on Saturday. Early."

Andre searched his face for a sign of truth. That he was remembering an actual incident, instead of wishing to remember, or wanting to be integral to the situation. Or even in cahoots with a vandal. "On Saturday? You're certain?"

"Yes, of course."

"But you didn't go in to see what was going on?"

"I was busy hooking up the trailer!"

That meant he'd gone behind the house, banged around and made noise a mere twenty feet from the roof vent, which may have spooked the thug.

Brodeur huffed and said, "I thought it was you moving the tables around. Doing your usual nonsense."

"I wasn't in. It was an intruder."

His shoulders bunched in an exaggerated shrug.

"Will you talk to the police?"

Brodeur's eyes narrowed. "No."

"Please, Monsieur, will you help?"

"I have no time for police nonsense."

Police nonsense? "Monsieur, please."

"There's a ladder behind the shed," he said and walked away, taking out his handkerchief again and blowing his nose.

After Andre got the ladder and secured it against the S2 house, he held it as Kateb climbed up. His lean body in his black uniform, flattened against the clouded sky, seemed like a grasshopper, its thin legs moving with exaggerated intention. Ten minutes passed. He noticed the light of Kateb's camera flash a few times before he clunked down and jumped off from the third rung. "We may be able to get prints off the plastic on the inside."

"Really?"

"Maybe." Kateb's expression solidified into resolve. "But I need to ask you, do you have anyone you're estranged from? Someone you may have had a long-term argument with?"

"Don't think so."

"Like an ex-wife or ex-friend? Anyone hold a grudge against you?"

In California? Yes, maybe. "No, not at all."

"And all of the plants you grow in here, they're legal?"

"Legal?" Was a sapling and a bunch of tree material taken from the mountains in Kazakhstan legal? Sort of. They had declared it, and the paperwork had been filled out. Bribes paid. "Yes, of course."

Kateb unzipped a chest pocket and pulled out a business card. "This seems like a revenge or hate crime to me. Think about who might have hard feelings toward you. I'll phone when I'm ready to return with a crew. In the meantime, don't touch anything."

After Kateb left, Andre sat for a while. He answered email and paced around, sprayed off the leaves and trunks of the surviving trees with water, hoping to cleanse whatever poison residue might remain. Soon, the clouds cleared, the sun emerged, the house brightened. As water sprinkled like rain from the hose wand, Andre moved from tree to tree, admiring the tiny thin-limbed souls. Their survival encouraged him. If Brodeur hadn't been working with the trailer on Saturday, they would all be dead.

Anyone hold a grudge...

He imagined Brodeur outside the house, hooking the trailer to the tow spike of the cart, hearing the noise inside the house, perhaps the awkward scraping sound of a wooden legs stuttering against concrete. Perhaps, the vandal had heard the rumble of Brodeur's trailer, loud and booming. It reminded Andre of the booming noise they always made at Suntime Orchards when loading the delivery truck.

Hold a grudge...

Who held a grudge? Well, more than one person in California. A whole family in fact. But they wouldn't travel to Europe to hurt him. Would they? Plus, that was over a decade ago. Still, his heart raced as he remembered Jason's mother, Teri, the office manager at Suntime Orchards. She'd once confronted Andre. He'd just loaded the truck with crates of lemons that were headed for Sacramento. As he took off his gloves and rounded the building, she cornered him.

"I just heard a rumor," she said. Her blue eyes were framed with heavy eyeliner. Her clenched lips with frosty pink lipstick. She held a ballpoint pen as if she'd rushed from the office mid-work. "A nasty one. It involved you. And Grandma Mel."

He froze. He knew she'd find out sooner or later, though he'd hoped never.

"I did everything I could," he said, trying to step past.

She blocked him. "Oh really? Later, you went to the police. but right there and then—"

"I tried to do the right thing, Teri."

"Oh. Well, maybe you should have done the right thing earlier. Before she died."

That hurt. Yes, he should have but didn't. With his boot, he scraped gravel toward a puddle. Someone had dropped a paper towel in a corner. It sagged, wet and gritty, in mud. "I wanted to, but I wasn't sure what was going on."

Her face, with its dipped nose and square chin, resembled Grandma Mel's. But Teri's face burned with red fury. "You weren't sure?" She scoffed. "Well, there's one thing *I'm* sure of, Andre." She pushed a finger at him. "You're a coward."

CHAPTER 13

Later that afternoon, when Renia saw the dead saplings, she moaned and clutched her stomach. "What a loss."

"I already pulled the survivors and transplanted them," he said with an apologetic tap as if he'd been responsible for crushing her mood.

She crouched to the cluster of dried trees in the corner, inspected the branches, fingered the trunks. "And you've checked the bark all the way to the base?"

"Yes, on all."

"And?"

He shook his head.

"Uckh." She bit her lip, hovered for a moment, seeming unsure what to do. "How did they get in?"

"Roof vent." He pointed at the ceiling.

She stared at the panel. After Kateb's crew had finished their examination, Andre had shimmied it wonkily in place.

"It was open when I got here," he said.

"Huh... I don't understand. The phone app should have notified you over the weekend. The temperature must have fallen during that first night."

He stiffened. The remote temperature device. She'd given it to him in January. When he'd taken it out of the packaging, he'd noticed the main unit needed batteries and had forgotten to buy some. Now, it sat under a pile of folders and receipts he hadn't gotten around to sorting. His face warmed. He wanted to kick himself. "Renia, I'm... such a jerk. I haven't installed it yet. Now I realize what a mistake that was."

A weary smile slipped on her face as if she specialized in bozo bosses who didn't remember integral details of their businesses. "I understand. You thought things were under control. So did I." She hooked her bag onto her shoulder. "I'll be back soon. I'm off to buy batteries. We'll set it up today, okay?"

Her voice rang with a sweet calm, a fair reassurance. "Yes," he said. "Of course."

"Do you need some medicine? Tissue? How do you feel?"

Weakly, he shrugged, "Better than those trees."

After she left, he got out his phone to call Edo. He hesitated. Outside, a crow squawked. This was exactly what his boss had predicted: trouble.

If only I'd installed that gage.

You were ill.

Finally, he sucked up courage and called, reported what happened, apologized for not being more careful, and expressed frustration at the harassment and stalking.

As they debated whether to tell Castel and Alba, Andre heard the wind whiff into Edo's phone, children yelling in the background, random squeals of high-pitched voices. He must have been at a playground. In the faint distance, a woman's voice playfully called out, "Where are you hiding?"

"Well, the fruiting trees are secure, yes?" Edo said.

"Yes."

"That is the main concern. And the Kazakh sapling."

"It's fine," Andre said. "It actually looks happy. Flower buds are forming."

"Al-hamdulillah," he said. "If the sapling is well, then the project is well."

"Yes, at least we'll get apples from that."

"And perhaps from the others," Edo said.

The grafted trees might produce less potent fruit or not produce at all. They might die after flowering. Disease could seep in. Moths. More vandalism. Who knew? There were a hundred things that could go wrong. And on that day, Andre had lost some faith in himself.

"But this, this… vandal is still on the loose," Andre said. "I'm thinking of buying a cot so I can sleep here."

"Don't be foolish. We will simply put locks on the roof vents. You'll have to rely on the louvered vents at night for circulation and secure the rest."

Andre wasn't crazy about that idea. The nights were warming. He didn't want heavy air in the house, too risky for disease. "I need to find out who's behind this. Why anyone would want to sabotage a medicinal tree project."

Quiet.

"Are you still there?" Andre said.

"I'm thinking about your question."

"I mean, why would anyone… that worker here, Brodeur. He wouldn't have meddled in this, would he? He's very prickly."

"No. I've known Monsieur Brodeur for many years. He's a difficult personality, but he respects the natural world."

"It couldn't be that test subject from the first clinical trial, could it?"

"That I do not know. I never found more information about him."

"Well, the sooner I find out who it is, the better. There must be *someone* who knows how to track down a stalker. It doesn't seem like the police are very concerned."

"Hmm. Well, I do know an attorney—distantly—his name is Etienne Lessard. He works for animal rights, but he also represents victims of harassment. He's a bit eccentric. He worked with some Africans I know in Clignancourt."

A spark of hope lit his heart. "Is he high-profile?"

"Yes, at least in the world in which he works."

"Are his services, you know, expensive?"

"Very."

Andre sighed.

"But I will speak with Directeur Bertrand about reimbursement," he said, "Contact him. He may be able to help."

On the following Wednesday at three o'clock, Andre took the metro to Montmartre. He walked the hilly streets in a white sunshine, checking the building numbers before finally arriving at the door of a narrow, crumbling building with weedy flower boxes and rusted railings. On the balcony, tattered towels were draped over an indoor air-cleaning unit whose front panel had been spray-painted with Cyrillic letters. Two empty litter boxes were stacked in the corner. On the front door, a scratched plaque said "E. Lessard, Avocat."

What a dump.

Andre approached a brass knocker in the shape of St. Francis, about to lift it when the door opened and Lessard appeared. With a short stature, pug nose, and squiggle of lips, he would've looked like a fairy dwarf had it not been for the thinning wisp of straw-colored hair and prematurely white beard. He wore cycling spandex pants, stained at the knees as if he'd been praying in a puddle or digging in the garden, and the sleeves on his greasy smock were too short for his long arms.

"Come in, come in," he said, waving with an anxious flap. "I've got the oven on and I don't like to leave it."

The dim vestibule smelled damp with a round window caked with mold and a burned-out sconce. Towers of plastic boxes were stacked against the walls. Various pipe wrenches lay in the corner. Lessard galumphed up a circular staircase littered with animal leashes and discarded hats and children's shoes.

Edo had said Lessard walked with a limp, but the odd cloppy gait seemed to be a result of his feet leaning into the inner sides of his soles, his shoes being those mushy athletics designed to protect the feet more than enable activity.

They hiked up three flights before he opened the door to a spacious room with large windows and a pyramidal skylight with tar patches. A desk, file drawers, bookcases, and sofa were clustered at one end, a small kitchen at the other. A dozen animals roamed about. It smelled like a barn. Two white cats lounged on a windowsill near an iguana in a tank. Three Toucans, one missing tail feathers, squawked in an enormous cage. Near the sofa, a three-legged German Shepherd slept on a heated mat.

"Here, here," he said, leading Andre to the kitchen and shutting off the oven, "I have to bake Enzi's treats," he said. "Otherwise, he'll throw up. Would you like a drink?"

"Oh, uh..."

"It's a hot walk up the hill."

Not wanting to seem rude, he said yes.

Lessard grabbed a jar and stuck it under the tap of a dye-stained sink, then handed it to him.

He peered into the glass. It seemed clean enough.

"Sorry, I don't have any soda or juice."

"That's okay," he said, "so Edo mentioned you might know—"

"Edo, yes, how is he? Such a kind man."

"He's well." A small animal lunged at Andre's arm. He jumped. His elbow had invaded the personal space of a nursing ferret in a cage.

"Come," Lessard said, "it's more comfortable outside."

He led Andre downstairs and out into a small courtyard. The cobbles were covered at the far end by hay and wooden structures and a hexagon-wire fence. A billy goat stood chewing beneath a chestnut tree, its wispy beard rotating with its jaw, indifferent to the visitor. In the opposite pen, a plump ostrich extended its neck forward to inspect Andre. The skin where its left eye should have been was wrinkled shut. It let out a squeak before pecking and scratching at the hay. A few hens roamed at its feet.

Is it legal to keep animals in Paris?

Lessard cleared two worn metal chairs of papers. "I have read your email," he said. "Very interesting." They sat down and Andre showed him the note card, photos of the greenhouse, and the vandalized trees. He looked over the photos cursorily, but examined the note and envelope closely, rereading several times. "And you say, this guy, or someone hired by him, followed you in the Latin Quarter last week?"

"Yes."

He nodded, loudly cleared his throat. "And do the police know?"

"They said to call if it happened again."

"Of course."

Lessard scratched at the small tuft of hair atop his head.

"Do you think it could be ecoterrorists?" Andre said.

Lessard blew out a long breath. "Perhaps. The threat is typical. The fact that it's from Brittany is not surprising."

"Really?"

"More than one extreme group has formed there. You've heard of the Nationalist Front?"

"Yes. But you don't think—"

"No, I actually don't. They wouldn't care about such small concerns as this. But other groups devote a lot of energy to policing people and practices they don't like."

"Do you know which one it might be?"

"I have a few ideas. The language here points to a religious organization, but I'm not sure. I can do a search in the database and see what comes up."

"There was an incident a few years ago in the United States," Andre said. "A group attacked a growing project in Oregon. Their team was experimenting with a special cultivar of apricots. The trees were sprayed with herbicide like mine."

"Ah, yes, I know that one."

"You do?"

He dug in his shirt pocket and pulled out a tissue, then wiped his forehead. "My God, this morning it's 17 degrees and now, 25." He dabbed the back of his neck. "Yes, the incident in America was assumed to be done by ecovandals, however, in the last news report I read, they hadn't made any arrests yet."

"Would they be in Paris as well?'

His face scrunched. "Hard to say. Those guys, they call themselves United Caring for the Natural or UCN. They like to destroy projects that exploit the earth and sometimes preserve it. They don't know the difference."

"The team in Oregon was doing good work."

Lessard balled up his tissue and shoved it deep in his sleeve. "Yes, I think the trees were for some sort of allergy research."

The goat lifted its leg and peed.

"Excuse me," Lessard said, then got up and untangled the rope around the goat's neck before limping back.

"I can confirm with the police report. Let's check."

He hobbled toward an arched wooden door, once painted purple, now faded to sooty lavender.

Andre followed him to a little room dank with sour air. One wall held buckets and feed supplies and tools, the other filing cabinets. Atop was an old desk monitor. He slid on crooked reading glasses and stood on tiptoes, typing a few words, scrolling through a list of summary titles. "Here's a brief. Okay, trial to research potential allergy reduction properties in apricots for future blah blah..." He read on in what seemed miniscule type. "Here, this is from a statement by a researcher who had worked on the project. Take it for what it is." He squinted. "On a trial with human research subjects for blah blah blah, they tested the effects of this apricot to curb allergies. The trial was quite effective, the results looked promising." He read on. "One subject, an older gentleman, who'd had a reaction to the apricot, maybe from an allergic reaction to ingestion of pit material, not sure, had fallen into a hallucinatory state, almost a speaking-in-tongues, religious experience." He paused. "What is speaking-in-tongues?"

"As if speaking in another language, but not really. Just fast jibberish."

"Okay, well, this man had to be rushed to the hospital."

"From apricots?"

"Yes. This says it was later determined to be an allergic reaction. But that information didn't seem to get out to the public. Rather, the video of him did in this jibberish state, when he was hallucinating. It happened outside in a parking lot. And it was quite frightening. He screamed, writhed around, beat himself with his own fists."

"Beat himself with fists? Great."

"Yes," Lessard said, still eyeing the screen at a close distance, "and apparently he bruised his face. But the worst news?"

"What?"

"The video had 330,000 views."

As he walked to the Metro, Andre couldn't shake the idea of a man convulsing from an allergic reaction. It kept flashing in his mind like an object's outline after a camera flashed. Disturbing. Unfortunate. He hoped the victim had recovered. Wondered who'd retaliated for him and sprayed Lisa Wight's trees. Lessard had searched for the video, but his computer started locking. Andre tapped down the stairs of the metro station, a paper copy of the report in his hand, yearning to speak with Lisa Wight. Once on the train, he read through the report three times. The man's unfortunate symptoms had created a magnetically chaotic scene. No wonder so many clicks. And LaRoche Naturel must have known about it. That's why they were so concerned about their troublesome trial subject. His story could go viral.

Later, at the Monge station, he trudged up the stairs, a bitter taste in his mouth.

His phone rang.

Dad.

"What's all this I hear about anonymous notes?" he said.

Andre stopped. Two pigeons were circling his feet. His dad knew, but how... Delphine. It had to be. The other Sunday when she'd visited while he was sick, he must have opened his yap, though he had no memory of it.

"Just some crazy person," he said. "I think, I think..." He stood before the window of a toy store. Inside a boy with red hair, maybe twelve years old, worked the remote on a little helicopter. It was white with the red markings of a hospital. "What happened was..."

He would have told him it was all an internal joke among colleagues, but Oskar cut him off.

"Aunt Dauphine said this threat came from Brittany."

Aunt Dauphine? In Bordeaux? Nosy Aunt Dauphine. Of course, she did. She'd heard from her daughter and now his mother and father were both alarmed about his safety and irritated that he hadn't told them.

Then, as if on cue: "Why didn't you tell us?"

"There was nothing to tell. The police are working on it." At least they didn't know about the sprayed trees, that the thug had followed him, or what he'd learned from Lessard.

"How's Mom?" he said. "Sorry I didn't call you back last week."

"No changing the subject," Oskar said. "What in the world is going on there?"

"Nothing really, I'm fine. It's just a kid fooling around. Maybe a student."

The helicopter hovered above the boy's head, flying in a small circle around the shop.

"A student?"

"Maybe, probably."

"But what if he does something worse?"

He already has. "I'm taking precautions."

"Good, because this weirdo may come back with more people looking for you. He may come tonight."

"I know that, Dad. I know."

"Can you set up a camera? Or an alarm system?"

"I don't have the money."

Silence. "Well, how much does one cost?"

"A lot."

"Well…"

The helicopter flew in a faster circle.

"I'm going to call your grandmother," Oskar said. "She may know someone in the Paris police department who can make this a higher priority."

"Paris police department?"

"She may know someone."

"No, Dad, she doesn't know anyone."

"She might."

"Dad, don't. Please don't. Instead, wait. They're working on it. They said they'll call me tomorrow, so hold off."

The helicopter zoomed toward the darkness of the shop. The boy laughed. His mother trailed him as he roamed through aisles of toys.

"Will you keep us posted?" Oskar said.

"Yes, for sure. Is Mom okay?"

"Yes. She almost fell again but caught herself on the counter."

"What? How?"

"She tried to make coffee without me. Got a nasty burn."

"A burn?!"

"It's on her leg. And it's healing. The kettle fell and hit her thigh. She's fine. In good spirits. Wants to see you whenever you can visit. But listen, about your project... you can't afford a second... just be careful, Andre."

The helicopter crashed into a wall of masks: unicorns, witches, the devil.

He walked on, leaving the toy shop behind. "I am being careful. Will you tell Mom I said I hope she feels better?"

"Yes, of course."

"I have to go, Dad."

They hung up. He felt like a ground up bean. Oskar would be outraged if he'd known someone had sprayed the plants and stalked his son. He would fly to Paris and sleep in the greenhouse with a baseball bat. Of course, sleeping in the greenhouse was the best precaution Andre could take.

A chill rang through his body. He'd passed a guy in a hoodie and jacket at the Monge station. But where? On the stairs, going down as he went up. The hood, charcoal gray, had been up, covering the face. He hadn't noticed Andre, but Andre had noticed him. He retraced his steps to the metro stairs, went halfway down and looked around. People walked up with backpacks, purses, and briefcases. Two white-haired ladies wheeled suitcases to the ticket kiosk. Buzzing, fluorescent lights. Stained floor. A map of Paris on the wall. The whishing sound of a train. Stale, blowing air. No thug. It must have been his imagination.

Once in a while, climbing the circular staircase that led to his apartment made him dizzy. This was why, when he reached his floor and saw what was at the end of the dim hall, he assumed it was a hallucination. A tree by the door in a black container. It seemed like a package delivery, but it wasn't boxed up. A short sapling. The thin trunk and branches had been chopped to pieces and left on the floor. A lower branch dangled at an awkward angle, attached by a string of bark. He took three fast steps. Dirt had been spilled, as if the pot had been knocked over and set upright again.

Near the tree, a small card lay on the floor. Stark white in the dark daylight. The same card as the mailed note. Faded typed letters read: "Because of the fruit, suffering is upon us. And now suffering is upon you."

He shivered.

How had the thug gotten hold of a Tengri? All were accounted for as of that morning. He'd come while Andre was gone?

His heart sank. *Linus.*

He stepped over the mess and grabbed the doorknob. Locked. A relief. He fumbled to unlock it and went inside, calling for the cat. Had he let him out that morning? The apartment was quiet, still. The empty bowl of muesli he'd eaten for breakfast sat on the kitchen counter, his pajama pants tossed at the foot of his unmade bed. But on the rumpled blanket or in the crook of a sofa pillow where the cat usually napped, the spots were bare and cold. With a tense gut, he whipped open each closet door and every tall cabinet, half-expecting a trapped cat to spring free. But each coat and every broom hung and leaned as they usually did.

"Linus!" He roamed the living room, checking behind the plants, rubbing his chin, unsure what to do. "Hey tiger, where are you?"

Maybe he's hiding. Give it a few minutes. He plopped on the couch, got out his phone and called the police, waited to be patched through to Kateb.

A woman answered.

Andre said, "I'd like to report a crime."

He gave his name and address. There was a moment of silence. The woman asked if he'd reported vandalism a few days ago. Yes, he said. He gave her the details and asked for Officer Kateb. She assured him he was on his way.

Afterward, he shook a bag of kitty treats as he scoured the roof deck, calling the cat. He checked the rear where it dropped off to a plane tree and the small courtyard. Linus could easily jump onto a branch, claw his way down the tree, and land on the cobbles. From there, he could slip between the buildings. But he never did. Andre searched through the potted trees and shrubs that stood like a random scattering of chess pieces with little hint of strategy. A spire of a king knocking against several squat round pawns. The odd shape of a vine, curving and dipping like a knight, the perfect spot for a hidden cat. He searched in random circles, calling Linus's name more loudly, peeking into every shadow and crevice.

But as the city clamored with revving engines, snippets of conversation, and hurried footsteps, the shadows and crevices remained quietly empty.

CHAPTER 14

A ndre, turgid with fear and wild scenarios, went through the apartment, about to search for Linus in the hallway. He stopped at the stairs. The police were on their way. *Should I leave? Where is he? How far could he go in a few hours?* He leaned against the wall in dejected surrender. Below in the foyer, the door opened. Voices bounced. The police. Officer Kateb and an older bald man trudged up the stairs. When they reached his floor, Andre shook hands and answered questions, waited as they took photos of the sapling. He filled out a report. Taking fingerprints was impossible since dirt coated the pot's surface already. The older officer, Mullins, wasn't impressed with a chopped-up tree as an act of vandalism, but when Kateb explained the anonymous note and greenhouse break in, he said, "Hmph. Possible hate crime," then grinned, "against florists."

Andre rolled his eyes.

Kateb crouched and picked up a branch with flowers. "And you're certain this is a tree from your greenhouse?"

"I thought so."

Mullins said, "Why not chop it and leave it at the greenhouse?"

The sapling stood like a broken tower. The trunk, still intact halfway down, stood amidst the cut branches, scattered where they'd fallen after being hacked. Something wasn't right. The branch Kateb held had bloomed with pink, not white, flowers. A few other branches had pink flowers as well. And the black container was a soft polypropylene, not a hard shell as he and Renia used at the S2 house.

"Wait," Andre said. "Can I see that?" He took the branch from Kateb and examined the series of short spurs with darkly pink flowers. "It's not the Tengri sapling. It's a different kind of sapling."

"Ah," Kateb said.

"Is it a close representation of the tree?" Mullins said.

"Yes," Andre said.

"Like an effigy, to send a message," Kateb said.

Mullins nodded. "Could be."

"It's an apple sapling," Andre said. "It looks like a Braeburn."

"Do you recognize the bucket?"

"It's not mine but used a lot in the industry."

Officer Mullins crouched down and pulled out a broken white tag hidden between the soil and the pot's wall. "*Alors*," he said, studying it. "It says 'Malice.' 'Edith Rose's Malice.'"

Malice? Another message? Andre took the tag. Of course. *Malus*, the genus. "Malus 'Edith Rose' is a kind of apple tree."

"Any idea where one could buy it?"

Andre shook his head. "A lot of nurseries sell fruit trees."

"Well, if you find any other evidence, or notice anything unusual, give me a call," Kateb said. He handed him the same card he'd given him previously. "Every time you experience another incident," he said, "the evidence builds. That's good for your case."

Andre gave a bitter smile. "So I should keep getting vandalized?"

"No, not at all. But it gives us more information." And with that, they walked around the mess and left.

At first, Andre thought he'd toss the tree in the outside waste bin, but decided to set it aside so he could take it to the S2 house and leave it at the door. He wanted the thug to know he'd seen it and wasn't intimidated, even though he was. Should he check on the Tengris again? He got out a pan and broom and swept up the dirt, set the branches back in the soil, and left the tree by the door.

Once inside under the light, the tag's black marker revealed the tree's name clearly, but on the flip side, faded letters spelled out its source and price. "Verdant Farms, 40 Euro."

Verdant Farms must have been the grower. A small operation. Otherwise, the company would have printed the labels with type and a logo. Where was Verdant Farms? The Netherlands? It was a British name, not French, written in English words. He didn't recognize it, had never heard of it, then realized who might know.

He got out his phone and dialed. "Nes, I need your help."

No reply. Clinking plates, a low rumble of background conversation. Jazz music with a fast, melodious trumpet. "Right, what's up?"

Andre explained what happened. "Where is Verdant Farms?" he said in a loud caw. He could hear a mug clack against a wood table. Silverware rang against ceramic.

"Verde? They're in Spain."

"No, Verdant. Verdant Farms."

"What?"

"Verdant."

"That's what I said, Verde," Nes said. "Verde Growing."

"Am I interrupting your dinner?"

"No, we're waiting for a table."

"I'm trying to figure out who carries Verdant Farms plants."

"Yeah, that's Spain, near Barcelona."

Andre paced in a circle. "Call me back when you're free."

He went to his bedroom to get his laptop, heard shouting. Outside the window and in the courtyard below, two boys, about eight years old, were on their knees, hunched over an iron plate. They folded paper notes, counting as they went, "*Un, deux, trois...*" stopping at the number five and tearing the notes into tiny pieces. Then, they jumped up, tossing the confetti in the air.

Andre opened the window. "*Ay,*" he called, "*qu'est-ce que tu fais?*"

The boys looked up and around, stunned by the voice. One

had brown hair and wore a tan windbreaker, the other was blonde in a ski jacket.

"*Rien*," they said. "*Nous devons eliminer le mauvais sang.*"

"*Le mauvais sang?*" Andre said. *Eliminate the bad blood?*

Dozens of white specks littered the soil around a tree.

He asked if they'd seen an orange cat and the boy in the ski jacket said he saw a cat in the wine shop but couldn't remember if it was orange.

Andre thanked them and closed the window.

The daylight had dimmed. It was 6:40, well past Linus' dinnertime. He took the treat bag and went downstairs onto the Rue Rollin, calling his name, shaking the bag. He went to the wine shop where a black cat lounged on the counter, then down a narrow pedestrian alleyway before rounding the block and going to the gate of a passage to his building. He scanned every nook, every doorway, every balcony for his tawny ragdoll. Nothing.

Yes, he could have taken him. That thug.

And locked the door? Maybe.

His mind raced with ghoulish thoughts. The cat's head bashed in. His neck slit. Drowned. Criminals used the things you loved to get to you. But that thug would have left Linus's body outside the door with the chopped sapling. Unless he intended to use Linus later as leverage. He walked faster, passing a rare bookstore whose antique copies of Leroux's *Mystery of the Yellow Room* and Bazin's *La Barriere* sat in the window. He jogged across the street where a grocer set a bulging brown bag in a scale that hung over a wooden bin of fruits of vegetables. "He's off from work today, sorry," he said to a customer. Clueless where to go, Andre stopped at every tiny street garden and alleyway, calling the cat's name. His voice echoed on the cobbles. What would he do without Linus, his tiger buddy of eight years?

His phone rang. Nes.

The restaurant noise was replaced by the sound of wood crackling and snapping, his voice clear. "Why are you so interested in Verde Growing?"

"I'm not. I'm looking for Verdant Farms, which I think is in Holland."

"Verdant? Oh yeah, for sure. Wait, Penny, love, would you put the screen up?"

"What?"

"An ember popped near your leg."

"Nes?"

"Sorry, got a fire going tonight."

"Do you know Verdant Farms?"

"Yeah, for sure. They're outside of Amsterdam."

Andre threw up a hand. He went left, then right, then decided to head home. The sky was indigo, the street lamps illuminated with soft light. As he walked, he passed a bistro whose two rows of cafe tables were enclosed by a thick black chain. A waiter lit a propane heater that sputtered, hummed, and burned blue. A chilly bite was descending on the city.

"Do you know who carries their apple trees in France?"

Nes was quiet. Andre could hear his wife's voice in the background. She spoke in an animated way to another female voice. Nes said to her, "No, it's squeezed in behind the table, hard to see," then in a louder click to Andre, "Well, Graines de Grace would carry them, but they're in the south. Maybe Le Soleil near Marseilles. Oh shite, what am I thinking? La Sculpture Verte. La Sculpture sells all the specialty plants. They buy from me on occasion. I'm sure that's it, it's only what, 50 or 60 kilometers from the city."

"Okay," Andre said, "good."

"Not really, because that snoot, Fanine, runs it. She's a queen and a half. You won't be able to fit through the door because her ego takes up all the space. Remember the Wilshire Prize at Chelsea? She won it, then dissed the whole show in the papers."

In a vague memory, Andre did remember this, some five or seven years ago. At the Chelsea Flower Show, a wild container arrangement had wowed the judges and public alike. After Fanine Rocher was awarded the prize, she proceeded to criticize the judges in a newspaper interview, calling them and show organizers old-fashioned and stodgy. On the closing night of the show, she got drunk in a pub and in a bold voice ridiculed the wealthi-

137

est donor.

"Do you think she'll help me?" Andre said.

"Not sure about that."

"What if I'm polite?"

"She's rarely in that nursery. Too special you know to show up and run the place. It would be work to get her to even come for a special appointment. And then, whether she'd help... maybe."

Andre stood before the wooden doors of his building. The two iron knobs centered on the wood reminded him of the glass eyes he'd once seen as a child on a taxidermied cat.

"What if I bring her something?" Andre said. "Is there a plant she wants but can't get a hold of?"

Long silence.

Nes laughed and said, "Oh, hell, how could I have missed it? Yes, of course, there is. Yes, there definitely is."

After he hung up, Andre unlocked the apartment door and tossed his keys on the entry table, dejected and blue. In the living room, a flash. Between a cataract palm and creeping fig, Linus's eyes shimmered gold from the hall light, his orange head and ears barely visible under the foliage.

"Linus!" Andre said, louder than he meant to.

The cat shot into the bedroom and hid under the bed.

Andre got on his knees and peered under the mattress. "Is that where you've been?"

The cat huddled in the farthest corner, watched him with a frozen vigilance.

"Come, on, let's go."

Linus meowed.

"I have tuna for dinner."

No movement.

"Treats?"

A turn of the head, away.

Andre got up and went to the kitchen. The cat was spooked. Maybe the thug had banged on the door to draw Andre out from the apartment.

He took a can of tuna from the cabinet, dropping it on the

counter with a loud whack. He rustled in the utensil drawer, making purposeful metallic noises, and found the opener. As soon as the lid lifted and the smell of fish wafted in the air, Linus darted in the kitchen and leapt onto the table, cheerily meowing.

That Friday, Nes came to Paris in the Plant Releaf van and they drove to La Sculpture Verte, a five-acre farm with a house, nursery, and shop near Rambouillet. Fanine Rocher sold the area's rarest plants and customers drove from as far away as Germany to see the stock. Fanine and Nes had a business relationship that stretched back a dozen years and from Nes's passionate thrashing of her, Andre wondered if romance had once sparked between them. When he and Nes had been in their twenties, Nes had spent a weekend with her in Amsterdam before he'd met Penny. Now the two maintained a business relationship. La Sculpture Verte needed Nes's plants from hidden corners of the world and Nes needed the nursery's far-reaching reputation to sell them at higher prices.

They parked in the gravel lot of an old stone farmhouse on a country road surrounded by fields of wildflowers and cultivated rows of plants. Red poppies sparked through swaths of bluebells and pink hyacinths. The dry smell of lavender hit Andre's nose as he got out of the van. By the entrance, framed by a giant arbor covered with sturdy grape vines, Fanine laughed loudly with a worker who arranged orange and yellow tulips on a wooden table. She was a tall hardy woman with a chestnut mane of hair in a loose pony tail. When she heard the door to the van slam, she turned, smiled and walked over, dangling a dead rabbit by its ears.

Nes nodded at it. "I see you're still treating the customers well."

She smiled slyly. "Dinner."

Nes made introductions and Andre waited for her to shift the rabbit to her other hand so she could shake his, but she didn't. Instead, she looked him over from boots to face, her height nearly matching his six-two frame. To Nes, she said, "Did you bring me a pretty?'"

"I might have a treat you want."

"Woody or green?"

"Bulb," he said.

A knowing smile slid across her face. "The 'Scarlet King' Cardiocrinum?"

"Yes."

She clapped her gloved hands together, the rabbit jiggling.

Andre knew the plant and the Canadian botanist who'd discovered it. It was a huge bulb native to South Africa that grew into a thirteen-foot, lily-like plant whose color was a velvety deep scarlet. She could probably sell each plant for 50 Euros.

"How many?" she said.

"Thirteen," Nes said, "Your lucky number."

She sported a happy yet grim expression as if to say, *You came through for me, you old asshole who I hate.*

"But listen, Fanny, we need your help," Nes said.

Her eyes shifted to Andre.

Nes said, "*I* need your help."

"Well, that won't be the first time, Nestor." She walked away.

Andre raised his eyebrows at Nes. He was unphased. They followed. Nes explained about the Kazakhstan expedition and the Tengri project. They wandered to a smaller house behind the main house and a woman came out wiping her hands on a canvas apron. Fanny handed her the rabbit before the three wandered through rows of potted shrubs.

"I won't go into the nitty gritty," Nes said, "but what it comes down to is this one bloke we know, he's been a real pain in the arse. We need to know if you sold him an 'Edith Rose' sapling in the past few weeks."

She paused, her arms folded. "An 'Edith Rose' apple?"

"Yeah."

"And he's a customer?"

Nes glanced at Andre. "We think of him as a competitor."

She smirked. "Those are the worst kind."

"We think he's tall, a big guy. Wears a gray hoodie, sometimes a cap. We're not sure, but we need to know who he is ... are you selling the 'Edith Rose' this year?"

"I have a few," she said. "They're small."

"Yes, this one was small."

They walked through the shrubs to a stand of potted trees. At the edge of the third row, amongst the pears and cherries, stood three Edith Rose saplings, all potted in soft-shell black pots, smelling sweetly of blossoms.

"That's it," Andre said.

"That's what?" she said.

He checked the tag. "This is the cultivar outside the door." His heart beat fast. "Do you have records of your sales?"

She looked away, avoiding his gaze.

Andre stiffened. *Too forward.*

"Fanny," Nes said. "We've got a tricky situation. We're working on a new apple tree."

At this, her face brightened.

"But it's become as hot as the devil. You see, this goon, he's trying to intimidate us. He already broke into Andre's greenhouse. And sprayed glyphosate on eleven saplings."

Her expression hardened.

She said to Andre, "This is true?"

He felt a mix of embarrassment and sorrow. "Yes."

"And he dropped off an 'Edith Rose' at Andre's door," Nes said. "Then, to send a message, he chopped the damn thing up like kindling and left it laying in its own dirt."

Her alert face melted to burning fury. She glared at Andre, as if outraged he could let this happen. Her intensity worried him. He thought she'd admonish him, perhaps send them away.

"It's true," he said helplessly.

At this, she stormed off, marching toward the larger house, stomping up the stone steps and through the door. They followed into a tall-ceilinged gift shop with gurgling fountains and garden tools. It smelled of smoky sandalwood though Andre couldn't find the burning incense stick. As she rounded the counter's corner, she whipped off her gloves and threw them down hard, then typed on a nearby desktop, pounding on an arrow key with her middle finger.

Nes grinned at Andre.

Andre stood quietly.

She scrolled through the records as a blonde woman in overalls and rubber boots passed by the open door outside, carrying a
tray of mini-roses.

"An 'Edith Rose' was purchased last Monday," Fanny said,
her face clenched. "The person paid cash."

Excited, Andre stopped himself from asking if she remembered the customer, lest she blow her top.

She stared at Nes, her umber eyes intense. "I don't remember
him, but Camille might."

They went outside to a nearby display table of tulips and
daffodils and grasses. The blonde woman in overalls was shifting
around containers to make room for the mini-roses.

"Camille, this is Monsieur..."

"Damazy," he said.

"Monsieur Damazy." Her voice trembled. "He received one of
our 'Edith Rose' saplings as a gift. Do you remember who bought
it? The customer purchased it a few days ago."

Camille swatted her gloved hands together, shaking off dirt,
her eyebrows crunched in thought.

"He would be a tall brawny guy in a sweatshirt," Andre said.
"A gray sweatshirt and jacket?"

"Yes, I remember that," she said.

"You do?"

"Yes. His accent was very rough. He wore a strange hat and
acted kind of weird. I was unloading a shipment in the driveway
and he came to me. He wanted an apple tree, he said. He spoke
so softly I couldn't hear him at first. I showed him where the trees
were and left him to shop, but he picked up the nearest one,
by the trunk," she shook her head, disapproving of the gesture.
"Then he walked behind me, very closely, all the way to the shop.
It was bizarre."

"Did he give you his name?"

"No... but I remember I asked if he had grown that apple tree
before and he hadn't. Once he had an apple tree, he said, at his
parents' house. I asked if they lived in Paris, just to figure out
the conditions, and he said they were in Brittany. So I asked if

142

he wanted the instruction sheet and he said no. He paid from a huge roll of Euros."

"A huge roll, eh?" Nes said.

"Yes, and he didn't wait for the change or the receipt, he just took the tree by the trunk again and walked out. There was a taxi waiting for him."

"Do you remember the name of the taxi company?" Nes said.

"No. The car was blue though. Is he your friend?" she said to Andre.

"Um," he said, "not really."

They thanked her and went to the van, and Nes got out the flat of *Cardiocrinums*. Each plant had four leaves shaped like hearts, glossy and gigantic. Fanine and Nes went in the shop to settle paperwork before coming back and Nes saying, "If any of your staff see him again, will you phone me?"

"If I see him again, I'll slit his throat," she said. "He destroyed a treasure. Verdant Farms gave me three of the five they grew this year. They've had trouble with moths lately. Now, one is gone for no good reason."

Andre considered trying to save the demolished sapling for her.

Suddenly she held out her hand, a faint smile at her lips.

Andre shook it. Her grip pinched.

"I hope your project is successful," she said. "Let me know if you'd like to sell your trees."

He thanked her and they got in the van.

Just as Nes fired up the ignition, Camille came hurrying out of the shop.

"Monsieur," she called. "Monsieur!"

Andre opened the door.

"He left this pamphlet on the counter the day he bought the tree. I kept it because I thought he might come back for it, but he never did."

CHAPTER 15

While Nes drove, Andre examined the pamphlet. On the front, a photo showed dramatically rolling clouds in the sky, outlined in silver, casting misty beams of sunshine. The font was looping and ornate, difficult to read. In English, it read: "The wages of sin is death. Romans 6:23." And on the back: "God so loved the world that he gave us his only begotten son. John 3:16. Don't be led astray. Let Jesus love you. Let Him fill your heart." At the lower right, an emblem displayed a cross slicing through raised flames, or maybe burning within them.

He set the pamphlet aside, then realized the thug's fingerprints might be on it and gingerly slid it in his bag. Outside the window, the open farmland changed into clusters of suburban buildings. On a local street, a teen girl walked a toy poodle on a leash. At a playground, a boy tried to spin a basketball on his finger. Briefly, Andre dozed before leaving a long text updating Officer Kateb. Soon, they arrived at Andre's building where he and Nes got out and clapped backs and Nes told him not to worry about "the wanker" because he was "all mouth and no trousers" but just in case he should install an alarm on the S2 house. Andre went upstairs, made sure the cat was in the apartment, and phoned Etienne Lessard.

The next Monday, Andre went to the Pigalle Café, and since it was warm but raining, he sat on the terrace beneath the awning. He ordered a sandwich and checked the temperature app on the S2 house thermostat before responding to student emails on his laptop. As he worked, a bulge from collecting rain formed in the awning above his head. It stretched the canvas. A steady drip of water fell at his right shoulder. After several minutes, a waiter in an apron came out with a broom and pushed the straw head into the bulge. The canvas resisted. He pushed harder and further, up, up, up before a splash of water crashed on the sidewalk. Through the drips, he saw Lessard crossing the street.

In a beret and raincoat, he limped along in a slow shuffle, carrying a soft briefcase with a peace symbol sticker. Beside him, a boy, about ten years old, strolled along. With a puffy jacket and baseball cap, he looked like a mini hip hop star.

"Excuse my tardiness," he said, "I had to pick up Gerard from ice skating."

The boy was thin, so thin that he looked ill. His complexion was pale and his eyes large with dark circles beneath. He sat in a quiet slump at the table. Lessard ordered them both soup. When it came, the boy eyed it with suspicion before shoving a spoonful in his mouth.

"Now," Lessard said. "Let's see this propaganda."

Andre handed him the pamphlet, which he'd stored in a zipped plastic bag.

"Papa, can I play?" Gerard said.

"One more," Lessard said.

Gerard hit his forehead in exaggerated exasperation.

Lessard held up a finger.

He picked up the spoon and swallowed.

"OK, you can play. On the street, not here."

Gerard pulled a bulky visor from his coat and strapped it on his head. He went just beyond the restaurant railing and switched on the headset. A blue light glowed from the eyepiece. With a serious expression, he played a virtual reality game. He jumped around with curled fists as if boxing. Hitting the air and dodging, hitting and dodging, tangled with an invisible enemy.

Lessard removed his glasses and stuck an eye close to the pamphlet, scanned the quote, the clouds, the cross. His eye seemed to move in slight shifts as if he had nystagmus. "Interesting."

"What is it?"

"This is unusual."

"What is?"

He tilted the bag toward the light. "It seems to be the symbol of a church logo. I've seen it or some variation. Do you see the fire and the dove?"

"A dove?"

"There's a cross slicing through the fire, but the tail end of it creates a new image..."

"Yes."

"It curves into a dove. Do you see the beak?"

"A small one."

"This is literature that's distributed by American churches. It's been a recent trend, within the last three or four years."

"American? But why not distribute a pamphlet in French?"

"That's what doesn't make sense," Lessard said. "Unless he's an American who moved here."

"He told the woman at the nursery his parents lived in Brittany."

"Hmph. Maybe a European who visited there." Lessard held the bag far from his face, then close to his eye. "Did you see the other side, this inscription? To M.F.?"

"No, I hadn't noticed that."

"In script, it says 'To M.F.'"

"The pamphlet was a gift?"

"Most likely."

"So his initials are M.F."

"Perhaps. But the pamphlet may have passed through a few people." He set it on the table, slurped his soup. "It probably originated in the Southern part of the U.S. It's the most common place to find these."

"In churches?"

"Yes. And they're the kinds of churches that dislike more kinds of people than they like."

They were quiet. Gerard still danced on the sidewalk, playing his game, punching at shadows.

"Should I show the police?" Andre said.

Lessard shrugged with one shoulder. "You could, they won't know it, I don't think. Although the initials *are* a clue." He ate his soup. After a few seconds, he said, "Hmph," and waved a finger. "Contact a colleague of mine. She's in America. Social worker who manages a nonprofit center. Does excellent therapy with hate crime victims." Lessard took out his wallet, a smashed piece of leather frayed at the edges. He sifted through a small clump of business cards.

The rain thickened into a noisy shower. Out on the sidewalk, Gerard didn't seem to notice.

Lessard turned over the wallet and checked a hidden slot, which held a dirty folded post-it note. "Ah, feed list," he said to himself. "Well, I'm unable to find her card, Andre."

In the awning above their heads, the rainwater bulge formed again.

"Does she know about this church?"

"I'm certain she does. What's more, she may very well know how it connects with your man in Brittany."

The canvas in the awning stretched and grew to the size of a boulder.

Lessard tapped his head, "But give me a few days. Unfortunately, at this moment, I can't remember her name."

Andre left feeling disappointed in Lessard's faulty memory yet grateful for a clue to the Breton's motives. He was part of a religious group, not an ecoterrorist. Either way, Andre had to be careful. Nes was right; his dad was right. He needed an alarm system. Questions about how to afford one and why he'd turned into a target in the first place tormented him. Over the course of the next several days, he dropped off the pamphlet at the Préfecture, worked in the greenhouse, crossed paths with Renia only once, and locked up each night feeling alert and tense. He'd had the roof vent fixed and hook locks installed, but whenever he was gone, that thug had an opportunity to spray the trees. He might return to the faculty offices. He might try to break in the apartment. Andre had kept Linus inside since the day he'd found the chopped tree but wondered if the cat would be safer outside where he could sprint away if needed. The fears gnawed at him until a couple of weeks later when he received an email from his mother.

"Have transferred $500 US to your account. Hope enough for alarm. Peas are ready for harvest. Love, M."

For Vivienne, typing was easier than speaking. Talking on the phone was worse since she could barely pronounce Andre's name. It was a struggle to string words together. Now, he'd grown used to the stilted rhythms and slurred sounds of her speech. She had improved over the last few years, but he missed her strong laugh. The laugh he knew as a child, as a teenager. Brash, unguarded. And the unguarded way she sang. In the car or in the choir at church. She had had a warm, dulcet voice. She'd sung to Andre, and to anyone, throughout her life, simple songs she liked, some folk, some modern, some choral. After the stroke, he realized over the course of several weeks, like dust settles in the creases of a noble statue, she'd never sing again.

"Wow," he wrote. "Thanks, Mom. Will put it to good use. How's the burn on your leg?"

As he sent off the mail, he imagined the conversation she and Oskar had before she'd sent the money. She, in garbled spurts of phrases, telling him Andre needed their help. Oskar, despite his concern for their retirement fund, had indulged her. Andre wasn't sure if 500 dollars, however that exchanged in Euros, would be enough for the size of system he'd need, but he might swing the difference from his savings, so he phoned a technician.

The next Friday, the tech arrived and worked all afternoon, hooking up elaborate wiring and motion-detector sensors. The control panel, installed at the back of the Chick's Nest, was a complex panel of choices. The tech taught Andre how to program it, how to call the police, how to call the fire department, how to set off a loud sound. It was a repetitive, abrasive buzzing noise that would drive whoever was in the house straight outside. They went over where the sensors were located. At all corners, at the temperature panel, near the drum fans, at the louvered vents, hanging from the center aisle rafters. Most certainly, at every roof vent. All wiring, with the exception of the connection to the circuit box outside, was done inside the house so intruders wouldn't be able to cut any lines. Together, they practiced punching in the shut-off code.

After the technician left, he opened his laptop and checked his email. His mom had replied with, "All is fine here. Burn not healing very quickly."

He sighed, covered his mouth with a hand. *Should I call?* The mail dinged. Renia with her notes from yesterday. She couldn't access the shed and later saw Brodeur come out, mumbling. He'd lectured her about pinching blossoms for fruit. Manu had borrowed a hose. She fertilized the Chick's Nest saplings. She also offered her analysis on the trees sprayed with glyphosate. She believed T9 had permanent damage from the spraying to a few branches, wanted Andre to look. Should they prune off? It was true. Four branches on T9's right side had dropped leaves while the bark had faded, so with careful cuts, he removed the branches down to where he found clean green-lined wood.

That night at eight o'clock, he finally found time to do his usual inspection of leaves. As he checked the tops and undersides for insects, he noticed a shadow wiggle by outside. In and out of the field's lamplight, along the west wall. At first, he thought it a branch. *No.* The shadow seemed to rise from the ground. He scanned the walls, but the shadow subsided. He rubbed his eyes, told himself he was imagining things. As he opened the Chick's Nest door, a shadow flew by the east wall. *A bird?* He watched it shrink from the size of a dog to nothing. His heart beat quickened. He waited. Watched. No movement. It had to be the shadow from a car's swiveling headlights in the parking lot. But it seemed human. *Brodeur?* He didn't walk in jerky, unpredictable ways. Andre froze, debating what to do. In a blip of frustration, remembering the light switch, he went to the door and poked his head out.

"*Allô?*"

The night air bit clear and cold on his face. The field was silent. Rows of hydrangeas sat in moody soft mounds. The hoop houses, now stripped of their plastic covering, looked like giant rib cages. Across the field, the office was dark. Several windows in the surrounding apartments were lit. He saw a young woman on an upper floor stirring a pot. The blue ring of gas fire on her stove, circular and pointed, looked like a supernatural crown. In the distance, the rolling traffic shushed in whispers. He closed the door, glad to have an alarm, nervous the police call button would somehow malfunction.

In the Chick's Nest, the saplings' leaves were healthy and sturdy. No insects. Each tree held multiple clusters of foliage with bold green leaves and bronze branches. The grafts had smoothed into tightly bonded tissue. A few miniscule flowers plumped on some trees, the appling showing the largest buds. As he examined S8, he noticed a questionable leaf with a faint gray spot. He took out his snips and with precision, cleanly cut the petiole. As he tossed the leaf in the main room's trimmings can, a shadow enlarged and shrunk on the wall, a mere seven feet away.

He swallowed. His heart raced. *What was it? A bat?* Or... Maybe it was a group of teenagers cutting through the passage to Rue Nicolas Houel. *Who are you kidding? It's the thug.* He stood, inhaling a deep breath and searching for a shovel or heavy tool to use as a weapon, finally grabbed his machete. At least it was sharp. He set a hand on the doorknob, his heart racing, telling himself that this might be an opportunity to change the guy's misguided mind.

Outside, all was as still and cold and dark as before. The buildings, the trees, the empty pavement of parking lot. In the field, a wheelbarrow leaned against a cinderblock, its handles splayed up, its ghostly shape resembling a wounded gorilla with arms reaching upward to the sky.

Andre inched around the S2 house, his eyes shifting to the shadowed nooks made from shrubs and walls and tree trunks. He passed the stalls of gravel and compost and bark. They were tall humps of material behind which a human could hide. The shed stood silently in the murky light, as if a threshold to the passage leading to Rue Nicolas Houel. Drooping branches cast long, impenetrable shadows. He strained to see through them, feeling his heart thump, his mouth dry, gripping the machete. As he came to the house's rear, he saw the cart and trailer parked in their usual snug spot. He walked beyond the thicket that formed the L'Enclos boundary and into the grassy corridor, passing a maple that blocked the light from the modern apartment building. Andre's breath billowed clouds of steam, obscuring his vision with every other step. Stillness. Nothing. He chewed his lip, wishing for a flashlight. Finally, when he saw the faint outline of the low white gate at the street, he turned around. Crunch. He stiffened, lifted the blade. A cloud of breath. No one. Crunch again. In a quiet vigilance, he crept toward the maple.

"*Allô?*" he said, cold sweat at his forehead. "Who's there?"

The distant roar of a truck answered.

He waited, looked around. Nothing.

Whoever had made the crunch must have been behind the greenhouse. So, he took a few steps into the shrub's thicket, his heart pounding. He maneuvered around a tumbling elderberry, a tall spiraea, a snowberry, laurel, more elderberry, more laurel. A branch scraped his neck. He jumped. Someone could hide in the foliage.

Crunch.

He stopped, shifted his weight. Crunch.

Under his feet, dry branches crackled and broke.

He tilted his face to the sky, letting go a relieved breath. "Silly," he whispered. He lowered the machete and walked to the greenhouse. A car idled at the far end of the parking lot. Silver. A compact Citroën he didn't recognize. After several seconds, it pulled away, its red tail lights shrinking as it rounded the drive. *A garden worker?* It had to be. Whoever it was, they had the code to open the gate, which meant they were authorized to be in L'Enclos, so he set aside his fear and opened the door to the S2 house.

The lights flashed. The alarm blared.

Crap. With a desperate hand, he punched in the code to make it stop. Wrong order. First, the numbers, then Enter. In a

151

fury, he tried again, hitting buttons harder. The blaring ceased. The white lights beamed. He tossed the machete on the counter and caught his breath. Combed a hand through his hair. *Okay. Calm down. Cool it.*

His phone dinged. He jumped.

A text from Lessard: "Call me. I remembered the name."

CHAPTER 16

That night, he walked home quickly, eyeing the streets, eyeing the people. Once inside his building, he dialed his dad, tapping up the stairs, making sure each landing's hall light was shining brightly. From the apartment below his, an orchestra played a dramatic score with screeching violins for what sounded like a thrilling movie. Behind the door in the apartment across the hall, a woman said, "And he was paralyzed by it, from the waist on." At his door, a sheet of paper lay on the mat. His heart skipped. He picked it up. A notice from the landlord about the installation of a new sewer line.

Inside, Linus jumped from the window sill and trotted toward him, meowing.

Andre refilled his empty food bowl.

When his dad answered, he told him about the alarm system, asked about his mom. "She told me the burn's not healing well."

"Hold on," Oskar said. The patio door clunked shut. Birds tweeted. In a lowered voice, he said, "Yes, that's true. I'm pretty mystified by it."

A crust of sadness accumulated at his throat. "What do the doctors think?"

"Her body may be resistant to this antibiotic."

Andre checked the roof deck. In the dim, his little statue of Saint Fiacre standing in the witch hazel seemed like a bent ogre. He switched on the outdoor light. "Can they try a different antibiotic?"

"They might. They're first checking her for lupus."

"Lupus?!"

"Well, she had some bruising on her feet. But I think it's because she was knocking around, trying to go downstairs."

Their basement stairs were narrow and steep. Andre scrunched his eyes shut. "Why is she going downstairs?"

"She wanted to do some laundry."

"Why?"

"She's bored."

Andre plopped on the couch, wondering how difficult it would be to smuggle Tengri apples into California. By September, he'd have some. He always thought he'd properly ship her some after the next clinical trial, but her body couldn't afford to wait. Could he fly with the appling so his dad could grow it at home? Maybe. With the right paperwork, he might get it through the Agriculture Department. Then again, if the department rejected it, they'd incinerate it on site. His head drooped. "I wish you two could come here."

Oskar cleared his throat. They hadn't been to France since before the stroke. "I know. She wants to. She wants to see all your work there. She wants to see Michel and Aunt Dauphine too. And all the kids."

Linus hopped onto his lap. He pet the cat's soft, warm, neck. Linus curled up and closed his eyes. "That would be nice. She'd like this project. And these apples might help her. In fact, I know they would, Dad. They helped... And I wish... I wish..."

"I know, son, there are a lot of wishes we both have."

The next Friday at six in the evening, in need of a decent internet connection, Andre went to his office. He opened his laptop and found the video conference website, dialed in, waited. Minutes later, the choppy image of a middle-aged woman with silver-blonde hair, round features, and a toothy smile appeared.

She sat at a wooden desk with unforgiving fluorescents overhead. To the left, framed diplomas and pictures of Lady Bird Johnson and Sally Ride hung on the wall. At the right was a window whose open blinds showed a feathery mesquite tree bobbing in the breeze. In the corner, a portable air conditioner hummed like a squeaking saxophone.

"Thanks for talking with me," Andre said.

Willa Oakes worked at the Breveford Advocacy Center in Austin, Texas, a nonprofit organization that helped victims of rape, incest, hate crimes, war, PTSD, and other trauma. As he waited for her to solidify on screen, he felt thankful Cloutier was gone, thankful for familiar voices in the hallway, and a door that closed and locked.

"So, Andre," she said, "to answer your email question, I *have* seen this pamphlet before. It's a pamphlet some of my clients know."

A Southern accent dominated her speech, which, with a tendency to speak in quick cadences, made it difficult for him to understand.

"The cross and dove represent Christ and the Holy Ghost winning the battle over the gates of hell and the devil," she said. "It's a symbol that sometimes appears on a pin worn by members of a church in Florida called East Valley. Now, Andre, they're not like 90 per cent of churches in America, they're not like my church, which is a welcoming place. This church isn't tolerant of certain people. Their beliefs are extreme. They are wary of people of color. Jews need to be saved, women should be submissive, gays reformed. They have a very refined list of issues they consider sinful."

"Oh, wow."

"Now, I hope I'm not offending you, Andre."

"What? No."

"I mean, because I'm a Christian myself."

He'd been raised Catholic but was more agnostic than anything. "Yes, me too."

"Great. Then we're on the same page. The East Valley Church often protests gay rights rallies and abortion clinics and even military funerals. Their leader's name is Bill Miller and he's very outspoken. But the congregation is small. And just to give you an idea of how small they are, most of the congregation is made up of his relatives and friends, about 70 people at most."

"I see."

"Yes, and even though they are small, they do some very big damage to folks whose beliefs they don't agree with. For instance, in your field of work, I believe he led the charge against the university in Oregon. The Southern Poverty Law Center believes this as well. Are y'all familiar with SPLC?"

"Yes," he said.

"Yeah, okay. Now many folks think that United Caring for the Natural sprayed those bushes, but they deny it and no evidence suggests otherwise. Plus, they learned their lesson years earlier when they vandalized another growing operation in Washington, which was actually on their side in creating sustainable timber. And what's more, most of the members were convicted in a court of law during that case. At this point, the organization is tiny, may not even exist."

"Oh. Good to know," Andre said.

"But East Valley learned about the man from the Oregon clinical trial. He was a test subject who had an allergic reaction and that's what drove them to action. Have you seen the video?"

"No, I haven't, but I know about the incident."

"Sure, well, let me tell you, in the video the man looks possessed. He's pretty debilitated. And the jumpy homemade nature of the video makes it all seem worse than it probably was."

He nodded, his mind churning with worry.

"And that has caused the church to be vigilant about other growing projects. They think it's like, witchcraft? As if the devil's behind it or something. So..." she slowed her speech, "considering that and considering your situation, like the break-in, the vandalism of your trees, the acts of intimidation, and the pamphlet, my opinion is that you are being targeted by the East Valley Church."

He rubbed his knees as if he were washing dirt off his jeans. "OK."

"That's just my best guess."

"Yes, I understand," he said. Her speech was a splashing cascade of words packed with information. "But how do they know about my work in Paris?"

"That's a good question and I am not sure," she said. "But I do know that they watch and listen for news all over the world. You're an American grower. Have you ever been on TV or published articles about plants in the U.S.?"

He had to think about that. "Yes, but a long time ago. I wrote an article for a West Coast journal on a new variety of pear tree. I doubt they would have seen it."

"Well, as I said, they monitor the news. Have you told your family about your work?"

Delphine. His parents. His grandmother. Yes, his grandmother. "I guess, several of them know. Yes." Even Aunt Dauphine knew.

"Well, I don't know how they may have found out, but if it's not East Valley, it may be a European group very similar to them. East Valley has some money, but I'm not sure they have enough to pay someone over there to do their work. Although I suppose it's possible. When you believe God is on your side, you will go to great lengths to carry out whatever you need to. Believe me, I've seen that firsthand."

"I'm sure," he said. "So, this guy, this guy who left the pamphlet, we think he's from Brittany."

"Yeah, that's interesting," she said. "I don't think American fundamentalists operate in Brittany. Is he a highly conservative Catholic? I know there are some of those in that region. And very traditional, conservative politicians."

"Oh."

"Well, I can ask a few of my sources if they have any ideas, but, for now, that's about all I can tell you. I will say that if there is a direct East Valley connection, then you are in danger. They don't hesitate to take action against people they believe are in conflict with their values, or God's values, as they would say."

"I see."

"I urge you to protect yourself, your plants, and any staff you may have."

"Staff?" *Renia.* Maybe he should call her. Yes, he should definitely call her. "I understand. We did install an alarm system."

"That's good. Make your facility as secure as possible."

"I'll do my best." Maybe he should stop by the S2 house tomorrow, and Sunday.

"Sure, and just remember," she said, "these people work off irrational emotion. They're fanatics. If you pinch them, they'll bite you. If you poke them, they'll punch. If you throw a firecracker, they'll set off a bomb. So, Andre, I will ask you to do one thing for me."

"Yes..."

"Do not engage or respond in any manner. Do you think you can restrain yourself from having an emotional response as things go on? Because it may escalate, you know."

He thought of Grandma Mel's house in California. That day, that terrifying day. Had he operated off emotion? Yes, but the emotion had been cowardice. He was trying his best now to be sensible, logical, rational, not scared or wimpy, though the idea that this guy knew where his office was, where the greenhouse was, and where his apartment was, made his skin shiver.

"Well," he said, "what I can promise is I'll try my hardest to do what's right."

After the call, Andre mulled over what Oakes said. The East Valley Church was best left unprovoked. He should buckle down and be safe. But the idea that their actions happened unchecked frustrated him. Those people had no justification for doing what they were doing. If he could just explain it, they'd see things differently, surely. He imagined himself talking reasonably with the guy from Brittany, saying, "What I'm working on may help your sick relatives. These apples show promise as medicine. They may cure people. Make people stronger, healthier."

And what would he say? "Oh, now I see, do you want to get a pint?"

He leaned his forehead on the desk's edge. Maybe he should set up a cot in the greenhouse—at least until harvest time. It was really the only way to ensure the trees' security. He checked the remote temperature app. All was usual. Should he have set up a remote camera to monitor it somehow? That must cost another small fortune.

In the end, there was no harm in doing a little research. He opened his laptop and searched for East Valley Church. The home page loaded. At the center, a photo showed Bill Miller speaking into a microphone before a small crowd at what looked like a park. The links were devoted to photos, videos, and sermons. At the right was a list of events the group had protested and would in the future. A list of things God hated with quotes from the Bible rotated at the bottom. Andre clicked on the videos but didn't find any information about the Oregon trial. He hopped over to a Christian video site and searched "East Valley Church, Oregon apricot project" and landed on something more useful.

A stilled video showed a heavyset man in a white shirt, khaki pants, and straw hat standing in what looked like a park. Behind him in the distance were palm trees and oleanders. Blue sky. A young man in board shorts throwing a Frisbee. The man in the hat held a small apricot for the camera, his mouth open as if about to speak. The caption read: "Pastor Bill Miller explains the dangers of natural medicines."

He hit Play.

"Now, this fruit," Miller said, "which may look like an innocent, everyday apricot is actually a deadly killer. Not everything is as it seems, my friends, and this is what you need to watch out for. I'm coming to you to enlighten you about a subject that's most pressing. There are researchers at fancy universities trying to grow this fruit and we, my friends, must stop them."

Andre whispered, "Am I one of those?"

"Now, they say their research will help the ill. But this claim is false. This is no ordinary fruit. Just like the forbidden fruit in the garden of Eden, this fruit is the work of the devil. The researchers may say this is all for the good of the people, but it's not. Because, my friends, the chemicals in this apricot almost killed a man. And, even though it almost killed a man, these," he held his fingers in quotes, "these so-called 'scientists' insist on continuing their work anyway."

So called botanist-scientist.'

The man paused as if to let his viewers absorb the point. "If you're unfamiliar with the situation I speak of, you need do nothing more than watch this footage of a poor soul in Oregon."

The video switched to a grainier film of a man in the driver's seat of a car. Maroon fabric on the seats and maroon plastic on the dashboard. He was in his fifties wearing a Raging Red Choir sweatshirt and jeans. He sat in the driver's seat and tried to put the key in the ignition but missed. His hands shook. His head twitched.

"Is it happening again?"

He didn't answer. Instead, he dropped the keys, grabbed the door handle and opened the door, but, instead of getting out, he slipped and fell across the seat, his arms stiff, his body convulsing. He struggled to sit up, his arms jerking. His head whipped around and forward into the steering wheel. He cussed. He reached out to the door handle to lift himself but missed, and his body tumbled on the ground.

Andre pinched his nose. The man was out of control.

"Oh God! Oh God!" the man said. His voice cracked. "Make it stop!" Offscreen voices said, "Get him up, get him up. Call an ambulance." His pleas for help descended into linguistic jibberish, almost as if he was speaking in tongues.

A woman knelt beside him and took his hand. She started speaking in a loud clap. "Scott! Scott, can you hear me?"

"I see flashes of light!" He made a fist and bashed it at his eyes. "I see it!"

Offscreen, voices said, "Call 911, call 911, get an ambulance."

"Scott, help's coming. Help is coming, don't leave me, stay right here, Scott. Don't leave."

Andre cringed.

The video, in an abrupt cut, went back to Bill Miller. "Now, thanks to the grace of our Lord and Savior, this man was rushed to the hospital and stabilized. But friends, the devil does not sit idle. He wants another victim; he's searching right now for another unsuspecting person to eat this apricot and be his next victim."

The camera cut to a close-up of Miller's face. He had full cheeks, a broad nose, and tiny eyes. "And there are other disreputable scientists, right now, as we speak, that are growing more of this fruit that they claim will help people but certainly will not. Now I ask you, what kind of medicine is this? What kind? Help us to help them see the light. They need our guidance to stop growing this harmful, tainted fruit. Now, we are working to stop this evil work. But we need your help to do it. If you can donate ten, twenty, even one hundred dollars to help, please send it as soon as you can to the address below."

The East Valley Church's P.O. box in St. Petersburg, Florida flashed on the screen in large white letters.

"Thank you and God bless."

Andre sat staring at the screen, his head in his hands, fingering the faint scar at his temple. With that footage of the poor soul and his allergic reaction, no wonder the thug from Brittany hated scientists. Of course, Miller hadn't mentioned that the test subject had eaten the apricot's pit, not just the fruit. Miller's small, penetrating eyes seemed to see straight at Andre. He had a determined shut mouth. On the collar of his shirt, he wore a pin. Andre zoomed in. In a fuzzy outline, there it was. The cross and flames symbol. A pastor in Florida had somehow connected with a follower in France. Together they were on a crusade.

A distraught torment surged through his body. He felt warm, closed his laptop, and packed up, wondering, as he hit the light, if he should divulge the harassment to Monique Castel. It was exactly what LaRoche had wanted to avoid. Then again, it was what they expected and may know how to deal with. Of course, dealing with it meant the Tengri project would be yanked from his control and he'd be fired. The last thing he wanted, after all of the work and worry and hope, was to give up the trees he'd worked so hard to grow.

CHAPTER 17

That weekend he went with Delphine to Bordeaux for Easter. He'd worried in a random blip of illogic that since he'd confirmed the thug was acting on behalf of an extreme leader, the thug would automatically act in retaliation. His heart clenched at the thought of the guy still being on the loose, still able to damage the trees. But Renia had offered to stop by the S2 house on Saturday and Monday and he took her up on the offer. On Monday night, they checked in by phone. Nothing of note had happened over the weekend. He taught class feeling thankful for Renia, feeling more than thankful, feeling, well... blessed.

On Tuesday, as he approached the S2 house, he buzzed with anticipation. Today was the day they'd pollinate flowers. In the morning, Renia had texted him, saying all of the trees had bloomed. *What a success.* After he opened the door and saw all that they'd done, how far they'd come, he laughed. Just laughed. Dozens of blossoms decorated the trees like white kisses. Everywhere. Renia stood in their midst, writing in the project notebook, dressed in a rose blouse and olive overalls, soft sunlight shimmering on her hair. He inhaled that fresh sweet scent, so pure. It beckoned, reassured, signaled this was a safe, beautiful place. They'd watched buds plumping for the last few weeks and the sapling flowers had opened sporadically, but today all of the trees had popped at the same time, as if they'd decided to offer a huge gift.

He roamed toward her.

She smiled. "I'm glad to see you're happy."

He marveled at how densely the trees had grown clusters of healthy green leaves. The white flowers blushed with a pink dusting, splayed open for whatever pollinators might come. Five-petaled, pure. Born to attract bees and birds and whatever animal might brush against them, announcing fruit about to emerge: food, rebirth, hope.

"Now, this is God's work," he said.

"It certainly is," she said.

They wandered around a few minutes, inspecting the healthy blossoms, chatting.

Finally, when they'd exhausted the admiration, counting five new flowers on the S8 sapling, she said, "Well, shall we try to create some fruit?"

"Yes. I'm ready."

With few words, they found the pollination wands and got to work. They wiped the anthers from the stock trees' flowers and dabbed the scion's pistils. The plan was to not pollinate all flowers in the main house, as much as LaRoche Naturel wanted them to, but allow some flowers to fade and fall. Those trees would use their energy to grow strong branches and bear more robust and plentiful fruit the next year. So they spread pollen on one flower per cluster, making sure to use some pollen from the stocks' blossoms and some commercial pollen before carefully recording what they had used on which trees in the notebook.

Inside the Chick's Nest, they applied the same technique to the new blooms, put away their brushes, and hoped for the best. They walked around with buckets, collecting the faded petals from the older flowers they'd already pollinated a week earlier.

"I think, with its new flowers, the appling will give us at least eight apples," she said.

He strained to find her face through the foliage. It popped from among the leaves like a sudden happy child. He went to the appling. Its tender branches had several healthy blossoms, its miniscule pistils and stamens like hairy stars. "I agree, maybe even nine." He pointed to a hidden bud on a lower branch, plump and about to open.

"An extra one for good luck," she said.

He smiled, then thought of the dream he'd had that morning. "Last night, I dreamt I accidentally kicked over the appling and it broke." He chewed his lip, inspecting the leaves. A sudden fright rang in his body. "I kind of have this recurring dream where the appling somehow gets stolen or dies, LaRoche cancels the project, and my dad calls and says my mom's in the hospital." He cleared his throat. "I know, it's silly."

She frowned. "It was diabolical to leave that destroyed tree at your door."

"Yeah, I guess."

"And clever, to pretend one plant is another." She gazed absently at the appling, as if marveling at the creativity of it. "But I believe we're cleverer than that brute is."

An hour later, they finished tidying up and watered the trees. As they secured the padlock to the Chick's Nest door, they chatted about a new café that had opened near Le Sanctuaire.

Renia turned, yelped.

Brodeur stood by the floor sink.

In an irritated snap, Andre said. "It would be helpful to knock next time."

Brodeur scoffed.

"How can I help you?" Andre said.

Brodeur's overalls were matted with mud, as if he'd been lying chest-down in wet earth. Slung across his shoulder was a hoe, dripping. He motioned to the padlock on the Chick's Nest door. "I need the combination to your lock."

"Combination?"

Renia headed out of the house with the trimmings bucket.

Brodeur's eyes tracked her, his body twisting, hoe flicking wet spray on the table.

"I'm not sure that's necessary," Andre said.

"It is highly necessary. The system panels are in there and an approved employee needs access to them."

"Then I'll give Manu the combination. He *is* the manager."

"But I'm here most often."

A bulbous fly zig-zagged between them. Andre swatted. *Now he's let in flies.*

Brodeur waited.

"I don't see why you need the combination," he said. "I haven't received a key to the storage house after two months."

Brodeur's eyes narrowed. "That is none of my concern."

"It isn't?"

His mouth clenched. "My concern is to maintain access to the S2 house's panels. It is against regulation if we do not have access."

Andre folded his arms, debating what to do. The image of Brodeur punching him popped in his mind.

"Monsieur," Renia said. She closed the door and went to the floor sink. Her smiled was gentle and reassuring. "We're happy to share the combination." She washed out the empty trimmings bucket and set it below the counter. "However..." she came in close to Brodeur, lowered her voice, looked around, "we can only share it verbally. We've had a bit of trouble with curious teenagers who've been up to high-jinks at our expense. I'm afraid they may get a hold of loose scraps of paper that aren't secure or official."

Brodeur's expression softened. "Ah. I understand. I see you are a more reasonable than—"

"Now, are you ready? I will recite it three times."

He straightened his shoulders. "Yes, of course."

As Renia repeated the numbers slowly and clearly, Andre wandered away, hiding the impressed smirk on his face.

That night after Renia zoomed away on her scooter and Andre reminded Manu one more time to make him a storage house key, he headed home to clean up for dinner with Delphine and Charles. Though he'd tried to cancel, Delphine insisted, saying she had news to share. Since they'd already announced their engagement, he guessed it could only be that she was pregnant.

At seven-thirty, they rolled up to Andre's apartment building in Charles's sleek black sedan. Delphine wore a burgundy blouse and Charles wore a burgundy shirt. They had matching earring studs, orange topaz that, in the street light, shimmered like sparks. Delphine's hair lay in a brushed curve that framed her face and Thomas's coal hair, always lay trimmed tightly, showing off his chiseled forehead. They were in a fantastic mood, singing along to the radio, holding hands, then ordering a bottle of champagne at the restaurant. When their meals came, they told Andre they'd found a beautiful apartment in Les Invalides. They were moving in early June. And could Andre help move a few of Delphine's things? Yes, of course, he said. The merriment continued for almost two hours as Andre drank wine and forgot about work.

When they asked what fun thing was new with him, he said Linus had pulled the corner of his food bag from under the pantry door and chewed through it, indulging in a huge feast. They laughed. He even laughed. Then he tossed back the last of his wine, the stem hitting the table hard. Without thinking, he said, "And I think I'm in love with my assistant."

They froze.

He swallowed. *Oops.* "I mean—"

Delphine squealed. "I'm so happy for you!"

Charles's face slouched in alarm. "We should get the check."

Outside, as they strolled to the car, Delphine hooked into Andre's arm, wanting to know all the details, who this mysterious woman was and how he'd found her and when could they meet. "Do you want to introduce her to your parents?"

"God, no. I've got problems, Delphine. Big problems."

"What? Don't be silly. You'll just have to find her other employment. A friend of mine did that when her boss proposed."

"Delphine," Charles said. "Don't encourage it."

"No, really," she said. "It could work. It could! Do you have a picture?"

"Well, I actually do. We took some for the project. I..." he searched his pockets for his phone. He'd forgotten it. Where? At home? No, at the S2 house. He debated whether to mention it, he didn't want to inconvenience them. Of course, grabbing it would be easy and he needed it in case Edo called again about another visit from Alba and Castel.

"I think I left my phone at the greenhouse. Do you mind stopping by? Or could you drop me off there?"

"Of course," she said. "We should definitely get your phone. I lost mine a few days ago. Now I have to pay a stupid fee to start my connection again. I'm waiting until I buy a new one. Let's stop in. Maybe you can show us your trees."

"Oh, sure. If you want." He thought of Renia that afternoon, her steady eyes studying the branches' scaffolding. "They're beautiful."

The chatter continued as they got in the car and drove down Rue Saint-Honoré. Delphine said, "love this song," and raised the volume on the radio. A woman sang in sultry English, "I pull, you push, I push, you pull. We go 'round, 'round, 'round…" The street bustled with diners, pedestrians, people on bikes, all in silent activity outside the car. Boutique windows glowed with wares of dresses or chocolates or jewelry in lush displays. Hotels seemed like bedrooms with thick drapes and velvet furniture. As they slowed at a corner, Andre thought a monk was carrying a basket of miniscule torches. The image morphed into a waiter in a long apron, carrying a tray of candles.

When they arrived at L'Enclos, the security trailer was dark, the driveway, empty, its conifers flashing alive by the car's headlights. The parking lot and office stood deserted. Behind the S2 house, the stairwell windows of the apartment building radiated a weak haze. Andre had never seen a person up there and no one was there now.

Charles parked in the closest space and they all got out. Andre led them across the field. As he neared the S2 house, he noticed a spot of light floating between the greenhouses. A flashlight. It swayed in random circles as if scanning the walls from the outside. *No wait, was it inside?* He wasn't sure. The house was dark, the lights off.

"Who's there?" he shouted.

The spot of light stilled.

Andre quickened his pace. As he neared, he saw, in the shadow created by the moon, a human figure.

He stopped.

The light jerked around like a flash on the sea's waves, jittering quickly.

Andre darted after it. "Hey!"

The light disappeared at the house's rear.

Andre sprinted between the houses and rounded the corner, knocking over a tower of stacked plastic pots. They tumbled onto the metal trailer, booming and rolling in random directions as they hit. He slowed to squeeze by the trailer and cart in a tight shifty walk. "Hey!" Branches scraped his arms.

A man scurried into the grassy passage.

Andre ran toward him, a spider web flattening on his face.

In the distance, Delphine shouted his name. He batted the air and cleared the web. The man raced toward the Nicola Houel gate.

"Stop!" He ran hard, knowing if he caught the guy, that thug, he'd end this whole thing.

In the rising streetlight, the guy's gray hood bounced at his back, exposing short sandy hair. He stumbled to a stop at the iron gate, secured with a chain, and paused to get hold of the top bar, but his foot slipped and he tried again. It gave Andre the extra second he needed. The thug scrambled over, his flashlight dropping in the grass. Andre took a running leap onto the gate's bar and threw himself over. The two crashed onto the sidewalk.

"Who are you?" Andre said.

He wrestled with him, trying to grab the huge arms. The thug had a square face, bulky body. His eyes slanted downward at his nose. His mouth, a thin resentful line.

Finally, the guy broke free, tossed Andre off, kicked him in the stomach.

Searing pain. He grabbed his abdomen, lost his breath. Collapsed and bumped his head on the curb. Above, a copper roof in the black sky spun, gargoyles leering at the corners. They floated in his vision. He tried desperately to suck in air.

The thug reared back with a fist to punch him.

"Andre!"

Charles.

The guy paused, spit in his face, and ran away.

Andre slumped with his cheek against the moist gritty cobbles, mucus at his nose and eye. In a slow dream, he rolled over, coughed. Windows shifted. The street bowed like a mound of sand. Far away, a car's headlights. He got to his knees and put a foot out to stand. It slipped and his leg buckled.

Charles's hands grabbed his armpits. His body rose. The smell of spicy cologne. The long horizontal lines of concrete balconies repeated in a broken, skipping image. He blinked to right his vision, hoped he wouldn't throw up. Delphine stood on the far side of the gate, a phone at her ear. Her speech rambled, her voice high-pitched, insistent, on the verge of hysterics as she explained. "*Non, il est mon cousin,*" she said, "*Ma famille,*" and then, "*Il est blessé.*"

That night at the police station, Andre's body felt injured but his spirit revived. His first impulse had been to wipe the spit from his face, but Delphine reminded him to leave it for evidence. A paramedic arrived first, checked his stomach and head while he was on the street. When the police came, they bagged the flashlight for fingerprints and took a sample for DNA from the saliva. At the police station, Andre relayed the incident to a muscled officer who looked like he could bench 200 pounds but typed like a snail with two fingers. Beyond the bullet proof glass in the lobby, Delphine and Charles sat on a wooden bench, waiting with hands locked. In the blaring clean light, they looked like a couple who'd walked out of a Louis Vitton ad into a TV crime drama. Delphine's face was shrunken in worry, Charles's in patient exhaustion. It was well after midnight when the three finally headed home.

The next morning, Andre struggled to sit up in bed. His stomach ached. He had a bruised lump below his ribs. A small hematoma, the paramedic said. Delphine had wanted him to go to the emergency room, but he resisted. The guy had gotten away, which frustrated him, but he hadn't gotten inside the S2 house. At least there was that. Through his phone app, he saw the house's temperature had stayed steady. The unfortunate part was that he might return until he figured a way in. As Linus jumped on the bed and curled up beside his legs, he debated whether to sleep on a cot in the greenhouse.

A knock on the door.

Strange.

He got out of bed and threw on sweatpants and a T-shirt before checking the peephole. Officer Kateb stood in the hall. His childlike hands resting on his belt.

Andre opened the door. "That was fast."

"What was?"

"I just left the station last night."

"Yeah, well, your evidence proved useful."

"Oh?"

"I was wondering if I could ask you a few more questions."

"Sure. Come in."

They went in the living room and sat down, Kateb's eyes scanning the clusters of plants inside and out on the deck. "Thanks for taking the time," he said. He smelled like deodorant soap and sat on the edge of the armchair, his body leaning forward as if ready to spring forth. He took out a pocket notebook and short pen, his belt and clipped vinyl compartments crunching. "Last night, at your greenhouse, did you actually see the man try to break in?"

Andre remembered the flashlight's halo, how it roamed along the wall, had landed on the roof. "Well, no. But his flashlight was scanning the house. Like he was looking for a way in."

"Did you see it go to the roof? To that vent where the original break in occurred?"

"Well, near it. I think anyway. I'm not a hundred percent sure but it was moving all around the walls, like he was searching for something."

Kateb scribbled on his notepad.

"So last night in your report, you claimed this person was the same person who broke into the greenhouse the first time."

"Yes."

"But you didn't see his face the first time."

Andre imagined the thug's disgusted face. The feeling of warm spit in his eye. "No, not the first time."

Kateb made another mark on his pad. "Was there ever another time you saw his face, previous to last night?"

"Well, he followed me for a few blocks some days ago. I didn't really see his face. Just his clothes and those were the same."

"Are you sure it was the same person who you confronted last night?"

"Absolutely sure. I mean, aren't you? Didn't the fingerprint from the flashlight match the fingerprint on the vent panel?"

"That's what we're checking on. And when you tackled him, he actually got up, but before he ran away, he kicked you and spit at you? *Before* he ran away. You didn't engage him after you tried to stop him?"

"No."

"And you never saw him actually do damage to the greenhouse last night?"

He scratched his ankle, where the Kazakhstan sprain used to be. "No, but I know it's the same guy. He probably would have broken in had I not shown up."

Kateb sniffed, ran a finger under his nose as he read his notes. "And your cousin and her fiancé. They did tell us what they knew yesterday, but is there anyone else who can shed light on this incident? Anyone else who may play a part from the past? Like someone who may hold a grudge?"

Andre thought of Jason in California. The group he ran in. "No, don't think so. Not..." He was about to say, "Not connected with this."

Kateb leaned in. "Not...?"

"No, I don't think so."

"Okay, thanks for your time."

He walked him to the door.

"We'll be in touch," Kateb said.

Linus circled the officer's legs.

Andre picked up the cat, encircling him in his arms so he wouldn't trot into the hallway.

171

"In the meantime," Kateb said, "I need you to thoroughly search your memory. Hard. Is there no one who may hold a grudge against you? Think about it. Anyone in your past who would have a reason to sabotage your project?"

"Not really. Is that common?"

"I've seen grudges held for 20 years."

Twenty years? "I see. Well," he swallowed, feeling his face warm, "I'll give it some thought."

CHAPTER 18

Andre locked the door and plunked on the couch, sinking his face into Linus's soft fur. Had he made mistakes? Of course. Related to this? No. Then again, maybe. There was an entire family who never wanted to see him again.

He remembered Grandma Mel's house in California. The heat, the rising barren hills. How the tall grass in the adjacent field had twittered in the dusty warm wind. So warm. Smell of cow manure. He could still feel how his T-shirt stuck in a soaked splat against his sternum. He'd drank a lot of water that day, picking the ripe pomegranates from each shrub. They were fresh and solid, his fingers red from a few split skins. He had one more bucket to load in his truck for the markets.

At the house, the windows were all open, curtains swaying, the bells of *The Price Is Right* dinging on TV. Earlier he'd waved to Grandma Mel as he'd backed up his truck in the driveway. She hadn't noticed. In an armchair, her head lolled to the side, her mouth open during a nap.

In the distance, a loud motor roared. Jason's friends pulled up in their SUV, a flashy ride with a paint job of flames and custom wheels, parking along the road. They got out and slammed doors but walked quietly to the house. Strangely silent. No chatter, none of the swearing and banter he heard when they'd crossed paths in a park or stopped by the orchard. The dusty smell of marijuana. The chain link gate clanged shut. Doorbell rang. Andre heard it through the house's windows, all wide open from the heat. Silence. Then hard pounding on the door.

The screen door creaked open. The sharp words of "Jason" and "where" and "too late now" rang out. The scratchy short responses from Grandma Mel. "You don't mind if we take a look, right?" The door clunked shut. Their rapid talk sounded like a train clicking over a railroad crossing, about to bellow a strong horn.

Andre was on his knees, contorting himself to grab berries from lower inner branches. From that low angle, he saw straight into the kitchen, the crayon drawings from the grandkids on the white fridge, a goggle of chipped plates and a mug with a unicorn in the dish rack. Three guys inched toward Grandma Mel, one with a trimmed goatee, one with pimples, one wearing a Sacramento Kings cap backwards.

The cap guy had on a sleeveless T-shirt, an elaborate skull tattoo on his shoulder. "No, *you* don't understand," he said. "We need our money."

He roamed toward Grandma, his hands out from his body as if ready to draw a gun.

Grandma Mel backed up until she bumped the sink. "I told you boys I don't want any trouble. I don't have money. I've got thirty-two dollars in my wallet. You can have that."

The goatee guy, who was stockiest and packed with muscles, left the room.

"And there's a carton of cigarettes in the cabinet. You can have it too."

"Where's Jason?" the Kings hat guy said.

"He's not here, hasn't been in two weeks."

"Oh yeah? Well, where is he? He ain't at his ma's house."

"I don't have any idea," Grandma Mel said, her voice wheezing with her breath. "He might be in Mexico. Last time, that's where he disappeared to."

"Yeah, well, we don't have time to go to Mexico. We just need our God damn money," the Kings hat shouted. "He owes me, and he told me the money was here, at Gramma's house."

Andre coughed, extra loudly, hoping to let them know someone was in the yard, but as he did, a truck zoomed by, muffling the sound.

"I don't have no money for you boys. You can take my thirty-two in the purse and get on your way."

The pimply guy, who was skinny with a beaky nose and stringy hair, slapped Grandma Mel's face.

She screeched.

"Look, Gramma," he said, "we had a deal and Jason skated on us. And now I need my money. Give us the money or you won't see little boy Jason ever again."

Andre froze.

The skinny guy pointed a gun at Grandma's head.

"My jewelry. My jewelry. There's a diamond ring. You can have it."

Andre swallowed. He watched, his pulse quickening.

"Where?"

They were going to shoot her. *Shoot her.* Andre walked to the kitchen window.

"Upstairs, upstairs in the bedroom," she said.

He lowered the gun and backed off, knocking a kitchen chair that fell in his path, batted it hard. It tumbled to the floor. She scurried toward the back door, but the goatee guy caught her arm.

"Ow!"

He shoved her body at the dining room. "Where's the ring?"

"It better add up to 3500 bucks," the cap guy said.

They bumped through the house, thumping sounds, then silence. Andre waited. Silence. Nervous, unsure, he carried his bucket to the truck, straining to see through the bay window in the dining room. The sheer curtain billowed. A wooden screen sat in the sill with a punctured hole, as if a bird had flown in and got stuck.

He shut the truck's tailgate. Buckets and buckets of red fruit, loaded, ready to be cleaned and counted and sent to the markets. He still had to sort for quality and weigh them. But Grandma Mel... He could rush in and defend her. But take on three thugs? With at least one gun? And get himself shot? Or maybe, slip out. They were getting the money. The goatee guy was on his way upstairs. They were upstairs, their voices lobbing back and forth. He tried to think of a distraction. What could get them out of the house? But what would he do if they came outside?

He checked his watch: eleven o'clock. He had to report in with the Stockton distributor about how much he'd picked. The man was waiting. He'd been eager to pick the fruit all week, woken up early to get started.

You can't leave Grandma Mel.

I have to.

He stood a moment by the dining room window. It was several feet higher than where he stood in the driveway, making it difficult to see in and out. Still, they might see him. Maybe knowing someone else was there would scare them.

He opened his tailgate and shut it again loudly. Nothing. No voices. No scuffle. The main floor was empty. He breathed in to calm his fast pulse. Everyone was upstairs. She was giving them her ring. She shouldn't have to. *Damn Jason. Loser.* But she'd be okay. They'd take the ring and leave. They wouldn't kill her. Even brutes like that wouldn't murder an old woman. Little did he know, as he started the truck and put it in gear, that though he was right about that, later he would also be wrong.

The next day, Andre came to the S2 house fully equipped. He brought a cot, a sleeping bag, a Swiss Army knife, a flashlight, a bottle of water and some snack. He'd wanted to buy pepper spray but wasn't sure where to find it. So, like a bizarre indoor camping site, he installed himself near the corner of the main room, not far from the door. What to tell Renia? She'd think he'd lost it. But now he knew nighttime was the most vulnerable time for a break-in. During the days when the gardeners were about, he'd make sure to roll up the bag and fold away the cot, go home, shower, and teach class. He told himself this wouldn't be for long, only until the thug tried to break in again. When he did, Andre planned on knocking him out with a shovel and tying him up until the police arrived. He was afraid to confront him, but Kateb had once said the police could be at L'Enclos in three minutes.

That Friday night, all was quiet. He slept well enough and on Saturday went to Delphine's for the day. He helped her pack boxes of clothes and shoes for her move before returning home to take care of Linus and leave again. On Saturday night, he had trouble falling asleep. He'd forgotten a pillow, so he balled up a sweater. With a thin mattress over a metal frame, the cot prevented him from stretching out comfortably. Though it was a foot from the ground, it might flip if he rolled over too fast. His back ached. He drifted in and out of fitful dreams. Every time the fans turned on he woke in a brief shock before falling back to restless sleep.

On Sunday, he woke at nine, tired, hazy. The daylight was bright. He threw on some clothes and headed to the office. Outside, the air was warm and clear. Birds chirped in an active song. He punched in the code for the door and went in the bathroom. In the mirror, his face looked worn. The stubble on his chin, scruffy and dark. He had a jagged, shimmery line along his temple from the fall in Kazakhstan and his eyelids drooped, making him seem sinister when he wasn't.

Disappointed, he dried off and headed to the greenhouse. His phone rang.

Renia.

In a shaky uncertain voice, she said, "Andre? Can you meet at the Antonia Café?"

"Uh, sure," he said. "Is something wrong?"

"Well," she said. Her voice cheeped. "I need to speak with you. Can you meet soon?"

His gut tightened. "I'll be there in fifteen minutes."

The Antonia Café's terrace was crowded with patrons. People drank coffee and ate breakfast. A few read books and talked on phones. You could always tell American tourists, he thought, they wore white shirts and white athletic shoes and often watched pedestrians and looked upward at architecture. He searched both arms of the corner patio, thinking she was at a back table, but despite the pleasantly warm morning, she wasn't outside.

Inside, he found her in a far-off nook, sitting in a snug booth against the wall. She sat slumped in a thick wool sweater, black visor, and sunglasses, her face angled down at her cup. The mirror behind her head showed a tan man in a wrinkled shirt with un-shaven face and sunglasses, wavy long bangs partly wet down on one side. When he realized he was seeing himself, he yanked at his shirt and combed fingers through his hair.

He slid in the booth and a waitress came by. He ordered coffee and croissant.

Renia stared at her tea, warming her hands against the cup.

"Are you not well?" he said.

"I'm fine now. A bit shaken."

She looked up, gave a tired smile, and took off her sun-glasses. She had a bruised eye and a cut on her chin.

He shivered. Sucked in air. "Renia…" He took off his glasses for a better look. Her eye was swollen, purple and blue. Her cornea bloodshot. She'd been punched. "Renia." He set a hand on her wrist, then lifted. He lowered his voice. "Renia."

Two well-dressed men stood from their table across the aisle and glanced over as they walked away.

"Renia. You're hurt. Does it feel as bad as…"

She nodded in a brief bob.

"Who did it? What happened?"

She sipped her tea.

"Please. Tell me. Who did it? Do I know? I think I know, oh God, I do know."

She grabbed his wrist, her head slightly quivering.

Her graceful fingers were intact, whole, okay. He spread his hand over them as if in protecting her hand, he could protect her entire person.

"Last night, I was walking to my door."

"After work? From the shop?"

She nodded. Her eyes glistened. She took a deep breath, sniffed. The cut on her chin, so deep and scarlet. Her lips, pale.

Anger knocked inside his soul, like a ball gaining heat with each bang.

"It was about nine o'clock," she said. "And a man jumped out from a tree with a knife."

"A *knife*?"

"He knew who I was. I mean, he said my name."

"What?"

"And he threatened me."

Andre's rage surged in his veins, a hot orange flame.

"No." She tilted her hand and gripped his fingers. "He told me we needed to stop the project. That we would be punished."

"Punished? He *already* punished you."

"I know."

His lip twitched. He wanted to shoot up and pace around. Punch a wall. She must have felt his hand jerk because she squeezed harder.

"Did he cut your chin with that knife?"

"No, I got that after he shoved me into the wall. I was turning, trying to get away."

He dropped his head, imagined the bull grabbing her from behind, one arm around her torso, the other holding a knife to her neck. In his bones, he felt her terror, his own hate. "Did he... did he, was that all he did? Tell me." If that scum had violated her, he would...

The waiter set down his coffee and croissant.

"Yes," she said. "That was all. Nothing else." She slurped, wiped her nose.

He fumbled to unfold his napkin and hand it to her.

She wiped her eyes. "He told me if we valued our lives, we wouldn't let the project continue," she said. "He didn't say the word Tengri, but he said 'trees.' He said we needed to stop growing the Devil's apples. That our hands were dirty with the blood of a man. That we were going to hell." Her eyes shifted to the window.

The perky chatter of the diners seemed like a bitter joke.

"He accused us of doing horrible things, Andre."

"What horrible things?"

179

She waved the thought away with a feeble hand. "Living in sin. He called me a whore."

Andre closed his eyes. "I'm so sorry."

She stared at her tea.

"He must have seen us in L'Enclos."

She shuddered. "And he had an unusual accent. I couldn't place it."

"Maybe Bretagne."

"Yes. Something like that."

He debated what to say. "I caught him at the greenhouse the other night, but he got away. The police know."

The sun shone on an unlit candle between them.

"I'm sorry I wasn't with you," he said. "I should have made sure you got home safely every night. What an idiot."

"No, no."

"Yes. I could have at least gotten you a taxi."

"My scooter has been fine. I park right outside my building every night. It was just an unusual circumstance. There were no spaces left for scooters. I had to park around the block."

He petted her hand with a thumb, as if that small stroke might smooth out the damage. "Did you tell the police?"

Quietly, "Yes. I filled out a report."

Regret sank like an anchor in his stomach. "I'm so sorry you were alone. You must be exhausted."

"I slept." Her eyes shifted from his eyes to his jaw to his shirt. "Did you?"

"It doesn't matter. Yes. Enough."

They were silent.

"And so," she vaguely shook her head, "I'm not comfortable working on the project anymore." She coughed into a small cry. "I'm sorry."

"Of course, no. No. I'm worried about you being out alone, I don't want to think—"

"I'll be fine. Really." She wiped her eyes, huffed out air. "I've dealt with men like him before. But can you manage, I mean with classes and such?"

"Don't worry about that. The botany class ends soon. I just want you to be safe. Would it, is it too much if, can I text you in the evenings? To make sure you're home okay?"

She let go a tender smile. "I'd like that. That way I know you'll be safe too."

"Don't worry, I'll be safe."

"Yes, I'm sure. But just in case, be careful."

"I will. I'll be very careful."

"It's important because..." Her expression darkened. She pulled in his hand with a taut grip. "He told me if he sees you again, he'll stab you."

A shiver ran through his chest. He exhaled an extended breath. His body churned, then settled like a cold stone. "Oh. Well, if I see *him* again, I'm going to kill him."

CHAPTER 19

On Monday, Andre bought a tiny video camera and went straight to the S2 house. He considered calling Nes to run the idea by him but decided there was no time to waste. He needed bait and needed it now. So, he recorded a long image of the healthy trees, the sturdy framework of the greenhouse, the locked Chick's Nest door. He moved through the center aisle, one table of Tengris giving way to the next until the video rested on one tree. In French, he said, "My name is Andre Damazy. I'm horticulturalist and botanist. The scions of these trees were found in the wild. They hold great medicinal promise. Early data shows they aid in recovering from illness and alleviating pain. In propagating them, I've obeyed all laws. But a cowardly person has physically attacked one of our staff. Viciously and unprovoked. The police are investigating. And while they do, I want anyone who wishes us harm to know that I will defend this operation with all of the energy I have. We expect to do our work in peace."

He only needed to film once. The video was smooth, the sound, clear. Later, at his office, putting it online was easier than expected. He created a YouTube account, uploaded the video, and added hashtags pointing to the East Valley Church, Bill

Miller, and Brittany. With an icy resolve, he hit the Submit button, whispering, "Come and get me. I dare you."

Hours later, Cloutier came in and the two did their usual bumping and avoiding while Cloutier talked rapidly on a phone call and Andre drafted an email to Nes. As he typed, he leaned forward, avoiding an animated elbow that poked his shoulder. On the phone, Cloutier explained to an architect that if a waterfall's flow was spread wider, the noise of its fall would soften, thus creating "a statement rather than thunder."

Edo appeared in the doorway.

"*Voilà! C'est ça!*" Cloutier said.

Edo wore a bright red sweater that blared like a traffic light. His face was locked in anger. "Andre, my office. Directly."

He followed Edo's quick march until his boss halted at his office and lifted a hand to invite him in. Andre ducked inside and Edo tossed the door behind them. It shut with a bang.

From a radio in the corner, a woman's voice read the news calmly. "Early this morning, a truck carrying 800 kilos of carrots overturned outside of Aubeterre-sur-Dronne, causing an automobile crash, which caused a pedestrian fatality..."

Edo clicked off the device and swiveled a laptop around on his desk. "What in God's name is this?"

A video frame showed a still of the S2 house's interior.

Andre hooked his hands together. "It's my response to the attack on Renia. Did you know she was physically assaulted on Saturday night?"

"Yes, I do know. She called me to officially resign. I'm sick with the news. But what do you think you are accomplishing here?"

The purple grow light illuminated the cactus garden. Andre marveled at how one cactus had a narrow, underwhelming shape but long bold prickles the color of blood.

"How did you find out?" Andre said.

"A student said he was searching on propagating apple trees and this showed up. He wondered what it was all about. Who was attacked? Why? Where you found the scions?" His mouth trembled. "I was horrified."

"What did you tell him?"

"I told him it was a drill. All fake. A misunderstanding."

Andre drummed his fingers in his folded arms. "Edo, this ass, and his friends at his *church*, if you can call it that, need to know we're not intimidated by their cowardly actions."

"That's another point. You tagged the video 'East Valley Church.' In doing so, you placed the video in a recommendations list with *their* insane videos. And you don't know for certain that they are behind these attacks."

"It's them, I'm sure of it. That thug gave one of their pamphlets to..." he thought of Fanine Rocher, "a business owner I know."

Edo paced in a slow burn. "And by responding to this nonsense you've lowered yourself to their level."

"I won't let the intimidation go unanswered."

"I pray Director Bertrand doesn't stumble upon it. You will remove it."

"Did you see Renia's face?"

"You will remove it. Today. Now."

"Did you see Renia's face? It's obscene. And this isn't the first time in her life she's been victimized. That, that cockroach physically assaulted her. A woman. Did you see her face?"

"No, but I assisted her in filing an incident report so I learned the details very well. She will be provided all of the resources the university offers. Now, let the police do their work and remove the video."

"The police haven't done anything! Renia gave them a description, I gave them god damn DNA. I've heard nothing back."

"They may be doing more than you realize."

"No, this, this ass needs to pay. And he needs to know we're not scared."

"He doesn't need to know anything about us. And thanks to you, he knows more than ever. In a moment of insanity, you posted a *film* of the greenhouse!"

"So? He's been in there already."

"But he, and whoever employs him, has not seen the state of the trees. And the layout of the systems. You've put the entire project in jeopardy. You're giving them information and provoking aggression."

Under the grow lights, a euphorbia's blue stalk displayed a rounded whorl of rubbery leaves, reminding Andre of an exotic ghoulish hand, waving.

"Fine, I'll take the video down, but I want access to the school's security footage. Thierry said that thug once came here, in our hallway, to ask about me. We can use the tapes to identify him."

Edo's face crunched into a frown. "You're in no position to demand anything. Only the police can request this and you're not the police, Andre."

"Well, I have to do *something*. Otherwise, he might go after Renia again. I'm responsible for *her*."

Edo shifted in a tight circle, his head slightly shaking.

"The next time he attacks me or the plants, Edo, I won't stand by and let it happen. I'm not going to blow it. I'm not going to let this project fail and go to hell."

The purple grow light buzzed in a steady pulse of energy.

"You are blowing it, as you say, right now," Edo said. "You need to return to your office and remove the video. If you do not, I will remove *you* from this project." His face hardened into a rigid glare. "What is your choice?"

Andre walked out of Edo's office resenting the threat. He'd almost broken his ankle, not to mention his face, to get that appling from Kazakhstan. He'd scrubbed a ruin of a greenhouse and brought the facility up to code. Cared for every tree, every branch, every leaf, every flower on those tables. Installed locks and alarms. Endured psychological and physical intimidation. Lost hours of sleep. And now this attack on Renia. This innocent pure woman. It was too much. Too much to let go. They needed to *pay*.

He went in his office. Cloutier was gone, his laptop displaying a photo of a Japanese cultural center's sparse meditative plaza, his suit coat neatly hooked around this chair. Andre dropped in his chair and launched the video. As he watched, he realized Edo had a point. Any viewer could see the lock on the Chick's Nest door and the control boxes in the frame. Where the vents were, even Andre's laptop. And his narration. It *was* provocative. Below the video box, the view count had reached 12. In so little time. He wondered who had seen it. How many of those were students, how many from the public? He hoped that Bretagne thug hadn't seen it, but a tiny part of him hoped he did. Andre wanted him to break in again so he could strangle him with his bare hands.

He hit the Delete button and after the video disappeared, he trotted back to Edo's office. The director sat fiddling with a pencil over a printed spreadsheet of numbers. Nearby, a cup of tea steamed, releasing a ginger lemon scent into the air.

"It's gone," Andre said.

Edo glanced up, his face remaining blank. "You chose well."

Andre paced, scratching his head.

"What is it?"

"What if I post notices, like flyers? What if I get a photo of the guy and post a request for information?"

He blew on his tea, sipped. "I don't like the idea."

"I'll do it with my personal phone number, nothing to do with the university."

"You should let the police handle it."

"Renia was punched in her *eye*."

A crease deepened in Edo's forehead. "Andre, I have seen a lot of aggression in my lifetime. Violence against women is one of the ugliest acts I've ever witnessed."

"Exactly."

"But revenge only brings hasty shallow rewards. Instead, we need justice."

"Edo, the project is in danger too."

He watched the steam curl from the cup. "Hmm..."

"How about one week? If I don't get any leads, I'll take them down, promise."

His eyes landed on his spreadsheet, then shifted to Andre, from the numbers to the person. "Are apples on the trees?"

The truth was the apples were tiny, if one could even call them that. But now, a few weeks after he and Renia had pollinated the flowers, the trees' ovaries in the Chick's Nest were swelling. Fruit droplets forming. With the exception of one, all saplings were growing apples. The appling had more robust apples than the others. Its branches had thickened, grown sturdier, the trunk, taller. Its leaves were still unblemished, whole. The project was about to be a success.

"Yes," Andre said. "A lot. The trees are healthy. It's everything we've worked for since last summer." In a nervous urge, he checked the thermostat app on his phone. Usual temperature.

Edo rolled the pencil in his fingers, his lips rumpled. "There *is* a lot of value there. Value the police may not understand."

Andre's fingers tingled. *If I could just nudge a bit further...*

"You have one week. If information comes from it, you will contact police immediately."

"Yes, of course."

"And you must be *very* discreet. No names, yours or the school's, nothing. Only a phone number. And say nothing more than he's been seen in the Latin Quarter for vandalism, and for, unfortunately, assault."

"Yes, right. Thanks, Edo."

"And Andre."

He stopped at the doorway.

"This conversation never existed."

In the hall, he walked to his office, about to clap his hands but shook a silent fist instead. *Yes.* Now he needed a photo or drawing of the Breton. He'd never forget that face, those small sinister eyes. If he had any talent, he could draw the face himself. But he didn't. He knew who did though. Renia. He'd seen the botanical sketches of plants she'd done. She sold them in her shop. They were amazing. Full of detail, true to scale. And she'd seen that creep's face clearly, so clearly it probably haunted her.

His phone rang. Kateb.

"We have a fingerprint match," he said.

Andre blinked. "And?"

"I'd like you to come in and take a look at a few photos of suspects. Do you have time?"

An hour later, Andre arrived at the Préfecture, wondering whether he should ask Kateb for a photo of the thug. Would he actually give him one? And for what reason would Andre say he wanted it? As these thoughts tumbled through his mind, he waited on the bench in the reception area. Soon, Kateb greeted him and brought him to a desk, asking if he wanted coffee or water, which Andre refused, too anxious to delay. A pen stuck with an orange-haired troll, dressed in a police uniform, stood at the head of the desk, near a mess of papers and Post-it notes. Kateb shuffled through until finding a sheet with nine photos of mug shots.

Andre scanned the men's faces, their slouched mouths, their dead eyes, all hollows of gloom. The thug's sharp pale face and unforgiving expression was at the top right. "That's him."

"Number 3. Are you sure?"

"No doubt. I remember his sneer."

"Great," Kateb said, flipping the paper over and scribbling.

"Is that the same person Renia identified?"

"We'll ask the questions."

"Oh," he said. "Well, I'm sure she would like to know. Can you tell me his name?"

Kateb stared with a chill, then his face softened. "I can tell you we have a warrant out for his arrest."

"Great. I'll let her know."

"She knows."

"She does?"

Kateb scribbled a second note on a different form.

"And you can't tell me his name?" Andre said.

Kateb held his eyes an extended few seconds. "All I can tell you, is that we have a warrant out for his arrest."

"What does that mean?"

A trace of a smile slipped onto Kateb's face. "This kind of arrest warrant is *public* information."

A bell chimed in his mind. "Oh. I see." Meaning he could look up information in a database? "So, what are the charges?"

"Assault, battery, harassment, vandalism..." As he said the words, he shrugged. "He's got a history."

"Is there a special website where this information is available?"

"Here." He scratched out a URL on a scrap of paper. His handwriting was like an illegible jumble of symbols. "Go to this site and find the guy's photo. You can search by date or location. And there haven't been that many warrants issued in the last week or so."

"So the warrant was issued in Paris?"

His face stayed neutral, unchanged. "Also, he may have been arrested for car theft in Le Havre."

Andre slipped the paper in his pocket, getting up. "Thanks a lot."

"Oh," Kateb said, "by the way, fun *useful* fact..."

"Yes?"

"Are you listening?"

"Yes."

"The police do not support vigilantism. Harming a person is illegal."

Andre hurried home, feeling as sharp and aware as an animal on the hunt. When he got to the apartment, he threw off his jacket and opened his laptop, searched the warrants database by date. He told himself it wasn't vigilantism to simply locate the guy. He found him right away: the face, the name, the crimes. Matthias Floch, age 39, the ML initials on the pamphlet, wanted for theft, vandalism, assault, battery, harassment. He'd been arrested twice in Amsterdam. "Never learned," Andre said, feeling bitter, wondering if the guy had ever worked an honest day in his life.

The next day, after downloading a photo, he went to a copy shop and laid out 50 black-and-white flyers featuring a crisp photo of Floch's face and a call for information to Andre's phone number. Afterward, he posted them in AgroPolyTech, on the bulletin boards, in the school café, near the labs, in the lobby. He posted on the boards at the Sorbonne, the other universities, the high school. Then he tacked them up in the Antonia Café, the Strada, and other restaurants in the Latin Quarter. He hung one in the office at L'Enclos and asked Delphine to post a few in cafés near her apartment in Montparnasse.

Later, at the S2 house, he rang Monique Castel, explained that apples were growing at a healthy rate and that since the trees were fruiting, they were more valuable than ever. He omitted any hint of harassment, vandalism, stalking. Renia's assault. How Floch had lurked outside the S2 house and tussled with Andre. Instead, he made the case for an extension to the budget so he could install two video cameras on the greenhouse. She encouraged him to manage as best he could with the funds he had, and to notify her and her only, not Monsieur Alba, if he ran into the slightest bit of trouble.

The slightest bit of trouble. What about far more trouble than he predicted? He hung up, feeling a muddy defeat, then called an alarm system company for an estimate and discovered adding to an already existing system meant installing an entirely new system. The price was beyond what he could afford, so he ordered three cheap security cameras online, all on a special for overnight delivery.

On Wednesday, he brought the cameras to the S2 house. Seeing the door securely shut, he smiled and whistled an aimless tune as he unlocked it. Inside, a forest greeted him, sturdy trunks with solid branches and big healthy leaves. *How could anyone vandalize such a wholesome endeavor?* He checked random pots for moisture and inspected leaf undersides for pests, marveling at how honest plants were. Give them the same light, water, air, and space as their native habitat and they grew. They didn't care where they were as long as it was similar to their native home. Home could be China, Chile, the desert, even the tundra. Plants did what they knew how to do. Grow and reproduce. Honorably. No deceit, no egos. He yearned for that honor in people. But people weren't honorable, and in his own small, regretful way, he felt like living proof of that.

He unpacked the cameras and looked over the directions and went to the storage house for a ladder. Locked again. *Damn it.* He jiggled the handle, pounded the door, called to Brodeur. No answer. *Crap.* He searched for Manu and found him in the field, on one knee, staking vine starts to a large iron trellis. He deftly pulled a piece of green ribbon from his dispenser, wrapped it around a stem, and tied, creating tiny manacled green arms.

When he saw Andre approach, he greeted him with a friendly smile.

"Manu, it's been months. I really need a key to the storage house."

His smile collapsed. "Oh gosh, I'm sorry, I have it. Here."

He reached into a front pocket, producing a small ring with a single key. "I got it weeks ago. Sorry, I've been so busy with the garden." He smiled that boxy smile, seeming like an old dear friend you couldn't stay angry at. Andre forgave him right there, sooner than he'd intended to.

He put the key on his own ring and went to the storage house. While unlocking the door, he learned the door needed to be slightly lifted so as to align the mechanism with the piece on the frame. Inside, the shed felt ghostly, unused. The space was a dark ten-by-ten-foot square jammed with rusty wheelbarrows, cracked pots, broken rakes, old power tools. All dusty, as if they hadn't been used in years. It smelled of dried dirt and lubricating oil. He looked for the ladder. There were several opened bags of chicken manure, perlite, peat moss, and soil. Hoes and shovels hung upside down on nails. Brooms slanted together amidst cobwebs in a corner. On a small counter were decorative pots and twine and rubbing alcohol. Ridges of sand dotted the edge. It didn't seem up to parks department regulations. The regularly used tools must have been in the larger garage.

Andre scanned the corners. Hidden behind an ancient roto-tiller was the ladder, laying at an angle, its one foot sunk in wet mud. Andre lifted it, holding it carefully away from his body so as not to dirty his shirt, and turned to leave.

A woman stood in the doorway.

She was a thin whisp with black hair fanning over her shoulders, tan complexion. She wore a camel-colored coat, a purple skirt, glossy ankle boots.

"Monsieur Damazy?"

"Yes."

"My name is Celine Du Mont. I work at AgroPolyTech in Enrollment. I left you a message this morning."

"Oh." He hadn't checked messages since... when? "Sorry, I haven't checked my phone lately." Vaguely he recognized the name. He'd seen it on a school email announcement.

"At lunchtime, I happened to see Director Bankole," she said, "who told me you were here working. I came because I saw the notice you posted in the library."

"The notice? About Matthias Floch?"

"Yes. That photo? I've seen that man."

"Really? Are you sure?"

"Yes. Very sure."

His heart thumped in his ears.

"And," she said, "I think I know where he works."

CHAPTER 20

Andre gingerly set the ladder against the storage house as Du Mont waited, her fingers politely locked and resting. In the daylight, he recognized her face as distantly familiar, like he'd seen it at a staff party or in the café. She had a touch of a friendly smile on her lips. Her eyes were guileless, orangish brown, the color of an oak leaf.

He pulled out a copy of the notice from his back pocket, unfolded it. "You're sure you've seen this man?"

"Yes. Certain of it."

"Great. Where?"

"In Belleville."

Suddenly, he felt the warmth of his breath shift in and out of his mouth. *Is it true?* "Where in Belleville?"

"On the Boulevard Voltaire. He works in a garage, on cars, and sometimes the door is open. Also, I've seen him several times at the Café en Flame, which is near the garage."

"He works at an auto garage?"

"Yes."

In the field, a gardener held a shovel upside down, its head pointing at the sky as he scraped the blade with a sharpening stone. A metallic scratch rang out.

"I saw him arguing with another man," she said. "Loudly. I thought they were going to fight, like with fists. So, as I walked past him, I went quickly. And then in the café, I saw him again. He was arguing with the owner. He was taking apart a piece of electrical equipment on the bar, I don't know what, and the owner wanted him to leave."

"Oh. Did he speak French?"

"Yes."

"Do you remember if he had an accent, like from Bretagne?"

"No, I don't remember."

"You said you saw him more than once at the café?"

She looked into the distance. "Yes, I've seen him once on a Wednesday and certainly on a Friday. Always evening. After eight o'clock. I'm certain about Friday because on Fridays I walk by that restaurant when I go to my mother's."

The scraping rang louder and faster, the clanging cutting the air.

"Why is he wanted for vandalism?" she said. "What did he vandalize?"

"Oh, uh. The trees in a project I'm working on."

Her nose wrinkled. "And assault? On a student?"

"No, no student... but a ... a friend of mine."

Her face collapsed in concern. "Oh no."

"Yeah, it was terrible. He hurt her."

She covered her mouth with a hand.

"But she'll be fine. And thanks to you, hopefully he won't hurt anyone else."

After Du Mont left, Andre clapped his hands and jogged to the S2 house, digging out his phone from his leather bag. His fingers shook as he scrolled for Nes's number. Outside, somewhere in L'Enclos, a horn beeped repeatedly. A male voice roared with an announcement, an explosion of laughter. Applause. Another man yelled, "*Ah oui, bon anniversaire!*" A chorus of the birthday song rang.

Nes answered. "What's up?"

"A woman who works at the university came to see me. She's seen our man."

"Ah, has she now?"

"Yes, in a Belleville café and in some garage where he works on cars."

"Belleville, eh?"

"Yes."

"Brilliant."

"I'm going tonight to find him."

"You?"

"Yeah, she said he's at this one café on Wednesdays and Fridays. Today is Wednesday."

"You can't get all up in this lout's face on your own. Call the *flics*."

"They hardly tell me anything. And I'm not waiting around for them, I'm going to settle this now. I want him to pay for what he did to Renia."

"But Andre, this guy... he's not like you and me."

"I know."

"No, I mean, he's vicious. He's not going to have a reasonable chat with you."

"That's okay. I don't want to chat."

"Andre, the man is *dangerous*."

He considered that. He didn't hesitate to punch a woman. "And he did threaten to stab me."

"Listen, hold off," Nes said. "Tell the cops what you know and leave it there."

"But if I don't confront him, he'll do more damage. Maybe even attack Renia again."

"There is that."

"I'm going after him tonight. Maybe in a couple hours, after I finish here."

"Wait a minute, just wait. Let me think." There was a pause. Andre could hear water running from a hose splashing onto a hard surface. "Look, you remember my friend, Heckie?"

"Maybe."

"Frizzy hair? Built like a wooly mammoth?"

"The contractor guy?"

"Yeah, well, I had a pint with him the other day. Pretty sure he's working tonight, but I'll bet he's not working Friday night. He owes me a favor… and I've got an idea."

On Friday night, Andre, Nes, and Heckie went to the Café en Flame. It was a shabby brasserie with washed-down graffiti and anarchy symbols on either side of the door. The neon "e" in "café" blinked in a random, intermittent pattern. It had a sticky door-knob and creaky door. Inside, the faded tan wallpaper had seen too many cigarettes and the wooden bar too many keys and sharp objects. The owner, a tired looking man in his sixties with greased hair, shuffled to the table in a slow gait and handed them taped menus. The food was traditional. The prices were cheap. The atmosphere dim and neglected.

They took a table in the far corner and ordered and talked over a round of beer. Heckie was a hulking man in his mid-twenties, 6'5" and 300 pounds. He had brown kinky hair that was puffy and wild though his beard was thin and spottily covered his cheeks. He dressed in a flannel shirt, saggy jeans, and leather cowboy boots. He told them about installing a new bathroom in a house in Belgravia that was owned by a Deutschebank executive. In a soft-spoken, sparsely worded story, he said one night the banker's wife had had too many drinks and invited him to "show her my tools in the bedroom."

"What did you do?" Andre said.

"Packed up the most important tool and left."

After what seemed a half-hour, their food came and they ate in unimpressed silence, faces contorting with expressions of sur-prise and mild repulsion. Brown-edged lettuce on Andre's salad, a dry bun on Heckie's burger, dripping grease on Nes's Croque Ma-dame. "I'm not sure this stuff is safe even for my iron stomach," Nes said, his elbows crunched in besides Heckie's broad frame. They ordered more beer to wash away the disappointment.

By nine-thirty, as they all agreed Matthias Floch must not be coming, he swung in and slid onto a seat at the bar. Andre's back was to the door, but Nes recognized him: tall, gray sweatshirt, tan hat. Andre peeked. Floch sat hunched over the bar, his hat low on his head so he could see out but others couldn't see his face.

Nes's mouth opened.

"What is it?" Andre said.

"Put your hood up," he said in low whisper.

"Why?"

"He noticed us."

Andre reached to put up a hood on his racer jacket, realized he hadn't worn a hoodie underneath. He sat motionless, tense, staring at the table, his heart beating hard, frozen with the realization that what he'd wanted was actually happening. Nes absently flicked his fingers against his empty plate, dotted with slick puddles of oil. Andre's fork lay in bits of limp carrot. Heckie's enormous hand sat wrapped around a beer bottle. It seemed like a toy rocket in his hand. A medical bracelet dangled off his wrist. Andre worried. *Are we putting him in danger?* He was about to ask why he wore a medical bracelet when Floch and the waiter exchanged words.

"What is he doing?" Andre said.

"Ordering," Nes said.

"Now what?"

"We have another round."

They waited a half-hour for Floch to eat steak and potatoes and drink two vodkas on ice. At 10:15, he paid his check and left. Right after, the three slapped Euro bills on the table and followed.

Floch went up the Boulevard Voltaire amidst a lean scattering of people. A heavy rain had driven most people indoors. The May air steamed warm and muggy. Most shops sat shuttered, their metal screens down: the pharmacy, the erotic shop, the chocolate bakery. The three hung some fifty feet back, staying quiet and in the shadows of awnings and trees. Andre kept a step hidden behind Heckie. He couldn't remember if he'd worn his racer jacket the night he'd caught Floch outside the S2 house and fretted he might recognize it.

Soon, at the smaller Rue Voltaire, Floch went right. Nes, who'd been mapping the neighborhood on his phone, pointed to the Dumas passage. "Let's get ahead and jump him at the intersection," he said. The walkway bordered an apartment building to the north, a courtyard garden to the south. They hurried into it, paralleling his path.

Andre's stomach sloshed. He felt a nervous, disorienting buzz from the beer. "What if he turns left, away from us?"

They paused, stared at each other, unsure what to do.

"We'll chase the wanker down," Heckie said.

They went past a row of cypresses, headless with branches splaying in all directions, past graffiti that said, "Feel this!" and "No master, no God," then past a heavy chain laying on the ground, attached to nothing. They veered left and came to the corner of the Rue Voltaire, pausing in a dark loading area. A rounded row of hornbeam trees screened the apartment windows above. Andre and Heckie set their backs against a wall. Heckie on the edge, Andre beside. Nes floated opposite them, leaning in the street to check if Floch was there. They waited. And waited.

To Heckie, Andre whispered. "Are you scared?"

Heckie wrinkled a confused brow, as if Andre were wearing a silly hat. "Only of my mother, mate."

Nes peeked into the sidewalk, hopped into the passage. "He's coming," he said and came around to ready himself beside Andre. Floch's footsteps clicked on the cobbles. His shadow jaggedly shuffled in the lamplight. He strolled by, head down, hands in pockets, unsuspecting.

Heckie jumped out, grabbed his shoulders, and spun to slam him against the wall, one giant arm pressing his collarbone, a giant hand binding his wrists.

Floch's eyes flickered in shock.

Nes waved at a boarded door and its deep stoop. Heckie, a hold of Floch, dragged him into it.

"So," Nes said, "are you Matthias Floch?"

Floch's eyes, those small eyes the color of a pinto bean, beamed in alarm.

Andre hid behind Heckie, a mix of panic and relief rushing through his body.

Nes reached into Floch's back pocket.

He flinched.

Nes took out the guy's wallet and combed through the cards and money. "Apparently it is Matthias Floch. We thought so. Interesting. You're from Brittany then, eh? or what?"

Floch breathed through a flaring nose, his mouth shut in a contorted clip.

Andre turned away, his panicked nerves creeping into regret. Edo was right. He should have let the police handle it.

Nes said, "It seems you haven't behaved very well lately."

Heckie, with his strong hands and meaty bulk, had laid into Floch so hard that Floch couldn't budge. He had one arm across the collarbone, pressing hard as if Heckie could headbutt Floch's forehead and kill him.

Andre chewed his lip, hoping his pressure wouldn't do just that.

"It seems you're upset with our operation here in Paris," Nes said. "You speak English? Or just French, *mon ami*?"

Renia's swollen purple eye appeared in Andre's mind. His anger smoldered. He took a breath and stepped from behind Heckie. He didn't care if Floch knew who he was. This was what he'd waited for.

Nes held out Floch's driver's license and said, "Ah, an expired license. You could get in trouble with the *flics* for that." To Andre, he said, "Want a picture keepsake?"

Andre took out his phone and clicked a photo. Nes replaced it and leaned in close to Floch. "Who do you work for?"

Floch didn't answer. His eyes were wide. He tried to wrestle out of Heckie's hold, but Heckie pressed his forearm deeper into the collarbone.

"Okay, call the *flics*," Nes said to Andre.

Andre tapped the police icon on his phone. Kateb's number appeared. Andre had texted him, told him he was "meeting Floch" that night. He would hit "Call," but not yet.

"I don't know what you're talking about," Floch said.

"Ah, he speaks English after all," Nes said.

"What is your god damn problem?" Andre said. "Why did you break into my greenhouse?"

Floch breathed in a heave, his eyes narrowed. "Your house?"

"Those are my trees in that greenhouse, you *con*."

His eyes shifted like blowing sand.

"The trees you sprayed," Andre said. "What is your problem with them?"

Silence.

"Fine. I'm calling the cops."

"Those trees you're growing…"

Andre paused.

"They're the devil's work. The devil soiled humanity with an apple and now you two are soiling the Lord's work again."

Andre and Nes exchanged a glance.

"You know this, yet you turn away from Him."

Andre drew in an exasperated breath. "You've got it wrong," he said, more tired than fierce. "Those apples are medicinal. I grow them to help people."

"That's not true."

"What are you talking about? Of course, it is!"

"It's not worth arguing," Nes said. "Call the cops."

Andre's face hardened. "Are you working for the East Valley Church?"

Floch was silent.

"Are you?"

Andre's voice hardened. "Do you have a connection to the East Valley Church? Yes or no?"

Floch clamped his mouth shut.

"What is the connection, damn it?" Andre said.

Floch swallowed, checked Heckie's face. Heckie's expression was calm, focused, as if he might be whittling a block of wood into a sculpture of a bird.

"And don't lie or you'll regret it," Andre said.

Floch's eyes blinked, betraying his fright.

Andre snapped a photo of him. He texted the photo to Kateb.

"Listen," Nes said. "It's over, mate. You might as well tell us. Otherwise, your future's further in the toilet. We could tie you up and dump you in the Seine right now. Do you think my friend here hasn't done it before?"

Floch's eyes went to Heckie, who smiled.

"I'm a proud member of East Valley."

"What Valley?" Nes asked.

"East Valley Church."

"Who's that?" Nes asked.

"Do you work for him?" Andre said. His heart felt cold, his mind, focused.

Silence.

"What is your connection to Bill Miller?" Andre said.

"He saved me," Floch said.

"What?"

"He saved me. Don't hurt him."

"Hurt him?" Andre said. "He's not even in France... is he? Where did he save you?"

He swallowed. "Florida."

"Is he paying you?"

"No, I think for myself... but he prays for me."

"Prays for you?" Andre said.

"Come on, how much is he paying you?" Nes said.

"Everything is *my* choice."

"Your choice?"

"It's the least I can do. I owe him my life. And you two..." He cringed at the pressure of Heckie's body leaning in.

Nes had a sour expression. "Loosen up."

"You guys are lost, pathetic lost souls."

"We are?" Andre said. "You attacked a woman! You—"

"She's doing the devil's work," he eeked out.

"Devil's work?"

The sound of sirens rose in the distance.

"How could you even *think* to hurt her?" Andre pushed his chest.

"Andre..." Nes said.

He got in Floch's face, his blood pumping fast. "If you ever touch her again, I will *kill* you, do you hear me?"

"Andre."

"You tell Mr. Miller that I will destroy anyone who vandalizes my work or hurts my staff. You tell him, do you understand?"

The sirens grew louder.

"Let's get him out," Nes said.

Floch's face trembled. "You're pathetic. And you'll pay in the end. You won't win. I'll make sure of it."

"Heckie, let's move him to the street," Nes said.

Heckie grabbed him in an abrasive, side-bear hug with Floch's neck in the crook of his elbow and dragged him from the doorway.

The blue lights of a police car flashed on the wall.

Floch went limp. Surprised, Heckie loosened his hold a half-second and Floch slipped out. He sprinted away, his hat tumbling down.

Andre and Nes tore after him. Floch ran into the Passage Dumas and through the courtyard. His body jagged left and right as he avoided trees, benches, and garbage bins. Andre, maybe from longer legs or determination, pulled ahead. The image of Floch bounced in wild jolts, his sweatshirt tail billowing. Just when Andre thought he could reach out and grab it, Floch turned in a slight sway, then jerked into the Rue Guenot, scooting between a dozen parked bikes, and into the narrow street.

Andre kept up, his heart racing, his lungs sucking air. The white lines of a crosswalk carouseled through his vision. Floch curved into the Boulevard Voltaire and Andre followed, avoiding a kiosk at the curb before hooking hard left into Montreuil. As Floch crossed the street, a scooter buzzed past. A beat later, Andre dashed in the street and the scooter rammed him. His body flew sideways, banged hard on the pavement. The scooter bumped over his arm.

The pain. The buzz of the motor.

Nes shouted unrecognizable words.

Andre yelled, "Go!" The pavement was gritty and smelled like oil. The sky floated in a murky black sweep, tufts of light from street lamps. A young man, an Asian teenager leaned over, his hair flopping forward, his face tormented. A sign that said *Delice* floated at his ear. It faded into the smell of Heckie's panting breath, meat, grease, ketchup, and the high-low whir of sirens.

CHAPTER 21

In the morning, Andre woke from a throbbing ache. A hot pulsing sensation in his arm. Was he in California? Wait, no, a hospital. No. His bedroom. In Paris. Outside, a truck beeped while backing up. A metal barrel clanged. Soft paws dabbed at his ankles. The room brightened, creating a grainy outline of his nightstand, the closet door, the clothes tree. The window shade hung to the sill, farther than usual. He usually left it half-raised since Linus liked to look outside in the morning. Nes must have pulled it. He looked at his phone. Above the photo of Linus grabbing a catnip mouse on a string, the date said May 28th, at least two mornings since they'd found Floch.

He groaned. How he, Nes, and giant Heckie had lost Floch in the streets of Belleville, he couldn't explain. *What a disaster.* And the result? He stared at the ceiling, the deco fixture like a sealed shell. A cast on his arm. Heavy, clunky like a robotic limb that didn't work. He got up, feeling sore, and went to the bathroom, splashed water on his face, dug around in the drawer for painkillers, and swallowed two. He remembered lying in the street, the rubber sound of footsteps, fingers poking through bike gloves. The kid patted his shoulder. "*Désolée. Désolée,*" he said, "*l'ambulance arrive maintenant.*"

He remembered shocking hospital lights, nurses speaking fast medical lingo, the shooting pain while his shirt was cut away. Then a doctor's methodical words: a fractured ulna, two months in a cast. Later, Kateb and that other cop had come in the room, interviewed him, taken notes. A clock ticking on the wall, the arms flicking toward 1:27, then hobbling into the apartment with Nes and Heckie. Sleep. They rolled into random sleeping bags and blankets on the couch and floor. The smell of burnt toast. With regretful faces, they caught the train late the next afternoon. TV. Linus. More sleep on Sunday. Now, a new day with a broken spirit and Floch still on the loose.

He checked the temperature app. The S2 house was stable, in the assigned "green" zone. He clicked off. The phone rang, startling him. He answered.

A sleek female voice said, "Monsieur Andre Damazy, *s'il vous plait.*"

"Speaking."

"I'm calling on behalf of Madame Monique Castel," she said. "She and Monsieur Alba would like to visit your project."

"Um," he sat up straighter, wiped his eyes, as if she could see him through the phone. "What?"

"Madame Castel and Monsieur Alba would like to visit on Wednesday. Is this possible?"

"Wednesday?"

"Yes."

"What day is it?"

"What day is it?"

"Yes. I mean, no. Wednesday would be fine. It's fine." *Is today Monday?*

"Do you have eight o'clock available?"

"Uh, eight o'clock in the morning? Yes, that's fine." After he said it, he winced at scheduling the appointment so early. He needed extra time to shower and dress with the cast. And feeding the cat. Even walking to L'Enclos would take more time.

"Alright, they will arrive at eight on Wednesday. And one more suggestion..."

"Yes?"

"Monsieur Alba will be coming from an early meeting he has in Paris-Saclay. Can you make available some breakfast refreshments?"

He hung up and double checked the day was Monday. *Okay. Go slow.* He stumped around, got himself dressed in a fresh shirt, filled a bowl with food for Linus, then considered sleeping at the greenhouse. He had to. Floch would be out for blood now. If he hadn't somehow vandalized the trees already. He shoved an extra shirt in his bag, then filled another bowl for Linus and scooped his litter box, petting his head. "See you tomorrow, buddy."

By the time he reached L'Enclos, he calculated he had two days to do the transplanting work next on his work list. And without Renia. At least the botany class had finished. Inside the S2 house, the trees stood undamaged and healthy. Smelled like earthy leaves. Floch hadn't retaliated—yet. He checked the temperature controls, alarm system, and new cameras he'd installed last week, all in working order. He found a note from Nes on the counter: "Saturday. Checked on the Tengri. All looks brilliant."

Andre had no memory of giving him the key or alarm code or combination to the padlock. Didn't matter. *What a friend.* He shuffled around, eyeing the trees. All indeed looked brilliant. He knew, though, from the vigorous burst of growth this last month, the roots needed more space. If he'd been able to plant outside, he wouldn't have had this problem, the trees would have been in open soil, free to spread in whatever direction they needed. Now, without his right arm or Renia, transplanting would be an awkward, messy task. The upshot was bigger containers made the trees stand taller, better to impress the LaRoche visitors.

In the Chick's Nest, he measured the apples on the fruiting saplings: over an inch in diameter, solid white and disease-free. If he fed the trees with potassium, the apples might plump up and appear more robust, even by Wednesday, so he went to the storage house and unlocked the door. Once inside, amidst the same dusty supplies, he couldn't find the bottle of fertilizer. He checked the counters, behind the trash bins, under the tarps, in the shelves. In the far corner, a small cabinet was attached to the side of the workbench, its door oddly facing the wall. *Why?* He threaded his hand through the short stool beside it and reached far back to the tiny knob and opened the door.

Clank.

In the dim, he strained to see inside so he felt around, hoping to avoid a mouse trap, hoping to find the fertilizer. Clank. A cluster of glass bottles. *Glass?* He maneuvered a bottle out.

Armagnac.

A near-empty bottle. The label stained with dirt. Beside it, an unopened one. *Wow. Brodeur. Drinking on the job.* He set both in place and closed the door, feeling like a kid caught in his parents' liquor cabinet. How long had that been going on? Years. Decades? It was why the old codger locked himself in. He was a drunk. With a heavy sigh, Andre went outside and locked up. At the corner behind a clay pot was the fertilizer, where he'd left it last week.

By nine that night, he'd transplanted 21 trees. Not nearly enough if he would make it by Wednesday. He went to the sink and washed his hands, careful to wash his right fingertips only gently as they were sensitive to being bumped, and he opened his laptop to check the last two nights of security footage. The scenes were mostly Brodeur going behind the greenhouse to drive out the cart and trailer before re-parking at day's end. Twice, he passed by to enter the storage house. On Thursday afternoon, he stayed inside a full half-hour, no doubt nursing his bottle of Armagnac.

Andre nibbled on bread and cheese, every hour his body feeling more like sludge. His arm pulsed in faint pain. His stomach ached. He fast-forwarded through the final hours of footage from the previous day. Nes had gone in and out at lunchtime on Saturday. From then on, nothing unusual. He was about to shut it off when the east side footage, the shed side, fizzled to static. Time stamp read: Today, 7:43 am. He fast-forwarded through the day. The camera showed static. He wanted to check on the camera, but he'd need a ladder. *Haul it and set it up with a left arm? No. Too beat.* He had to leave it be.

206

That night at ten o'clock, he rolled himself in a blanket and fell in a hard sleep on the cot. In the darkness, the wind howled like a wolf before ceasing when the rain poured, creating a fast violent ticking on the roof. The fan spun to clear the humidity. The hum woke him. For a while, he stared at the pattern of streetlights and shadows dancing across the walls of the house. They bounced and reared as if jousting. He contemplated what he'd do if Floch broke in. Call the police? Fight him with one good fist? A week ago, he was sure he'd strangle him with his bare hands. Now he was barely capable of standing straight. Worried Floch might break through the door, he hoisted up and searched his tools on the counter, found the machete, and set it, unsheathed, on the floor beside the cot, feeling a touch more relaxed.

He lay on his back, hands folded on his stomach like a corpse, listening to the rain hit like bullets. Grandma Mel became a corpse in California sixteen years ago. He remembered her funeral. Her body flat in that modest casket. She was dressed in a yellow sweater, the color of butter, with a necklace of pearls. The same necklace Jason had stolen? Or a new one? Andre didn't know. A rosary wound through her clasped hands. Her gray hair had been pinned in a tighter, more formal style than she usually wore. Everyone knew Grandma Mel had lived a rough life, her ex-husband having been not only a cad, but occasionally violent. She hadn't spoken about that to Andre, but he knew the stories. Drunk and mean on Saturday night, meek and pious on Sunday mornings. She often laughed and said, "I've been to hell and back and back is better!" In the casket, she seemed childlike and at peace, with a worn face holding an impish smile that implied she knew a secret.

Andre approached the casket, surrounded by vases of flowers. It was the first time he'd seen her since that day he'd driven off, bailed, escaped like a wimp. He'd apologized a hundred times to her in his head, had even gone to church and prayed. Now, she was before him and he didn't know what to do. So, he softly set his hand on her forearm. The skin was thin, the bone sturdy. "I'm sorry, Grandma Mel," he whispered. "I didn't know. I didn't think..." and in his mind the words trailed off like a beetle that

207

scurries away in a frenzy. He swallowed, wanting a few more minutes, but the couple behind had small children. The boy rocked back and forth on his heels, dressed in a little powder-blue suit. He danced and tugged at his mother's hand. Andre let go of Grandma Mel's arm and moved from the light of the casket into the church's darkness.

The pews gently bustled with family and friends, murmuring to each other, fanning themselves with the ceremony's program. Teri wept in the front row with Jason's brother Karl and two younger sisters, Jason himself absent. At seeing her, Andre hung his head. He marched straight out the door, past a statue of Jesus and a statue of Mother Mary, his face warming with shame.

Outside, the concrete steps baked in the hot autumn air. Near the street, crispy leaves spiraled from an oak tree like sad confetti. He went to a bench beneath the tree and sat, curling his arms around his stomach.

Oskar emerged from the church, walked across the lawn. He didn't own a black suit so he wore a gray suit with a black tie. As he neared, he said, "Are you sick?"

Andre combed his fingers through his hair again and again. "No. I mean, maybe. Yes."

His dad gripped his shoulder with a heavy hand. "I didn't think you'd take this so hard."

"I'm trying not to."

"She was a sweet old gal. I think Teri turned out so well because Melody was around to make sure she did." Teri had worked at Suntime Orchards for twelve years. She was one of his dad's best employees.

Andre shot up, paced. "Stop it, just stop it."

"What?"

He was unsure what to do, unsure where to go. Get in a car and drive away? That meant leaving Dad and he didn't want to leave him without a ride. "I need to get out of here."

"Alright, let's go home."

"No, I mean out of Sonoma County." He walked around the bench. A fly zoomed and nearly bumped his face. He scratched his forehead, then wiped it, then rubbed it. He caught sight of his dad with fresh eyes. His age. His descent into weakness. Oskar was rugged, but his mouth sagged. His eyes had deepened in the last few years. They were the color of cocoa, large with a practical expression, the same eyes Andre had inherited from their Polish ancestors. He couldn't keep secrets from his dad.

"Dad, I did it," he said. "I let Grandma Mel die."

His face soured, doubtful. "What?"

"It's true."

"Don't be silly."

"On the day those gangsters came to her house, *I* was there."

His father's face turned lax, spreading like a pile of uncooked dough.

"It's true," Andre said.

"You're sure?"

"Yes."

"But you're not in a gang... are you?"

"No, I'm not," he said. "I was... I was in the backyard."

"With Jason?"

"No, by myself. I was picking the last of the pomegranates."

His bottom lip wavered, unsure. "You were?"

"Yes." He paced in a circle. He felt like if he could walk fast enough, he'd walk out of his body and disappear from life. "Those guys were looking for Jason."

His father examined the ground as if the scattered leaves could reveal an answer.

"Did you notice Jason wasn't here today?" Andre said. "He's still in Mexico. He owed those guys money, lots of money, Dad. Drug money."

"Oh. No, I didn't."

"And I saw them mess with her and I left. I started the *God damn truck* and I left."

He dropped to the bench, feeling like wet crumpled paper.

"Andre..."

"I thought she'd be okay. They threatened to beat her up, but she gave them a ring. They all went upstairs, and I didn't know they were going to tie her up and leave her there. I didn't know, Dad."

"No, I'm sure you didn't."

"And I didn't know she had a heart condition. If I'd known that, I would've stayed. I swear I would have."

He rocked a little into himself, wishing he could be an anonymous person in an anonymous situation. "And then she had a heart attack and now she's dead and I can't change it and oh God, I can't *change* it."

He covered his face.

Oskar pressed on both his shoulders. "Listen, you listen to me. Yes, you should've gone in. But there were what, three of them and one of you?"

"Yes. And I had so much to do that day. I was so obsessed with my dumb crop. I wanted the money. Oh God, why did I drive away?"

"Andre, they could have had guns, they could've killed you."

He chewed his lip frantically. "They did have a gun."

"See."

"It's no excuse."

"Of course, it is. You did the right thing."

"But I could have saved her."

"You could have ended up dead."

He moaned.

"Look," Oskar shook his head as if convincing himself, "it didn't happen that way and that's all there is to it."

Inside the church, the mourners sang a hymn. The music of voices vibrated the air.

"If you want to do something," he said, "go to the police and tell them you saw the guys."

"But then Teri will find out I left and she'll hate me."

Oskar frowned, staring at the gleaming cars in the parking lot, washed and shimmering in the sun. "But could you give them a description?"

"Probably... yes."

"That's helpful. Do that. No one besides the police needs to know you were there."

"She'll find out. I know she will. What if they catch these guys or worse, what if they don't? How can I live here? I can't live with myself as it is."

CHAPTER 22

On Tuesday, Andre woke up and went straight home, worried about Linus, worried about Renia. He wanted to be in two places at once. He needed to be. Floch's words rang in his memory. *You won't win. I'll make sure of it.* He texted Renia, asking if she was safe and if she'd seen any unusual characters in her neighborhood. She only replied with a couple words: "Safe, *merci*." He told her he was worried about Floch being on the loose, sheepishly admitted he and Nes had confronted him, but he'd gotten away. "Oh no! You're hurt?" He wrote: "Not badly." *A tiny lie.* "Don't worry, I'm at greenhouse. Everything will be fine." He waited. "More later, busy today," she wrote and nothing else.

As he took a hot slow shower and ate a slow breakfast, his jaw aching from stress, he felt a lump of regret grow in his stomach. All those years ago, after Grandma Mel's funeral, he had gone to the police. Thanks to his descriptions, they arrested one of Jason's gangster friends. Most of the orchard workers who heard that forgave Andre except Teri and her family. Instead of thanking him, they shunned him. Teri never physically handed him his paycheck again. It went from being tossed it at his chest with a glare to being left discreetly on the counter. He said nothing, felt like he deserved it. But his dad noticed and finally talked with Teri, reasoning that Andre was only seventeen. Andre over-heard her say, "Yeah, well, I know other seventeen-year-olds with a lot more integrity."

As he waited for the L'Enclos gate to open, he exhaled the regret. Teri had quit Suntime Orchards six months later, after selling Grandma Mel's house. Her co-workers never mentioned where she'd moved to and Andre never dared to ask.

Inside the S2 house, the light on the alarm keypad was dark. He punched in the code, but the numbers didn't light. He searched for Floch, expecting to see him with a scarf tied on his face, spraying trees with a bottle of herbicide. But all was quiet. No one about. The Chick's Nest, locked. Oddly, a steady wind blew. The fans spun at high speed, circulating cool air. The trees' leaves fluttered in a fury. He jogged to the control panel and hit the Off button. Nothing. He tried again. No change. Then the On button, Off, Auto, Enter, and any button, but nothing changed. He darted to the electrical box in the Chick's Nest, flipped the circuit. No change. He switched off another circuit, another. The lights went out. The fans spun fast. He heaved the master switch. The unruly wind died.

He leaned against the wall, pinching his nose. The alarm had been disabled, but the fans switched on. *For how long?* He'd left a few minutes after nine. It was now noon. Floch must have sab-otaged the wiring outside. In the actual daylight. Maybe even as Andre was leaving. *My God. Had he been waiting for the chance all night?*

The trees looked shaggy and tired. The leaves drooped as if they'd been driven down a highway in open air. Some had fallen, scattered on the tables and floor. In the Chick's Nest, the saplings looked okay but needed water. *Forget transplanting.* The sprin-klers were tied into the electrical system, so he went to the floor sink area and turned on the hose's spigot. The hose sputtered and shot a weak stream before petering out. *Shoot.* Floch had not only hijacked the electrical, but had rigged the water too.

The water line valve was by the hoop houses, in a box covered by a steel plate. After a brief struggle of tugging at the handle with his left hand, he opened it and found the valve. Shut off. He

needed a plumber's wrench to switch it on. Who was around?
Manu, gone. As was Brodeur. No gardeners nearby. He went to
the office. A gardener he hadn't seen before was at a desk in the
interior office, a squat plug of a guy typing deftly on a computer.

"Excuse me. Do you know where I can get a wrench?" Andre
said.

The guy's gaze landed on Andre's cast. "Sorry, no."

"Someone shut off the water valve."

"Oh, strange. Try the storage house."

At the storage house, a new padlock hung from the door
handle.

What? A bloody padlock? He yanked at the handle. *A bloody,
stupid padlock.* Brodeur must have done it in response to Manu
giving Andre a key. *Unbelievable.*

Damn the old fool.

Andre stormed to the office. As he burst in, he asked who
had the key to the storage house padlock.

The gardener half-shrugged. "Probably Manu."

Outside, a crow squawked.

"Is he back yet?"

"No, he was hedging in the garden. Maybe he's eating lunch,
I don't know."

The crow cawed, again and again.

Andre imagined searching the huge public garden. It would
take at least a half-hour to find Manu. "What about Brodeur?"

"He's in the Jardin Ecologique."

By the time Andre reached the Jardin des Plantes, the last
of the night's clouds had cleared and the sun shone in a radiant
haze. The promenade that led to the Museum of Natural
History seemed like a jagged puzzle, the conifers hedged
straight, the pond sharply angled, the corners of the borders a
cacophony of color. Andre stormed by fiery coreopsis and pointed lupines. Magenta coneflowers blasted up like missiles aimed
at the sky. Unsuspecting tourists strolled the paths with maps,
stopping to read a plant sign and get in everyone's way. He

passed a bed of craggy acanthus and red-hot poker from which stalks of giant reed grass rose up like crossed spears.

Brodeur had insisted on playing psychological games since Andre's first day at L'Enclos. In the last seven months, he hadn't once deferred on any decision Andre had made on the S2 house. And now he'd locked him out of his dumb shed so he could drink booze in peace. What a lousy human. His condescension was endless. The outrage burned as hot in Andre's heart as the pain in his arm.

He found the old grump along the Allée Jussieu near a wooded corner. With another gardener, he carried a tarp loaded with cuttings and weeds. At the trailer, the two lifted the tarp and folded it onto the flat bed.

Noticing Andre, Brodeur crossed his arms. His co-worker drove the trailer down the path.

"Excuse me," Andre said. "Did you put a lock on the storage house door?"

Brodeur squinted. "What do you want?"

"Did you do that? I have a key now, but you put a lock on the handle. Why?"

"I don't have to explain myself to you."

"I have permission to access the storage house."

"Anyone who is not an employee of the Parisian parks system cannot access it."

Andre kicked at the grit. He wanted to knock that dirty canvas hat off his head and beat him until he bled. "I have a damn document with the parks system seal and signatures. I need to get in there *today*."

"Why? What is so urgent?"

He hated to provide an explanation. To this person who had no right to an explanation. Had no authority over him. "Someone turned off the water last night. I can't water my trees."

"I didn't touch it," Brodeur said.

"No, but I need to water my trees."

Brodeur dug in his pocket and pulled out a heavy ring crammed with keys. "Where is Manu? Manu will give you the key. I can't lend you my ring. I need it for the vehicle."

"I can't find Manu," Andre said.

"He's in the office."

"No, he's not. I was at the office."

Brodeur shifted his eyes around the garden. "Then he has gone to eat lunch. You must wait." He put the ring in his pocket.

"Wait."

"Yes."

"My trees are dried out."

"You must wait."

"They will die. Seven months of work will die."

"Then they will die."

Andre circled around, his blood racing. "You know, since the day I started, you've fought me. You act like you're my boss, my superior. If there's an opportunity to make my job harder, you take it. I wouldn't be surprised if you're helping the guy who vandalized my trees."

Brodeur's face tightened. "I did no such thing!" He stepped closer, his mouth crumpled. His bushy brows cast a shadow over his milky eyes. "Since you came along, you act like you're the king of L'Enlos Vert. You take over the S2 house though you're not employed here, and every few days, you demand assistance. More, more, always wanting more, like a king."

"I haven't bothered you for anything except a dumb key to a crappy shed, whose lock, now that I have a key to it, has been rigged so I can't even use it!"

Brodeur stomped away.

Andre marched alongside. "The only reason I needed to go in that building in the first place was because you insisted I store my..." he blanked on the word for 'fertilizer' in French so he said, "plant food there when it would have been fine in the greenhouse."

"That is against regulation."

"And by the way, why are you in the storage house for such a long time? What are you doing in there with the door locked?"

Brodeur stopped, his face boiling with suspicion.

"The other day I was in there and found Armagnac. Whose is that?"

The old man's face reddened. For a second, his eyes shifted around the garden. The coworker was digging in the soil yards away. No one nearby. His eyes burned. His mouth twitched. In an explosion, he said, "You young fools don't know what it means to have loved and lost *love*. I, too, once had a beautiful wife."

Wife? What?

"But I lost her. I lost my... chrysanthemum. She *died*, in a crash. And I tried to steer left, but it rained and we slid to the right and hit that ridiculous tree. And the car hit only on the right, not the left, not the center, but on the right where *she* sat. Oh, I wish God had taken me instead! And now I'm left here in this mad world with the likes of you!" His eyes flamed. "Is it a crime for a man to mourn in his own way?"

Brodeur's face was charged with broken agony. Full of contorted cracks. Each crack another year of grief. At any moment, it would burst like a cloud of rain. Andre remembered Brodeur leaving the storage house while wiping his mouth, his eyes, and his forehead with a handkerchief. On another day he'd taken off his hat and wiped his nose with a sleeve. Always wiping his face. Always wiping... tears.

The inferno in Andre's heart drained. He let go a long sympathetic breath. "Monsieur," he said in a quiet snap, "Forgive me."

Far out on the stately lawn, two teenagers blew bubbles, laughing.

"I didn't know of your loss," Andre said. "I'm sorry. I'll wait for Manu to gain access."

With that, he walked away and didn't look back.

Andre went in the S2 house and collapsed on the cot. He stared at the dreary, dim space below the counter and above the floor. Once, a long time ago, Brodeur had been a young man. Probably in the 1970s. In love. Kissing a woman. Smiling. A strange sight to imagine. André had fallen in love once during a semester in college. Since then, he'd been too busy with work to try much. That may have been why his last girlfriend, Claire, had moved to Ireland. Now, his intense devotion to Renia must have publicly sizzled like a neon sign. Brodeur had assumed they were married. *If only.* He cringed at calling out the old man for his drinking to his face. Not a polite action to take with a Frenchman. If Brodeur had lost even a scrap of what Andre felt for Renia and wanted to drink on the job, so be it. He wouldn't judge.

He took out his phone and called the electrician, left a message, then wedged the front door open to let in cooler air. He'd have to risk insects, the house was warming. And the trees were in dire need of water. He found a watering can and went to the office, filled the can in the bathroom sink and gave ten saplings a drink. Then he looked up larger electrical companies on his phone and made some calls before finding an independent contractor who would come at three o'clock for twice the cost.

On his laptop, he reviewed the security footage. The storage house camera glittered with static. Had Floch done that? Probably. Floch felt like a known evil friend. A proud demon. He whapped shut his laptop and closed his eyes. A sudden pain shot through his forearm. He was sweating. And thirsty, hungry. The air, so warm. High humidity might help the trees recover a bit, but with the electrical offline, he couldn't bring in fresh air. As he searched his bag for an old crust of baguette he'd brought to eat, Manu stuck a head in the house.

"Brodeur radioed me. He said you need access to the storage house."

"Yes. Please."

They went outside.

"Sorry about the lock, Andre. Monsieur Albert is kind of old-fashioned."

"I know. It's okay."

"I find it so strange someone would turn off the water." Despite the break-in and police visit and all else, Manu had been fairly clueless about the project's problems.

Andre gave a weak shrug. "Not sure. Someone also sabotaged the electricity. The fans were blowing."

"Today?" Manu asked.

"Yes."

He stopped, staring at the mottled bark of a plane tree. "Why would she do that?"

"Who?"

The sunlight shifted, beaming on the bark, illuminating the intersecting splotches of olive and cream and copper.

"I thought she left the job on good terms," Manu said.

"Who?"

"Renia. She was here this morning."

CHAPTER 23

"Renia was here? Today?" Andre said.

"Yeah. I thought you knew."

"I wasn't here. When?"

"Earlier. Maybe nine o'clock?"

Were they supposed to meet? What appointment had he forgotten? She must have arrived right after he'd gone home. "Was she filling out paperwork in the office or something?"

"I don't think so. I was in the hoop house and saw her go in the S2 house and come out with a box. I assumed she forgot a tool or something that belonged to her."

Andre blinked. "So you didn't speak to her?"

"No, she just waved as she drove off on her scooter."

After getting the wrench and turning on the water valve, Andre held his breath and tried the sprinkler system. The black watering spikes stood motionless in the pots. Dead. He'd predicted that. Until the electricity was fixed, he'd have no irrigation. Thankfully, the hose worked. He watered all the trees, called Kateb, and waited an hour before he arrived and surveyed the damage. He asked questions, took photos of the electrical wiring and alarm system, and told him not to get his hopes up because the other night in Belleville had been their best chance of hauling Floch in for questioning. Most likely, he'd stolen a car and headed to Spain. Then Kateb shook his hand, revved up his motorbike, and bounced over the L'Enclos field.

At three o'clock, he ate the chewy baguette, expecting the electrician any minute. The saplings had already absorbed the water and their leaves had perked up, hanging in a level horizontal way again. He transplanted a couple trees, accidentally tipping a container and nearly breaking a branch with three apples.

By four o'clock, the electrician had still not come.

At five-thirty, his phone dinged.

A text from Delphine.

"I need help. Please come now!"

Shoot. Her move to the new apartment. Of course. He'd promised to help and it was the end of May. Or was she moving on June 1st? Regardless, today must have been the day, and in the hectic whirl of finding Floch and recovering and this watering emergency, he'd forgotten. Had she texted him over the weekend? He keyed through old messages. Nothing. Oh well. What good he'd be with a fractured arm, he wasn't sure. He gulped a pain pill without water, then clipped his jacket collar to his teeth and slid his left arm in. A sharp pang shot through. Any bump to his forearm made his brain burst with pain. With a shove, he shut the door and locked it, wondering if he should tell Manu an electrician might be on the way.

He checked the office and hoop houses before spotting a person behind a clump of potted magnolias. "Manu?"

Silence.

"He's gone for the day."

Brodeur knelt by the cold frames, screwing a tiny hinge on the lid.

Andre debated what to do.

"Did you get the water started?" Brodeur said, wandering over.

"Yes, thanks. But the irrigation is down because the electricity is off. I was waiting for an electrician, but..."

"Those scoundrels are never on time."

"Yeah, well, I had no choice." He felt tired. As heavy as the sagging bag of soil near his feet. "Someone rerouted the wires. Where, I can't tell."

"How long have you waited?"

"Over two hours. And I have to leave. I have to help my cousin move."

Brodeur eyed the S2 house as if he were judging its quality. Beads of sweat clung to his speckled forehead. The sun slanted into his eyes, illuminating their deep gray color. The day was melting toward a warm muggy evening.

"Go on," Brodeur said. He swiped his gloved hands together. "I'll look at your box and see what I can do."

"You know electrical systems?"

"I've worked on some. I don't know if I can get this one to work, it might be too fancy, but I can probably get the alarm to operate for the night."

In the summer light, Brodeur's face took on a softer, more noble cast.

"Well, that would save me. I'm so grateful, Monsieur. If you can get it to work, will you call me?"

"If I must."

Andre scribbled his number on an old receipt. "Here it is. Thank you. You have a key to the door, right? Of course, you do. And you know the padlock combo. Thank you. Thank you so much," he said and jogged toward the gate.

At Delphine's building on Rue Francois Bonvin, Andre waited at the door. He buzzed twice. No answer. Odd. A bee whizzed by, headed for a nearby flower box, empty save for one geranium with a few flopping wands. He pressed the button again, waited. And again. He waited for fifteen minutes, thinking she and Charles were out of hearing range. He called her name into the intercom. Silence. *Must have left for the Invalides apartment.* He settled on the stoop and called her. As he listened to her phone ring, he realized the striped insect crawling on the flower box wasn't a bee but a hornet.

Across the street, at a restaurant called Le Tourniquet, a No Access sign hung on a chain across the door. The windows were covered in brown paper. Pieces of iron fencing were stacked against the wall. A silver BMW pulled up and parked and a man got out. He undid the chain, opened the restaurant door, and went in, leaving the chain to lay on the stoop. After seven rings, Delphine didn't answer.

Andre texted her. "Are you at the new place?"

No reply. Probably because she was carrying boxes up and down a stairwell. But unless he knew where the new apartment was, he couldn't help. He texted: "Where are you?"

No answer. He waited another fifteen minutes until well after seven o'clock, feeling a mix of helplessness and confusion, then headed to the metro.

As he waited for the train in the Jussieu station, his phone rang.

"Hey there, how are you?" Delphine said.

The train arrived, creating a high-pitched, whirring sound.

"How am I? What do you mean?"

The doors opened and Andre got in.

"Like, how are you doing? Haven't heard from you in a while. Do you want to join us for dinner tonight?"

"Dinner? No. Wait, what do you mean? I just called you and texted you two times."

The train jerked forward, Andre grabbed a pole. An ad along the ceiling read, "Pick up litter. Keep our planet green."

"You did? I didn't get them."

"That's strange. I texted, let me check," he tapped his messages and checked the list. "I texted the 0054 number."

"That's my old number. Remember I told you I lost my phone? I have a new number."

"Did you ever give it to me? I don't think I have it."

"I'm sure I've texted you since."

"Oh. Well, I was just at your place in Montparnasse. Do you need help moving?"

"Yeah, I do need help."

The train swished fast through the tunnel, dim lights accelerating.

Frustrated, he snapped his tongue. "I just got on the metro to go back."

"I don't need help *today*."

"No?"

"No. I need help this *Saturday*."

He rubbed his forehead. "Okay, I'm confused."

"I am too. But how about I give you my *new* number right now and you can delete the old one, okay?"

He typed in the number and she asked about the "baby tree project" and they chatted a few minutes. He updated her about Floch and his broken arm and said he didn't have time for dinner that night but would help her on Saturday. After he hung up, he slouched in a seat, his arm thumping with pain. It filled his awareness like a river's overflowing rapids. No pause, no relief. As the train slowed into the station, the car grew quiet. A high beep rang out.

He yawned.

The beep rang again. A young man in headphones, leaning on a pole, glanced at him. Was it his phone? Yes. He pulled it out. The app for the S2 house temperature. The central number flashed pink, registered 80 degrees. *Eighty degrees*? The train shuffled on. He checked the settings. At the next station, the pink numbers blinked in magenta: 86 degrees. He stared, mystified. The temperature must have fluctuated from Brodeur's attempt to fix the electricity. As the train slowed to Censier-Daubenton, the app beeped again. If Brodeur hadn't fixed the electricity, the gauge wouldn't be working in the first place. The train halted and he walked onto the platform, up the stairs. The app beeped again, over and over, in bright red now, numbers blinking: 95 degrees, 95, 95, 95...

He came out of the stairwell into the waning daylight of the Rue Censier. *What the hell?* The evening air was warm but not warm enough to create 95 degrees inside a greenhouse. If Brodeur had fixed the electricity, the HVAC unit should have automatically switched on to cool the air. Maybe Brodeur had got the electrical system working but only the heating had started. Maybe the app was buggy, not communicating accurately with the sensor.

Then, like a flat stone dropping in a pond, he realized what was happening.

And in a panic, he ran.

Andre raced down the sidewalk, swerving around people, nearly crashing into a lamp, almost tripping over a dog. Cars and shops rushed by in a blur. He rounded the corner onto Rue Mirbel, where two women watched him dash by, probably wondering if he had robbed a bank. The city flashed in snippets: black posts, cement snake head, cane chairs, motorbikes, iron grate, crosswalk, person, person, person.

His lungs burned. He came to an intersection against the light, but free of traffic and turned, clogging into a dense crowd of people in the street. A mass. *Damn.* A protest outside the Sorbonne. The crowd marched with signs that read "*Cumule des Professions*" and "*Absence de Formation.*" University students, protesting the lack of wage increases for student workers. He leapt this way and that, wherever a free inch of space allowed him to push through, but the throng was unforgiving, absorbed in their own goal. He bumped shoulders again and again, smelling sweat and mint gum, cigarettes, leather, body odor. Step by step, he squeezed through the crush of poster signs and bodies.

Finally, he got free and on to the sidewalk at Rue Buffon. A cluster of policemen escorting at the rear passed by. A few last students beat drums. He darted around a group of young men, laughing as they tried to light cigars with a lighter that wouldn't catch. At the L'Enclos gate, the security trailer was closed and dark. He punched in the code. The gate slid open in a slow crawl. When it rumbled wide enough, he slipped through the opening, bumping his cast against the metal. *Ow.* He paused, closing his eyes to let the stars he saw fade, then stumbled on, fiddling in his pocket for keys.

In the distance of a darkening blue sky and tuft of maple trees, smoke streamed upward.

It rose in a steady billow. Smelled dry. He rushed down the driveway, around the corner, into the parking lot. The office was empty. Door shut. Everyone had gone home. His app still beeped,

he could hear it faintly but frantically in his pocket, signal-
ing over and over, in emergency mode. Across the field, the S2
house was bright but not from lights. Smoke jittered out of the
roof vents. The door was ajar. He ran to it, smelling a smell he
hadn't smelled in years. Like from a barbecue. Gas. Lighter
fluid.

Inside, gray smog obscured his vision. A dozen trees, on fire.
The door to the Chick's Nest, open. He sprinted to it, hearing a
metal can bang against wood. In the far corner was Floch. In a
black shirt with black knit cap and black leather gloves. Three
saplings, already in flames. He poured lighter fluid on the others.

"No!"

Floch glanced up, then frantically jiggled his can over more
trees. He lit a match and tossed it. Flames billowed up and
engulfed the branches. Andre stumbled back, shielding his face
with the cast. Floch scurried toward the door where trees hadn't
caught yet, sloshed fluid on them in random, awkward strokes.
He threw a match again and flames burst upward. Instantly the
wood of the table caught fire. The small white apples blackened.

In the far corner, the appling stood untouched. The flames
hadn't reached it, but it was only a matter of seconds before
they would.

The fire illuminated the house in a dastardly light. Andre
covered his head with his jacket, the heat scorching his skin. He
coughed, ran a few steps forward, unsure which direction was
safest, and saw, on the floor beneath the electric panel, Albert
Brodeur, unconscious.

He lay on his back, bleeding from the head. Andre surged
with fury. Coughing, he lurched to the counter and grabbed
his machete. As Floch doused the larger trees and ignited them
with every few steps, Andre lurched over a table and swiped the
blade at Floch. It sliced through his sweatshirt. Blood spurted
from his upper arm. Floch winced, roared. Andre braced himself
to slice again but Floch heaved the can at Andre, the last trickle
splashing out and catching fire in mid-air. Andre ducked and
with his good shoulder, pushed over a table to block Floch's
path, but the vandal slipped through the doorway.

More heat. So hot. It seared his face. Andre dropped and crawled to the Chick's Nest. The fire caught another sapling. Flames shot up. He lifted an arm to protect his face. He could save the appling if he went for it now, six steps and he'd be there. He could take it and get the hell out. But Brodeur also lay six steps away. The appling looked pure, grown. More apples had fruited than he remembered. He moved a few steps to it, but there, in the orange light of fire, he saw the old man on the ground, his hat knocked off, his hair matted, the blood on his forehead so fresh.

He thought of his mother. Her crooked hand. Her slanted smile. He could grab the appling and salvage the project. For her. Have something to show for it. He'd be the man who'd saved his special tree for his mom, for the sick. But what would his mom want him to do?

He threw his jacket further over his head and crawled, his arm throbbing, to Brodeur. Andre shook the man's shoulder, but he didn't wake, so he hooked his left arm around Brodeur's beefy chest, then stood as best he could and walked backward, dragging him, coughing. The old man was compact and heavy, at least one hundred-eighty pounds. Poof. Another tree shot up in flames. Then the one next to it, singeing Andre's face. He wrenched Brodeur around the table. Backward, dragging, dragging, a few feet then pausing, a few feet more. His app screamed in a steady, fast beep. The tables and plants curled and crackled in flames. The smoke burned his eyes. So hard to breathe.

As he came out of the Chick's Nest, he felt a jolt of heat. Sparks flew and charred twigs landed on Brodeur's shirt. He batted them away. His jacket was slipping off his head, the heat searing his nose. *So tired. Can't breathe. Keep moving.* Finally, he bumped the front wall. The door at his left. The overturned table burned, the trees on the floor, charred. He coughed, slipped his cast arm out of the sling and locked both around Brodeur's chest. With a heave, he stumbled backwards into the open air.

He landed hard on his back, Brodeur atop. The old man's hair was singed, his face red. Still unconscious. Andre checked his chest. Heart still beating. He got up, sucking in air, his head in a daze. A strong chemical smell. The polycarbonate roof was melting.

Inside, the flames had died on the west side of the house. His bag lay plainly on the counter. He could squeeze in that way and get the appling. The tree might be crisp from the heat but not burning. Its pitch not boiling yet. He charged to the house.

A hefty arm hooked his torso. "*Arretez!*"

Andre wrestled against it. "You don't know," he said. "We need that tree!"

The fireman locked his torso. Andre writhed out of his hold until another set of arms locked his shoulders and hurled him away. "*Arretez! C'est dangereux.*"

The house cracked and snapped from the heat. Flames licked out the roof vents. Billowing smoke. The plastic melted like an alien creature dying. That awful, chemical smell. There were pillars of flames as each tree burned, lined up in the geometric way he'd arranged them. Now, with the burning tables, the entire house looked like a terrarium of orange torches, growing brighter and brighter against the twilight sky.

From heavy hoses, water sprayed high. Police officers criss-crossed the field. Two firemen dragged another hose to the front door and began spraying the interior. People pointed, talked on giant walkie-talkies. The word "Police" in white letters on coats flitted everywhere. The red lights of an ambulance, a cacophony of the French language.

Brodeur, smeared with soot, lay on a gurney, a clear mask over his nose and mouth. A paramedic knelt before Andre, asked him questions he didn't know the answers to. He coughed at the grit, wanted to speak but couldn't. He wheezed, heard himself croak, "It's all gone to hell," and dropped to his knees, watching what he loved melt away, his awareness fading like a warm balloon rising in frigid air.

CHAPTER 24

The next morning, he came in the kitchen and saw Delphine by the sink drying dishes. He couldn't remember if she'd slept over or had come to the apartment early in the morning. She wore designer jeans and a chic short-sleeved blouse and high-heel boots, makeup of mascara and lipstick, tiny dangling earrings, hair in a slick ponytail. As he lowered his showered aching body to the bistro table, he guessed she'd come in the early morning.

She dried dishes with a rote efficiency, stacked plates neatly beside a straight row of glasses draining on a towel. "You don't have much in the way of food," she said, "so I went to the bakery."

She set a plate of pastries before him. The buttery smell made his mouth water. He ate a pain au chocolat, thinking it the most delicious thing he'd tasted in his life. Linus jumped on his lap. He scratched the cat's neck as it kneaded his legs. Its sharp nails dug into Andre's jeans and he thought it a small gift compared to the previous night. He'd spent what seemed like hours in the ER, being treated for minor burns on his hands and cheeks, filling out a police report, calling Edo, Renia, and Delphine, relaying the story over and over. Had he sobbed on the phone with Renia? He might have.

He remembered Delphine arriving at the hospital in Charles's coat and her own slippers, with a panicked expression, ready to bring him home. As he shook Kateb's hand, the officer patted his shoulder, saying, "At least we apprehended the suspect. He created a trail of blood that led us straight to a dumpster. We'll need your assistance once you're feeling better."

Now, a soft knock sounded at the door. Delphine answered. Renia slinked into the kitchen, her face frozen with sympathy, those sparkling eyes. Beside her, Delphine's alert face with concerned eyes. For Andre, to see them together was a bizarre dream.

"Renia's here to take you," Delphine said.

"Where am I going?"

She smiled. "Don't you remember, silly? That's okay. Do you have a coat you can put over your cast?"

"I think so. In the closet."

Renia opened the entry closet door and looked through the clothes.

"By the way," Delphine said, "your phone rang super early this morning. Like at seven o'clock. It startled me. I didn't know if it was the police or what, so I answered. It was a woman named Lisa, spoke English. I was only half-awake and told her you were sleeping. She said she'd call back."

"Lisa?"

"Yes, Lisa W. she said. She wouldn't give her last name. Very secret." Her eyes grazed Renia. "Who is... well, we can talk later."

He noticed Delphine's attempt at discretion. "I'll call her back. She's a colleague in the U.S., a grower, a researcher, went through something similar. I'm sure we'll have a lot of notes to compare."

Outside, Andre winced as he put a leg over the Vespa. He lowered his weight on the cushion, feeling a pinch under his ribs, his face radiating warmth, his shoulder aching, his cast tucked under a buttoned wool coat. Renia clicked a helmet strap under his chin, tightened it, and tightened her own. Her eye had completely healed. *Thank God.* She slipped on a pair of retro aviator sunglasses.

"How's your eye?" he said. "How are you feeling?"

"I'm recovering."

He nodded, guilt clenching his gut.

"You look tired," she said.

He thought of his face in the mirror last night. Hair singed, scarred face caked in soot, shadowy beard from not shaving for three days.

"Still feel hazy. But I slept."

"I'm sorry about the Tengri. After all of our work, it's a terrible loss."

He choked up, swallowed.

"At least Monsieur Brodeur is okay," she said. "I talked to him this morning."

"You did? Did he have your number?"

"No, he called Manu and Manu called me. I called the hospital. He was happy to hear that you were okay."

Pain shot through his forearm. He winced.

"*Are* you okay?" she said.

"Yes."

"Well, I need to show you one thing and then I'll take you home so you can rest."

"The cat," he said alarmed. "Linus. He's outside."

"No," she said. "Linus is inside. Delphine is upstairs."

"Delphine is upstairs?"

"Yes."

"In my apartment?"

"Yes."

"And so is Linus, for sure?"

"Yes, he was on the sofa when we left, chattering at birds."

"Oh. Good." His body sagged a little, his gaze wandering up to the apartment windows. "He's my tiger buddy."

She smiled and started the scooter. "Hold on tight," she said and wrapped his good arm around her waist. They drove south. The wind on his face felt icy, refreshing. She headed down Rue Saint-Jacques for several miles before crossing the highway and coming into Montrouge. Feeling more alert, he called out over the motor's whirr. "This isn't far from Edo's apartment."

She nodded.

The cars flying past at high speeds rattled him, but when they slowed onto a narrow street, he relaxed. After a few more turns, he realized they were actually going to Edo's. They parked before a mammoth 19th-century building and a broad courtyard filled with palm trees: blue Mexican fan, windmill, saw palmetto, needle. Renia gripped his hand as he maneuvered off the bike and they went in the lobby. It was a grand foyer with a tile floor and Beaux-Arts lamps. Renia hit the bell and they waited. Andre knew the apartment, having been there twice for dinner parties. A woman's voice answered, and they went through a buzzing lobby door and into a roomy elevator. On the third floor after walking the long hall, Renia waited for Andre to catch his breath before knocking on the door.

Edo's wife appeared. She had wavy black hair, cocoa complexion, a motherly smile. Andre vaguely remembered her name: Chinara. In a beaded, multi-colored shirt and dark slacks, she greeted them, her face crunching in sympathy. "I'm glad you weren't seriously hurt. Come in."

They went through the entry and into the kitchen where Edo was chopping vegetables. He was in dress pants and a plum turtleneck, shined shoes, looking as if he were going to the ballet or a music performance.

When he saw Andre, he did a doubletake, set aside his knife, and wiped his hands. "Perfect timing."

They followed him down a hallway.

"We have to speak quietly," Edo said. "Beatrice is taking a nap."

They went to the last door and Edo put a hand on the knob. "Andre, do you know how clever Renia is?"

Andre glanced at her.

She half-smiled, biting her lip.

"I think I do."

"Well," Edo said, "you'll appreciate her even more when you see this." He opened the door to a small, bright office. Behind the desk, a tall acacia stood in the corner beside a dense ixora, a hibiscus, a slew of exotic plants Andre didn't recognize, and a hanging pot of trailing purple heart. A lone grow light was against the wall, shining on a flat of tiny cacti and blue gravel. There, sitting on a low table before the window was a small apple sapling. At the end of its branches were clusters of leaves and eleven white apples.

"This looks like a Tengri," Andre said.

"It is the sapling from Kazakhstan."

"...what?" He imagined the tree in the S2 house, about to burn in flames. "But it caught fire."

"Actually," Edo said, "what you saw in the house was a 'Light Delicious.' This Tengri has been here since yesterday."

Andre burst into a smile. "Really?"

"After Floch put his own false Tengri at your door," Renia said, "it gave me an idea. Edo bought the other tree and I switched them. I didn't have a chance to let you know. The store was so busy yesterday."

Andre gawked at the appling, absorbing her words. "Alba and Castel," he said. "We should tell them."

"Yes," Edo said, "well, this is not such a happy point of discussion. I spoke with Madame Castel a few hours ago. They're very upset, as you can imagine. As is the Jardin des Plantes director, but that's a park system matter, we'll deal with it. Monsieur Alba though has decided to sever the contract. He said it drew too much controversy."

Andre swallowed, his heart dropping. "Of course. That's what I expected. The trees... all destroyed."

"But an interesting thing happened when I gave her the news. I started explaining about saving the sapling, but she said they weren't interested in hearing explanations. She expressed extreme disappointment with starting over and was unsure if they would invest in this again. She ended the call rather abruptly. So..." he shrugged, "it's fallen through the cracks so to say."

Andre admired the tree. Its graceful branches were now strong and horizontal, covered in fresh leaves. The apples, round and unblemished. He marveled at how Renia had safely transported the plant to Edo's without damaging it.

"And I spoke to Directeur Bertrand today," Edo said.

"Is he upset?"

"He's not happy, but I think he's relieved that no lives were lost."

Softly, Renia said, "I am too."

"In fact," Edo said, "he sees this as an opportunity to draw in funding. The goodwill toward the university is high today. If all goes as he thinks it will, he wants to grow a new crop of Tengris. And this time you can grow them in the field at the Bois de Vincennes with Renia or Lucille or Nestor, whoever you'd like to help you."

Andre searched Edo's face for a false tone, a joke. There was none. Only clear, reliable eyes.

"In the meantime, my friend," Edo handed the sapling to Andre, "this little diamond is yours."

With the tree in his arms, Andre felt loose like a fool. A happy, goofy fool. "Edo, this is..."

A child cried out, moaning. "Daddy."

"Ah, Beatrice. She's been ill. Excuse me."

Edo closed the door, leaving Andre to face Renia.

"Renia, I can't believe... you saved me, saved us. The sapling, the Tengri... its potential, I mean..."

A sly smile slipped onto her face.

"There're even apples still on the tree, I—"

She giggled, inching in, cupping his cheek. "Isn't it wonderful?"

He shivered, hooked his hand on hers and squeezed. "Yes, I can't think of anything more wonder..."

Her face floated in gently, lightly, her sweet breath warming his nose.

"Well, maybe..." she whispered.

With a racing heart and a moment of uncertainty, he tilted his face down.

She kissed him.

SUMMER
CHAPTER 25

In August, he visited his parents in California. As he walked up the path to the old farmhouse, he snapped off a leaf from the enormous bay tree that grew by the porch. It smelled spicy, of the earth. The tree's dense sweeping crown gave the living room the shade it needed in summer and screened the view of the lemon orchard. If the tree hadn't been there, his mom had always said, she would have been constantly reminded of all the work they had to do at Suntime Orchards.

He climbed the wraparound porch steps and knocked on the wood screen door, wheeled suitcase at his side.

Oskar appeared. He wore a plaid shirt and jeans, sneakers instead of work boots. His fingernails were clean, as today was Saturday. His dark eyes, framed by lines and wrinkled brows and gray hair that faded into brown, skipped from Andre's face to his clothes. "You're so thin."

He laughed. "This is the best shape my body's been in in months."

Oskar opened the door and touched the faint scar on Andre's jaw, his temple. "You got these in Kazakhstan?" he said. "And how's your arm?"

"Yeah." He swiveled his arm. "It's a bit sore but still works."

His dad pressed up and down his forearm lightly, his face betraying his worry. He swallowed and wrapped a tender hand around Andre's neck, bringing him in, clapping his back. "I'm glad you're home."

"Me too."

"She's been waiting for you."

He went inside, letting Oskar take the suitcase, and found his mom dozing in a chair by the window. She was a slim woman with henna-colored hair streaked with gray, her eyes deep set and observant. Her body, dressed in a maroon athletic jacket and matching pants, lay crooked in the chair, the left side of her face in a slight sag.

"Mom," he said, kneeling.

Her eyes fluttered open and her face brightened. Her mouth dropped, smiling in a slant, awkwardly leaned forward and hugged him. She smelled of apricot jelly.

He unhooked his leather bag over his head. "I brought you something."

She gasped. "No. Really?"

"Yep."

"How did you get them through customs?" Oskar said.

"Well, let's just say on the certificate they're known as 'Light Delicious.'"

He smiled. "Nice work."

Andre pulled out a large wax paper bag stuffed with tissues for padding, took out a Tengri apple. It was the size of a small baseball, creamy white, hard and crisp. "This is it?"

Oskar crouched. "Oh my, white as snow."

"Isn't it?"

"And the taste?"

Andre cocked his head. "Tart. But not too tart."

He unfolded the fingers on his mom's damaged hand and placed the apple in her palm. "This is for you."

"It's so smooth. Oh, love," her face slowly crinkled in sympathy, "how thoughtful." A shadow crossed her face. "But it's okay if... it doesn't work. At this point, I'm used to... this all now."

"But you'll feel better, I know you will."

"I'll get a knife," Oskar said and went to the kitchen.

Her speech was slow, deliberate. "You do? You have... faith, huh?"

"Well, I have faith yes, but right now, even better, I have data. The trial data *and* the personal data that proved its worth. When I ate these in Kazakhstan, the next morning I was able to walk on a sprained ankle."

Oskar took the apple and cut a thin slice, handed it to Andre.

"What do you think?" Andre asked as he carefully set it in her mouth.

She chewed in a laborious rhythm. Her eyes widened at the taste. "Mmm. Yes, strong," she said, squeezing his hand, her eyes glittering, "just like you."

On a warm September morning, Andre, Nes, Samal, and Vlad hiked up the ridge in the Tian Shan mountains, leading two donkeys with packs. When they reached the top, Andre relaxed into the expansive sight of the valley. From the west all the way east, the land spread in a rugged terrain of boulders and herbs and trees, a winding creek meandering through, the Tengri on its hill, a jagged line of powder-dusted mountains on the horizon. In the early morning sun, their peaks were misty, but Andre knew once the fog burned off, the day would be clear and he'd enjoy the view they'd missed the year before.

As they wandered into the valley, he noticed the Tengri stood in full green leaf, more imposing than he remembered, fuller and denser, casting a large shadow. His father was right. It did have the sturdiest trunk he'd ever seen. And Renia... he took a photo for her. She would love how lushly the tree showed off its fruit. White apples covered the crown like pearls on an ornate dress.

After they crossed the creek, lower from a late summer drought, they tied the donkeys in the shade and unpacked the camp.

Nes strolled toward the hill's foot. "This looks like a good place for lunch." He tossed down his pack and climbed on a boulder, facing the Tengri.

Andre clamored up and sat nearby. "Yes, not a bad view."

Nes unwrapped a wedge of cheese and some apples he'd collected a mile back. "Want one? I think it's a 'Kazakh Beauty,' one of the sweets."

"No, thanks, I'll try this." He showed Nes the white apple in his hand, one he'd recently picked up off the ground. It was small, a brief handful, but free of bruises and solid. He bit into the mealy flesh, sour with a bright aftertaste. He took another bite, and another, his mouth jammed with tart pulp.

"Harvesting the Tengri already?" Nes said.

Andre chewed, tasting the complexity that had challenged him, forced him to grow, given him courage, taught him that everyone makes mistakes and that anyone can change. This white apple, full of promise. He rotated it, considered its brilliant color, as brilliant and elegant as the Kazakh language itself, as the meaning of the word *Tengri*.

"Yes," he said, "I am harvesting, harvesting the *Sky*."

ACKNOWLEDGEMENTS

This story, like a sapling, grew into a tree because of the following people:

My husband Ethan whose easy belief in me and unwavering support is amazing. He not only read several versions of this book but listened to me chatter on about my ideas too many times to count! Also, I feel intense gratitude for my beloved friend and fellow author, Natasha Oliver. Her sharp insight and loving support always convinces me I can accomplish anything. Thanks to my dear friends Gretel Hakanson and Ann Hedreen for feedback on an early version and to my children who always impress me with their maturity and patience when I'm occupied with work.

To the team at Woodhall Press, thank you for reviving The Forgetting Flower and for going full speed ahead with this follow-up novel. Thanks to the sweet Angie, Hemu, Kimberly, and Roxana who make up my writing group, and to the larger community of writing friends and colleagues who share a passion for the written word.

Lastly, I'd like to again thank my old horticulture teacher and friend Timothy Hohn for his botanical eye, and all of my fellow plant geeks who share a passion for green life.

ABOUT THE AUTHOR

K aren Hugg is also the author of _The Forgetting Flower_ and _Song of the Tree Hollow_. Born into a Polish family and raised in Chicago, she later moved to Seattle and worked as an editor in tech, which gave her the opportunity to live in Paris for a short time. Afterward, she became a certified ornamental horticulturalist and master pruner. Her work has appeared in _The Big Thrill_, _Crime Reads_, _Thrive Global_, and other publications. She lives with her husband and three kids near Seattle.

For more information about Karen, visit her website www. karenhugg.com. To get updates about her new writings, sign up for _A Vine of Ideas_.

If you liked _Harvesting the Sky_, please help spread the word by posting a few sentences about it on Amazon or Goodreads.